THE
McBAIN BRIEF

Also by Ed McBain

THE 87TH PRECINCT NOVELS

Cop Hater

The Mugger

The Pusher

The Con Man

Killer's Choice

Killer's Payoff

Lady Killer

Killer's Wedge

'Til Death

King's Ransom

Give the Boys a Great Big Hand

The Heckler

See Them Die

Lady, Lady, I Did It

The Empty Hours

Like Love

Ten Plus One

Ax

He Who Hesitates

Doll

Eighty Million Eyes

Fuzz

Shotgun

Jigsaw

Hail, Hail, the Gang's All Here!

Sadie When She Died

Let's Hear It for the Deaf Man

Hail to the Chief

Bread

Blood Relatives

So Long As You Both Shall Live

Long Time No See

Calypso

Ghosts

Heat

Ice

Lightning

Eight Black Horses

Poison

Tricks

Lullaby

Vespers

Widows

Kiss

Mischief

And All Through the House

Romance

Nocturne

The Big Bad City

The Last Dance

Money, Money, Money

Fat Ollie's Book

The Frumious Bandersnatch

Hark!

Fiddlers

MATTHEW HOPE NOVELS

Goldilocks
Rumpelstiltskin
Beauty and the Beast
Jack and the Beanstalk
Snow White and Rose Red
Cinderella
Puss in Boots

The House That Jack Built
Three Blind Mice
Mary, Mary
There Was a Little Girl
Gladly the Cross-Eyed Bear
The Last Best Hope

ED MCBAIN—OTHER NOVELS

The April Robin Murders
  (with Craig Rice)
The Sentries
Death of a Nurse
Where There's Smoke
Guns

Another Part of the City
Downtown
Driving Lessons
Learning to Kill
Women in Jeopardy
Alice in Jeopardy

EVAN HUNTER NOVELS

The Evil Sleep!
Don't Crowd Me
The Blackboard Jungle
Second Ending
Strangers When We Meet
A Matter of Conviction
Mothers and Daughters
Buddwing
The Paper Dragon
A Horse's Head
Last Summer
Sons
Nobody Knew They Were There

Every Little Crook and Nanny
Come Winter
Streets of Gold
The Chisholms: A Novel of
  the Journey West
Walk Proud
Love, Dad
Far From the Sea
Lizzie
Criminal Conversation
Privileged Conversation
Candyland
The Moment She Was Gone

MEMOIR

Me and Hitch
Let's Talk

CHILDREN'S BOOKS

Find the Feathered Serpent
The Remarkable Harry

The Wonderful Button
Me and Mr. Stenner

SHORT STORY COLLECTIONS

The Jungle Kids
The Last Spin & Other Stories
Happy New Year, Herbie
The Easter Man (a Play)
   and Six Stories
The McBain Brief

McBain's Ladies: The Women
   of the 87th
McBain's Ladies, Too
Running From Legs
Barking at Butterflies

WRITTEN AS EZRA HANNON

Doors

WRITTEN AS RICHARD MARSTEN

Rocket to Luna
Danger: Dinosaurs!
Runaway Black
Vanishing Ladies

The Spiked Heel
Even the Wicked
Big Man

WRITTEN AS CURT CANNON

I Like 'Em Tough

I'm Cannon—For Hire

WRITTEN AS HUNT COLLINS

Cut Me In

Tomorrow and Tomorrow

WRITTEN AS JOHN ABBOTT

Scimitar

THE
McBAIN BRIEF

ED McBAIN

wm

WILLIAM MORROW
An Imprint of HarperCollins*Publishers*

THE MCBAIN BRIEF. Copyright © 1982 by Hui Corporation. All rights reserved. Printed in the United States of America. No part of this book may be used or reproduced in any manner whatsoever without written permission except in the case of brief quotations embodied in critical articles and reviews. For information address HarperCollins Publishers, 195 Broadway, New York, NY 10007.

HarperCollins books may be purchased for educational, business, or sales promotional use. For information please e-mail the Special Markets Department at SPsales@harpercollins.com.

A hardcover edition of this book was published in 1982 by Arbor House Publishing Company.

FIRST ARBOR HOUSE PAPERBACK EDITION PUBLISHED 1984.
FIRST WILLIAM MORROW PAPERBACK EDITION PUBLISHED 2016.

Library of Congress Cataloging-in-Publication Data has been applied for.

ISBN 978-0-06-264401-5

16 17 18 19 20   DIX/RRD   10 9 8 7 6 5 4 3 2 1

*This is for
Ed and Alyce Kalin*

Contents

A Brief Introduction

The peculiar thing about the following collection is that only one of the stories in it has ever been published under the Ed McBain byline, and even that—if memory serves—*first* appeared under my own name, Evan Hunter, as did several of the other stories. For the rest, I used either the pseudonym Richard Marsten (from the surnames of my three sons, Richard, Mark and Ted) or else Hunt Collins (derived from my alma mater, Hunter College in New York). Since McBain writes exclusively about matters criminous, you may well ask why *his* name did not appear on any of these stories that most certainly deal with crime.

I wish I knew.

The oversight might seem understandable in view of the fact that some of the stories appeared in print *before* 1956, when the Ed McBain byline first saw the light of day with the publication of *Cop Hater*. But many of these stories were written *after* the debut of the 87th Precinct novels, and still Ed McBain was rudely shunted aside by Hunter, Marsten and Collins, a trio of literary muggers to rival the infamous Totting Hill Triplets (whom I made up this very minute). As a drawing-room detective might have muttered over her knitting needles, "It's all very baffling."

Is it possible that the reasoning at the time may have gone something like this: *Well, this McBain chap writes police novels, so let the shoemaker stick to his last, let's not confuse the reader by giving him a McBain story that has nothing whatever to do with cops.* All well and good, except for the fact that many of these stories *do* deal with policemen and police work. (Oddly, the only one that McBain's name adorned before now was *not* a police story.) Or is it possible that those three hoodlums—Hunter, Marsten and Collins—once commanded higher prices in the literary marketplace than did poor, struggling, honest Ed McBain? Was a venal agent, editor, publisher, all or any of the above, responsible for the malfeasance? If so, is there no higher court to which an appeal can be made? Must Ed McBain, in the face of such despicable strong-arm tactics, continue to hide his light under a bushel for the remainder of his days? Is there no way to rectify what has surely been a gross miscarriage of justice?

There *is* a way.

This is the way.

You may well argue that using the McBain byline to foist upon an unsuspecting public the crime-related stories that follow is an offense even more heinous than the one perpetrated by those three gangsters whose names I refuse even to *mention* again. I hope not. I hope indeed that you will enjoy reading these stories as much as I enjoyed writing them (however many *other* literary thugs may lay claim to that distinction). I am, in fact, rather fond of the little tales that follow, including the one I wrote when I was eighteen years old and serving as a radarman aboard a U.S. destroyer in the middle of the Pacific Ocean. (If you guess *Hot,* you're cold.) I also like . . . but that's another story.

I promised you a "brief" introduction. And so, ladies and germs, I give you, for the first time together anywhere in the entire universe, the one, the only (I hope) . . .

Ed McBain

THE
McBAIN BRIEF

First Offense

He sat in the police van with the collar of his leather jacket turned up, the bright silver studs sharp against the otherwise unrelieved black. He was seventeen years old, and he wore his hair in a high black crown. He carried his head high and erect because he knew he had a good profile, and he carried his mouth like a switch knife, ready to spring open at the slightest provocation. His hands were thrust deep into his jacket pockets, and his gray eyes reflected the walls of the van. There was excitement in his eyes, too, an almost holiday excitement. He tried to tell himself he was in trouble, but he couldn't quite believe it. His gradual descent to disbelief had been a spiral that had spun dizzily through the range of his emotions. Terror when the cop's flash had picked him out; blind panic when he'd started to run; rebellion when the cop's firm hand had closed around the leather sleeve of his jacket; sullen resignation when the cop had thrown him into the RMP car; and then cocky stubbornness when they'd booked him at the local precinct.

The desk sergeant had looked him over curiously, with a strange aloofness in his Irish eyes.

"What's the matter, Fatty?" he'd asked.

The sergeant stared at him implacably. "Put him away for the night," the sergeant said.

He'd slept overnight in the precinct cell block, and he'd awakened with this strange excitement pulsing through his narrow body, and it was the excitement that had caused his disbelief. Trouble, hell! He'd been in trouble before, but it had never felt like this. This was different. This was a ball, man. This was like being initiated into a secret society some place. His contempt for the police had grown when they refused him the opportunity to shave after breakfast. He was only seventeen, but he had a fairly decent beard, and a man should be allowed to shave in the morning, what the hell! But even the beard had somehow lent to the unreality of the situation, made him appear—in his own eyes—somehow more desperate, more sinister-looking. He knew he was in trouble, but the trouble was glamorous, and he surrounded it with the gossamer lie of make-believe. He was living the storybook legend. He was big time now. They'd caught him and booked him, and he should have been scared but he was excited instead.

There was one other person in the van with him, a guy who'd spent the night in the cell block, too. The guy was an obvious bum, and his breath stank of cheap wine, but he was better than nobody to talk to.

"Hey!" he said.

The bum looked up. "You talking to me?"

"Yeah. Where we going?"

"The line-up, kid," the bum said. "This your first offense?"

"This's the first time I got caught," he answered cockily.

"All felonies go to the line-up," the bum told him. "And also some special types of misdemeanors. You commit a felony?"

"Yeah," he said, hoping he sounded nonchalant. What'd they have this bum in for anyway? Sleeping on a park bench?

"Well, that's why you're going to the line-up. They have guys from every detective squad in the city there, to look you over. So they'll remember you next time. They put you on a stage, and they read off the offense, and the Chief of Detectives starts firing questions at you. What's your name, kid?"

"What's it to you?"

"Don't get smart, punk, or I'll break your arm," the bum said.

He looked at the bum curiously. He was a pretty big guy, with a heavy growth of beard, and powerful shoulders. "My name's Stevie," he said.

"I'm Jim Skinner," the bum said. "When somebody's trying to give you advice, don't go hip on him."

"Yeah, well what's your advice?" he asked, not wanting to back down completely.

"When they get you up there, you don't have to answer anything. They'll throw questions, but you don't have to answer. Did you make a statement at the scene?"

"No," he answered.

"Good. Then don't make no statement now, either. They can't force you to. Just keep your mouth shut, and don't tell them nothing."

"I ain't afraid. They know all about it anyway," Stevie said.

The bum shrugged and gathered around him the sullen pearls of his scattered wisdom. Stevie sat in the van whistling, listening to the accompanying hum of the tires, hearing the secret hum of his blood beneath the other louder sound. He sat at the core of a self-imposed importance, basking in its warm glow, whistling contentedly, secretly happy. Beside him, Skinner leaned back against the wall of the van.

When they arrived at the Centre Street Headquarters, they put them in detention cells, awaiting the line-up which began at nine. At ten minutes to nine, they led him out of his cell, and the cop who'd arrested him originally took him into the special prisoner's elevator.

"How's it feel being an elevator boy?" he asked the cop.

The cop didn't answer him. They went upstairs to the big room where the line-up was being held. A detective in front of them was pinning on his shield so he could get past the cop at the desk. They crossed the large gymnasium-like compartment, walking past the men sitting on folded chairs before the stage.

"Get a nice turnout, don't you?" Stevie said.

"You ever tried vaudeville?" the cop answered.

The blinds in the room had not been drawn yet, and Stevie could see everything clearly. The stage itself with the permanently fixed microphone hanging from a narrow metal tube above; the height markers—four feet, five feet, six feet—behind the mike on the wide white wall. The men in the seats, he knew, were all detectives and his sense of importance suddenly flared again when he realized these bulls had come from all over the city just to look at him. Behind the bulls was a raised platform with a sort of lecturer's stand on it. A microphone rested on the stand, and a chair was behind it, and he assumed this was where the Chief bull would sit. There were uniformed cops stationed here and there around the room, and there was one man in civilian clothing who sat at a desk in front of the stage.

"Who's that?" Stevie asked the cop.

"Police stenographer," the cop answered. "He's going to take down your words for posterity."

They walked behind the stage, and Stevie watched as other

felony offenders from all over the city joined them. There was one woman, but all the rest were men, and he studied their faces carefully, hoping to pick up some tricks from them, hoping to learn the subtlety of their expressions. They didn't look like much. He was better-looking than all of them, and the knowledge pleased him. He'd be the star of this little shindig. The cop who'd been with him moved over to talk to a big broad who was obviously a policewoman. Stevie looked around, spotted Skinner and walked over to him.

"What happens now?" he asked.

"They're gonna pull the shades in a few minutes," Skinner said. "Then they'll turn on the spots and start the line-up. The spots won't blind you, but you won't be able to see the faces of any of the bulls out there."

"Who wants to see them mugs?" Stevie asked.

Skinner shrugged. "When your case is called, your arresting officer goes back and stands near the Chief of Detectives, just in case the Chief needs more dope from him. The Chief'll read off your name and the borough where you was pinched. A number'll follow the borough. Like he'll say 'Manhattan one' or 'Manhattan two.' That's just the number of the case from that borough. You're first, you get number one, you follow?"

"Yeah," Stevie said.

"He'll tell the bulls what they got you on, and then he'll say either 'Statement' or 'No statement.' If you made a statement, chances are he won't ask many questions 'cause he won't want you to contradict anything damaging you already said. If there's no statement, he'll fire questions like a machine gun. But you won't have to answer nothing."

"Then what?"

"When he's through, you go downstairs to get mugged and printed. Then they take you over to the Criminal Courts Building for arraignment."

"They're gonna take my picture, huh?" Stevie asked.

"Yeah."

"You think there'll be reporters here?"

"Huh?"

"Reporters."

"Oh. Maybe. All the wire services hang out in a room across the street from where the vans pulled up. They got their own police radio in there, and they get the straight dope as soon as it's happening, in case they want to roll with it. There may be some reporters." Skinner paused. "Why? What'd you do?"

"It ain't so much what I done," Stevie said. "I was just wonderin' if we'd make the papers."

Skinner stared at him curiously. "You're all charged up, ain't you, Stevie?"

"Hell, no. Don't you think I know I'm in trouble?"

"Maybe you don't know just how much trouble," Skinner said.

"What the hell are you talking about?"

"This ain't as exciting as you think, kid. Take my word for it."

"Sure, you know all about it."

"I been around a little," Skinner said drily.

"Sure, on park benches all over the country. I know I'm in trouble, don't worry."

"You kill anybody?"

"No," Stevie said.

"Assault?"

Stevie didn't answer.

"Whatever you done," Skinner advised, "and no matter how

long you been doin' it before they caught you, make like it's your first time. Tell them you done it, and then say you don't know why you done it, but you'll never do it again. It might help you, kid. You might get off with a suspended sentence."

"Yeah?"

"Sure. And then keep your nose clean afterwards, and you'll be okay."

"Keep my nose clean! Don't make me laugh, pal."

Skinner clutched Stevie's arm in a tight grip. "Kid, don't be a damn fool. If you can get out, get out now! I coulda got out a hundred times, and I'm still with it, and it's no picnic. Get out before you get started."

Stevie shook off Skinner's hand. "Come on, willya?" he said, annoyed.

"Knock it off there," the cop said. "We're ready to start."

"Take a look at your neighbors, kid," Skinner whispered. "Take a hard look. And then get out of it while you still can."

Stevie grimaced and turned away from Skinner. Skinner whirled him around to face him again, and there was a pleading desperation on the unshaven face, a mute reaching in the red-rimmed eyes before he spoke again. "Kid," he said, "listen to me. Take my advice. I've been . . ."

"Knock it off!" the cop warned again.

He was suddenly aware of the fact that the shades had been drawn and the room was dim. It was very quiet out there, and he hoped they would take him first. The excitement had risen to an almost fever pitch inside him, and he couldn't wait to get on that stage. What the hell was Skinner talking about anyway? "Take a look at your neighbors, kid." The poor jerk probably had a wet brain. What the hell did the police bother with old drunks for, anyway?

A uniformed cop led one of the men from behind the stage, and Stevie moved a little to his left, so that he could see the stage, hoping none of the cops would shove him back where he wouldn't have a good view. His cop and the policewoman were still talking, paying no attention to him. He smiled, unaware that the smile developed as a smirk, and watched the first man mounting the steps to the stage.

The man's eyes were very small, and he kept blinking them, blinking them. He was bald at the back of his head, and he was wearing a Navy peacoat and dark tweed trousers, and his eyes were red-rimmed and sleepy-looking. He reached to the five-foot-six-inches marker on the wall behind him, and he stared out at the bulls, blinking.

"Assisi," the Chief of Detectives said, "Augustus, Manhattan one. Thirty-three years old. Picked up in a bar on 43rd and Broadway, carrying a .45 Colt automatic. No statement. How about it, Gus?"

"How about what?" Assisi asked.

"Were you carrying a gun?"

"Yes, I was carrying a gun." Assisi seemed to realize his shoulders were slumped. He pulled them back suddenly, standing erect.

"Where, Gus?"

"In my pocket."

"What were you doing with the gun, Gus?"

"I was just carrying it."

"Why?"

"Listen, I'm not going to answer any questions," Assisi said. "You're gonna put me through a third-degree, I ain't answering nothing. I want a lawyer."

"You'll get plenty opportunity to have a lawyer," the Chief of Detectives said. "And nobody's giving you a third-degree. We just want to know what you were doing with a gun. You know that's against the law, don't you?"

"I've got a permit for the gun," Assisi said.

"We checked with Pistol Permits, and they say no. This is a Navy gun, isn't it?"

"Yeah."

"What?"

"I said yeah, it's a Navy gun."

"What were you doing with it? Why were you carrying it around?"

"I like guns."

"Why?"

"Why what? Why do I like guns? Because . . ."

"Why were you carrying it around?"

"I don't know."

"Well, you must have a reason for carrying a loaded .45. The gun *was* loaded, wasn't it?"

"Yeah, it was loaded."

"You have any other guns?"

"No."

"We found a .38 in your room. How about that one?"

"It's no good."

"What?"

"The .38."

"What do you mean, no good?"

"The firin' mechanism is busted."

"You want a gun that works, is that it?"

"I didn't say that."

"You said the .38's no good because it won't fire, didn't you?"

"Well, what good's a gun that won't fire?"

"Why do you need a gun that fires?"

"I was just carrying it. I didn't shoot anybody, did I?"

"No, you didn't. Were you planning on shooting somebody?"

"Sure," Assisi said. "That's just what I was planning."

"Who?"

"I don't know," Assisi said sarcastically. "Anybody. The first guy I saw, all right? Everybody, all right? I was planning on wholesale murder."

"Not murder, maybe, but a little larceny, huh?"

"Murder," Assisi insisted, in his stride now. "I was just going to shoot up the whole town. Okay? You happy now?"

"Where'd you get the gun?"

"In the Navy."

"Where?"

"From my ship."

"It's a stolen gun?"

"No, I found it."

"You stole government property, is that it?"

"I found it."

"When'd you get out of the Navy?"

"Three months ago."

"You worked since?"

"No."

"Where were you discharged?"

"Pensacola."

"Is that where you stole the gun?"

"I didn't steal it."

"Why'd you leave the Navy?"

Assisi hesitated for a long time.

"Why'd you leave the Navy?" the Chief of Detectives asked again.

"They kicked me out!" Assisi snapped.

"Why?"

"I was undesirable!" he shouted.

"Why?"

Assisi did not answer.

"Why?"

There was silence in the darkened room. Stevie watched Assisi's face, the twitching mouth, the blinking eyelids.

"Next case," the Chief of Detectives said.

Stevie watched as Assisi walked across the stage and down the steps on the other side, where the uniformed cop met him. He'd handled himself well, Assisi had. They'd rattled him a little at the end there, but on the whole he'd done a good job. So the guy was lugging a gun around, so what? He was right, wasn't he? He didn't shoot nobody, so what was all the fuss about? Cops! They had nothing else to do, they went around hauling in guys who were carrying guns. Poor bastard was a veteran, too, that was really rubbing it in. But he did a good job up there, even though he was nervous, you could see he was very nervous.

A man and a woman walked past him and onto the stage. The man was very tall, topping the six-foot marker. The woman was shorter, a bleached blonde turning to fat.

"They picked them up together," Skinner whispered. "So they show them together. They figure a pair'll always work as a pair, usually."

"How'd you like that Assisi?" Stevie whispered back. "He really had them bulls on the run, didn't he?"

Skinner didn't answer. The Chief of Detectives cleared his throat.

"MacGregor, Peter, aged forty-five, and Anderson, Marcia, aged forty-two, Bronx one. Got them in a packed car on the Grand

Concourse. Back seat of the car was loaded with goods including luggage, a typewriter, a portable sewing machine, and a fur coat. No statements. What about all that stuff, Pete?"

"It's mine."

"The fur coat, too."

"No, that's Marcia's."

"You're not married, are you?"

"No."

"Living together?"

"Well, you know," Pete said.

"What about the stuff?" the Chief of Detectives said again.

"I told you," Pete said. "It's ours."

"What was it doing in the car?"

"Oh. Well, we were . . . uh . . ." The man paused for a long time. "We were going on a trip."

"Where to?"

"Where? Oh. To . . . uh . . ." Again he paused, frowning, and Stevie smiled, thinking what a clown this guy was. This guy was better than a sideshow at Coney. This guy couldn't tell a lie without having to think about it for an hour. And the dumpy broad with him was a hot sketch, too. This act alone was worth the price of admission.

"Uh . . ." Pete said, still fumbling for words. "Uh . . . we were going to . . . uh . . . Denver."

"What for?"

"Oh, just a little pleasure trip, you know," he said, attempting a smile.

"How much money were you carrying when we picked you up?"

"Forty dollars."

"You were going to Denver on forty dollars?"

"Well, it was fifty dollars. Yeah, it was more like fifty dollars."

"Come on, Pete, what were you doing with all that stuff in the car?"

"I told you. We were taking a trip."

"With a sewing machine, huh? You do a lot of sewing, Pete?"

"Marcia does."

"That right, Marcia?"

The blonde spoke in a high reedy voice. "Yeah, I do a lot of sewing."

"That fur coat, Marcia. Is it yours?"

"Sure."

"It has the initials G.D. on the lining. Those aren't your initials, are they, Marcia?"

"No."

"Whose are they?"

"Search me. We bought that coat in a hock shop."

"Where?"

"Myrtle Avenue, Brooklyn. You know where that is?"

"Yes, I know where it is. What about that luggage? It had initials on it, too. And they weren't yours or Pete's. How about it?"

"We got that in a hock shop, too."

"And the typewriter?"

"That's Pete's."

"Are you a typist, Pete?"

"Well, I fool around a little, you know."

"We're going to check all this stuff against our Stolen Goods list, you know that, don't you?"

"We got all that stuff in hock shops," Pete said. "If it's stolen, we don't know nothing about it."

"Were you going to Denver with him, Marcia?"

"Oh, sure."

"When did you both decide to go? A few minutes ago?"

"We decided last week sometime."

"Were you going to Denver by way of the Grand Concourse?"

"Huh?" Pete said.

"Your car was parked on the Grand Concourse. What were you doing there with a carload of stolen goods?"

"It wasn't stolen," Pete said.

"We were on our way to Yonkers," the woman said.

"I thought you were going to Denver."

"Yeah, but we had to get the car fixed first. There was something wrong with the . . ." She paused, turning to Pete. "What was it, Pete? That thing that was wrong?"

Pete waited a long time before answering. "Uh . . . the . . . uh . . . the flywheel, yeah. There's a garage up in Yonkers fixes them good, we heard. Flywheels, I mean."

"If you were going to Yonkers, why were you parked on the Concourse?"

"Well, we were having an argument."

"What kind of an argument?"

"Not an argument, really. Just a discussion, sort of."

"About what?"

"About what to eat."

"What!"

"About what to eat. I wanted to eat Chink's, but Marcia wanted a glass of milk and a piece of pie. So we were trying to decide whether we should go to the Chink's or the cafeteria. That's why we were parked on the Concourse."

"We found a wallet in your coat, Pete. It wasn't yours, was it?"

"No."

"Whose was it?"

"I don't know." He paused, then added hastily, "There wasn't no money in it."

"No, but there was identification. A Mr. Simon Granger. Where'd you get it, Pete?"

"I found it in the subway. There wasn't no money in it."

"Did you find all that other stuff in the subway, too?"

"No, sir, I bought that." He paused. "I was going to return the wallet, but I forgot to stick it in the mail."

"Too busy planning for the Denver trip, huh?"

"Yeah, I guess so."

"When's the last time you earned an honest dollar, Pete?"

Pete grinned. "Oh, about two, three years ago, I guess."

"Here's their records," the Chief of Detectives said. "Marcia, 1938, Sullivan Law; 1939, Concealing Birth of Issue; 1940, Possession of Narcotics—you still on the stuff, Marcia?"

"No."

"1942, Dis Cond; 1943, Narcotics again; 1947—you had enough, Marcia?"

Marcia didn't answer.

"Pete," the Chief of Detectives said, "1940, Attempted Rape; 1941, Selective Service Act; 1942, dis cond; 1943, Attempted Burglary; 1945, Living on Proceeds of Prostitution; 1947, Assault and Battery, did two years at Ossining."

"I never done no time," Pete said.

"According to this, you did."

"I never done no time," he insisted.

"1950," the Chief of Detectives went on, "Carnal Abuse of a Child." He paused. "Want to tell us about that one, Pete?"

"I . . . uh . . ." Pete swallowed. "I got nothing to say."

"You're ashamed of *some* things, that it?"

Pete didn't answer.

"Get them out of here," the Chief of Detectives said.

"See how long he kept them up there?" Skinner whispered. "He knows what they are, wants every bull in the city to recognize them if they . . ."

"Come on," a detective said, taking Skinner's arm.

Stevie watched as Skinner climbed the steps to the stage. Those two had really been something, all right. And just looking at them, you'd never know they were such operators. You'd never know they . . .

"Skinner, James, Manhattan two. Aged fifty-one. Threw a garbage can through the plate glass window of a clothing store on Third Avenue. Arresting officer found him inside the store with a bundle of overcoats. No statement. That right, James?"

"I don't remember," Skinner said.

"Is it, or isn't it?"

"All I remember is waking up in jail this morning."

"You don't remember throwing that ash can through the window?"

"No sir."

"You don't remember taking those overcoats?"

"No, sir."

"Well, you must have done it, don't you think? The off-duty detective found you inside the store with the coats in your arms."

"I got only his word for that, sir."

"Well, his word is pretty good. Especially since he found you inside the store with your arms full of merchandise."

"I don't remember, sir."

"You've been here before, haven't you?"

"I don't remember, sir."

"What do you do for a living, James?"

"I'm unemployed, sir."

"When's the last time you worked?"

"I don't remember, sir."

"You don't remember much of anything, do you?"

"I have a poor memory, sir."

"Maybe the record has a better memory than you, James," the Chief of Detectives said.

"Maybe so, sir. I couldn't say."

"I hardly know where to start, James. You haven't been exactly an ideal citizen."

"Haven't I, sir?"

"Here's as good a place as any. 1948, Assault and Robbery; 1949, Indecent Exposure; 1951, Burglary; 1952, Assault and Robbery again. You're quite a guy, aren't you, James?"

"If you say so, sir."

"I say so. Now how about that store?"

"I don't remember anything about a store, sir."

"Why'd you break into it?"

"I don't remember breaking into any store, sir."

"Hey, what's this?" the Chief of Detectives said suddenly.

"Sir?"

"Maybe we should've started back a little further, huh, James? Here, on your record. 1938, convicted of first degree murder, sentenced to execution."

The assembled bulls began murmuring among themselves. Stevie leaned forward eagerly, anxious to get a better look at this bum who'd offered him advice.

"What happened there, James?"

"What happened where, sir?"

"You were sentenced to death? How come you're still with us?"

"The case was appealed."

"And never retried?"

"No, sir."

"You're pretty lucky, aren't you?"

"I'm pretty unlucky, sir, if you ask me."

"Is that right? You cheat the chair, and you call that unlucky. Well, the law won't slip up this time."

"I don't know anything about law, sir."

"You don't, huh?"

"No, sir. I only know that if you want to get a police station into action, all you have to do is buy a cheap bottle of wine and drink it quiet, minding your own business."

"And that's what you did, huh, James?"

"That's what I did, sir."

"And you don't remember breaking into that store?"

"I don't remember anything."

"All right, next case."

Skinner turned his head slowly, and his eyes met Stevie's squarely. Again, there was the same mute pleading in his eyes, and then he turned his head away and shuffled off the stage and down the steps into the darkness.

The cop's hand closed around Stevie's biceps. For an instant, he didn't know what was happening, and then he realized his case was the next one. He shook off the cop's hand, squared his shoulders, lifted his head, and began climbing the steps.

He felt taller all at once. He felt like an actor coming on after his cue. There was an aura of unreality about the stage and the darkened room beyond it, the bulls sitting in that room.

The Chief of Detectives was reading off the information about him, but he didn't hear it. He kept looking at the lights, which weren't really so bright, they didn't blind him at all. Didn't they have brighter lights? Couldn't they put more lights on him, so they could see him when he told his story?

He tried to make out the faces of the detectives, but he couldn't see them clearly, and he was aware of the Chief of Detectives' voice droning on and on, but he didn't hear what the man was saying, he heard only the hum of his voice. He glanced over his shoulder, trying to see how tall he was against the markers, and then he stood erect, his shoulders back, moving closer to the hanging microphone, wanting to be sure his voice was heard when he began speaking.

". . . no statement," the Chief of Detectives concluded. There was a long pause, and Stevie waited, holding his breath. "This your first offense, Steve?" the Chief of Detectives asked.

"Don't you know?" Stevie answered.

"I'm asking you."

"Yeah, it's my first offense."

"You want to tell us all about it?"

"There's nothing to tell. You know the whole story, anyway."

"Sure, but do you?"

"What are you talking about?"

"Tell us the story, Steve."

"Whatya makin' a big federal case out of a lousy stick-up for? Ain't you got nothing better to do with your time?"

"We've got plenty of time, Steve."

"Well, I'm in a hurry."

"You're not going anyplace, kid. Tell us about it."

"What's there to tell? There was a candy store stuck up, that's all."

"Did you stick it up?"

"That's for me to know and you to find out."

"We know you did."

"Then don't ask me stupid questions."

"Why'd you do it?"

"I ran out of butts."

"Come on, kid."

"I done it 'cause I wanted to."

"Why?"

"Look, you caught me cold, so let's get this over with, huh? Whatya wastin' time with me for?"

"We want to hear what you've got to say. Why'd you pick this particular candy store?"

"I just picked it. I put slips in a hat and picked this one out."

"You didn't really, did you, Steve?"

"No, I didn't really. I picked it 'cause there's an old crumb who runs it, and I figured it was a pushover."

"What time did you enter the store, Steve?"

"The old guy told you all this already, didn't he? Look, I know I'm up here so you can get a good look at me. All right, take your good look, and let's get it over with."

"What time, Steve?"

"I don't have to tell you nothing."

"Except that we know it already."

"Then why do you want to hear it again? Ten o'clock, all right? How does that fit?"

"A little early, isn't it?"

"How's eleven? Try that one for size."

"Let's make it twelve, and we'll be closer."

"Make it whatever you want to," Stevie said, pleased with the way he was handling this. They knew all about it, anyway, so he might as well have himself a ball, show them they couldn't shove him around.

"You went into the store at twelve, is that right?"

"If you say so, Chief."

"Did you have a gun?"

"No."

"What then?"

"Nothing."

"Nothing at all?"

"Just me, I scared him with a dirty look, that's all."

"You had a switch knife, didn't you?"

"You found one on me, so why ask?"

"Did you use the knife?"

"No."

"You didn't tell the old man to open the cash register or you'd cut him up? Isn't that what you said?"

"I didn't make a tape recording of what I said."

"But you did threaten him with the knife. You did force him to open the cash register, holding the knife on him."

"I suppose so."

"How much money did you get?"

"You've got the dough. Why don't you count it?"

"We already have. Twelve dollars, is that right?"

"I didn't get a chance to count it. The Law showed."

"When did the Law show?"

"When I was leaving. Ask the cop who pinched me. He knows when."

"Something happened before you left, though."

"Nothing happened. I cleaned out the register and then blew. Period."

"Your knife had blood on it."

"Yeah? I was cleaning chickens last night."

"You stabbed the owner of that store, didn't you?"

"Me? I never stabbed nobody in my whole life."

"Why'd you stab him?"

"I didn't."

"Where'd you stab him?"

"I didn't stab him."

"Did he start yelling?"

"I don't know what you're talking about."

"You stabbed him, Steve. We know you did."

"You're full of crap."

"Don't get smart, Steve."

"Ain't you had your look yet? What the hell more do you want?"

"We want you to tell us why you stabbed the owner of that store."

"And I told you I didn't stab him."

"He was taken to the hospital last night with six knife wounds in his chest and abdomen. Now how about that, Steve?"

"Save your questioning for the detective squadroom. I ain't saying another word."

"You had your money. Why'd you stab him?"

Stevie did not answer.

"Were you afraid?"

"Afraid of what?" Stevie answered defiantly.

"I don't know. Afraid he'd tell who held him up? Afraid he'd start yelling? What were you afraid of, kid?"

"I wasn't afraid of nothing. I told the old crumb to keep his mouth shut. He shoulda listened to me."

"He didn't keep his mouth shut?"

"Ask him."

"I'm asking you!"

"No, he didn't keep his mouth shut. He started yelling. Right after I'd cleaned out the drawer. The damn jerk, for a lousy twelve bucks he starts yelling."

"What'd you do?"

"I told him to shut up."

"And he didn't."

"No, he didn't. So I hit him, and he still kept yelling. So—so I gave him the knife."

"Six times?"

"I don't know how many times. I just—gave it to him. He shouldn't have yelled. You ask him if I did any harm to him before that. Go ahead, ask him. He'll tell you. I didn't even touch the crumb before he started yelling. Go to the hospital and ask him if I touched him. Go ahead, ask him."

"We can't, Steve."

"Wh . . ."

"He died this morning."

"He . . ." For a moment, Stevie could not think clearly. Died? Is that what he'd said? The room was curiously still now. It had been silently attentive before, but this was something else, something different, and the stillness suddenly chilled him, and he looked down at his shoes.

"I . . . I didn't mean him to pass away," he mumbled.

The police stenographer looked up. "To what?"

"To pass away," a uniformed cop repeated, whispering.

"What?" the stenographer asked again.

"He didn't mean him to pass away!" the cop shouted.

The cop's voice echoed in the silent room. The stenographer bent his head and began scribbling in his pad.

"Next case," the Chief of Detectives said.

Stevie walked off the stage, his mind curiously blank, his feet strangely leaden. He followed the cop to the door, and then walked with him to the elevator. They were both silent as the doors closed.

"You picked an important one for your first one," the cop said.

"He shouldn't have died on me," Stevie answered.

"You shouldn't have stabbed him," the cop said.

He tried to remember what Skinner had said to him before the line-up, but the noise of the elevator was loud in his ears, and he couldn't think clearly. He could only remember the word "neighbors" as the elevator dropped to the basement to join them.

Skin Flick

We'd *still* be shooting that damn movie if it hadn't been for Harry. And I want to tell you it was *me* who at the very beginning said Harry would be no good for the project, and don't forget it. That's because Harry is a dope. I am not talking about his acting ability. He probably was as talented in his own way as the rest of us put together. I am only talking about his capacity to understand a very good deal that could have made everybody extremely happy, if only some dope wouldn't fall in love with a dizzy broad the way Harry did. I will never forgive Harry. I don't know where he is right now, but someday I'm going to meet him someplace, I'm going to spot him coming down the street with his skinny face and his eyeglasses, and he'll probably have that dumb blonde on his arm, and I'm going to walk up to him and say, "Hello, stupid, you happy now? You happy you blew the whole thing?"

I don't want to hear anything about morality; there's no such thing as morality when you are making a pornographic movie. In fact, the only thing obscene was that Harry went off the deep end for that girl, and ruined my idea. Yes, it was my idea from the beginning, though I've been hearing around town that Ben says it was *his* idea. I don't like to hear that kind of talk. It breaks my heart to hear that kind of talk. I give credit where credit is due, and Ben was the one who thought of the empty loft, but that was *after* I got the idea of doing the movie. Anyway, it was that dumb bastard Harry who blew it all, so what difference does it make *whose* idea it was in the first place, even if it *was* Ben's? Which it wasn't.

And I admit that Solly was the one who found the girl, I'll even admit he did the preliminary talking, he's a very smooth talker, Solly, and a good dresser besides; I'll tell that to anyone who'll listen, you'll never hear me bad-mouthing a friend. But it was *me* who convinced the girl we could make her a star. Even Solly will admit it was me who finally sewed up the deal that day in the R&M Cafeteria when she was sitting there at the table nibbling on a jelly doughnut and driving us all crazy just from the way she licked powdered sugar from her lips. She was no beauty, but she had something, all right; she had *star* quality. Solly recognized her star quality while she was giving him a massage in that place on Eighth Avenue. Solly's got a good eye, no one can take that away from him.

It was raining the day she came in the R&M, and she was wearing this soaking wet black raincoat, and she apologized for being late, but she'd just come from dance class. She took off the coat, and what she was wearing underneath was this black leotard with a short leather skirt wrapped around it, and black boots, and right away I got an idea for a scene in the picture, but I didn't tell her about it just then because what we were there to do was sell her on becoming a porn queen. I did most of the talking; I'm the one who sold her. Ben was the one who explained the project to her, but I'm the one who finally nailed down the deal. In fact, it wasn't even Ben who told her what we planned to do. It was Solly. Yes, that's absolutely correct, what's right is right.

They had got to talking in the massage parlor, and she had apologized for not being so good at this line of work, but she was really an unemployed actress and had just taken the job to make ends meet. Solly had immediately told her we'd been looking for somebody exactly like her to play a role in a low-budget movie we were doing, and this had got her interested, and she'd agreed to talk it over with us the next day. And it was Solly who picked up the ball the minute she came to the table shaking rain out of her frizzy blonde hair and saying she was always starved after dance class, could she order something to eat, would that be all right? She ate like a friggin horse, that girl. I hope Harry, wherever he is, is spending a fortune on food bills. Solly explained that we were three movie buffs who'd managed to save a little money, not a lot, and who were now ready to take a chance on a lifelong dream, which was to produce a quality motion picture which, if everything went okay, would make us all millionaires, God willing. He went on to say that he himself had written a pretty good screenplay . . .

"It's a *great* screenplay," Ben said. "Don't knock it."

. . . and Ben would be cameraman on the picture, and I would be directing. We had none of us had too much experience, but we were sure we could make a movie that was a lot better than some of the junk being shown around these days, though plenty of *those* pictures, too, were making tons of money.

"Like I told you in the massage parlor," he said, "we've been searching for a girl about your age and build, who also has that nice quality of looking innocent and sophisticated at the same time together."

"Thanks," the girl said. She had listened to all this while first she demolished a big bowl of clam chowder, and then a plateful of pot roast, boiled potatoes, and stringbeans, with two buttered rolls. She thought it over now while she sipped at a glass of milk and nibbled at a sugar-covered jelly doughnut—Jesus, that doughnut. Then she said, "How big is the part, and how much are you paying?"

Now *that* was when Ben came in, I remember it distinctly, I always give credit where credit is due. It was Ben who put her on the defensive by telling her we naturally wanted somebody with acting experience, and preferably acting experience before a *camera* because after all we were going to be shooting a movie here and not doing some crumby little play downtown in some grubby little theatre. And I remember she got very offended when he asked her what her acting credits were. She told him she'd been doing plays even when she was a high-school freshman, and since her graduation four years ago, she'd done a lot of summer stock and could even show us some of the really very good reviews she'd got if we cared to see them. She'd never been before a camera except in home movies, but she was only twenty-two, and she figured she had plenty of time yet. Of course, things weren't going exactly her way just then, which is why she'd taken the job in the massage parlor, but a girl with her talent was sure she'd make it sooner or later, so what was the hurry? And besides, how big was the part, and how much were we ready to pay her?

Solly almost blew it right then and there; I think he was very premature in asking whether or not she had any objections to doing nude scenes. For a minute, I thought she was going to get up and walk right out, especially since by now she'd also finished the doughnut and the glass of milk. But she looked Solly straight in the eye, and she said in this very tiny sort of breathless voice she had, "What do you mean? Do you mean I'll have to take off my clothes in front of a camera and everything?" And that was where I stepped in, and saved the day. I figured there was no sense kidding this girl, she had to know sooner or later what the project was. If we lost her, we'd just have to look for someone else.

"Miss," I said, "this is a pornographic movie we have in mind here."

The girl blinked and said, "Could I have another doughnut and glass of milk, please?"

I sent Ben up to the counter, and while he was gone I patted her hand gently and told her I knew this must come as a terrific shock to her, but she shouldn't think for one minute that we were going to make a *dirty* movie, so-called. The sex scenes would be explicit, yes, but Solly had written a beautiful screenplay with plenty of socially-redeeming value, and the film we planned to make would be something that no one would be ashamed to take his wife or his sweetheart to, or maybe even both together, something in fact that might be beneficial to poor unfortunates who had sexual hang-ups as well. I told her that the film would be shot on a closed set, no exteriors, we would never even *consider* asking her to take off her clothes in public. There'd be only her on the set, and a few actors, and Ben cranking the camera, and Solly there to make any necessary script changes, and me, of course, directing. I told her I was a man of sensitivity who would most certainly be aware of her innermost feelings, and the feelings of any actor working with her, and besides I'd be the *first* to take offense at any line or gesture that seemed merely dirty or obscene without being also artistic and socially-redeeming. This was going to be a story of quiet beauty and delicacy, I told her, and she said, "Gee, I don't know, I've never fucked in front of a camera before."

Ben came back with the milk and the doughnut, and he

began talking about the kind of salary she could expect. He explained that some very fine dramatic actresses like Linda Lovelace and Tina Russell and Marilyn Chambers had got their start in pornographic movies of taste and distinction, but that their salaries were very low when they were just starting out—Georgina Spelvin, for example, had got only five hundred dollars for the extraordinarily sensitive work she did in *The Devil In Miss Jones*—but of course now that she was a star, now that they *all* were stars, they could call their own tunes and were even being sought after for work outside skin flicks. Considering the circumstances, and realizing that we were interested primarily in turning out a quality film, which would mean making sure that every inch of footage was in good taste and carefully shot, the most we could offer her was *double* what these other actresses had got. In short, we could offer what was a high salary for a beginning actress in a starring role in her very first big movie, and that was one thousand dollars from the start of principal photography to the day of completion.

"Gee, I don't know," she said.

"We'll pay you an advance of one hundred dollars on signing," Ben said.

"How long will it take to make this movie?" she asked.

"Twenty weeks," I said.

"Twenty weeks is a long time for only a thousand dollars," she said. "I make more than that in the massage parlor."

"You can't become a star in a massage parlor," Solly said.

"That's true," she said, "but . . ."

"I can understand what she means," I said. "We're offering her a thousand dollars for twenty weeks' work. That only comes to fifty dollars a week."

"That's right," she said.

"And suppose we run over?" I said.

"We won't run over," Ben said.

"How do you know we won't?"

"What do you mean 'run over'?" the girl asked. "What's 'run over'?"

"That means if it takes more time to shoot than we planned."

"More than twenty *weeks?*" she said. "This must be some long movie you've got in mind here."

"We want to do a quality job," I said.

"Well, I can tell you one thing," she said. "If it runs over twenty weeks, I want fifty a week for as long as it takes. That's *if* I decide to take the job, which I haven't decided I'll take it yet."

"Well, take your time," Ben said.

"Who's going to be in this picture with me?" she asked.

"We haven't found a leading man yet," I said.

"How much will you be paying him?"

"All we can afford is five hundred dollars."

"Mmm," she said. "So that's fifteen hundred for both of us, right?"

"That's right."

"And you guys expect to make millions on this picture, right?"

"Yes."

"Then I want a percentage," she said. "I want twenty-five percent of the profits."

"No," Ben said. "That's out of the question."

"Just a minute, Ben," I said.

"Out of the question," he said.

"And also I want script approval."

"No script approval," Solly said.

"Okay, I'll forget about script approval, but I still want twenty-five percent."

"Make it five," I said.

"Make it ten," she said.

"Boys?" I said.

Solly and Ben looked at each other.

"This is highway robbery," Ben said. "There must be a thousand young actresses in this city . . ."

"Ben," Solly said, "I want this girl for the part. She's perfect for the part."

"Do you know what ten percent of a million dollars is?" Ben asked.

"Yes, it's one hundred thousand dollars," Solly said, "and I'm willing to give her that if she turns out to be only *half* as good as I think she'll be."

"I think she'll be very good, too, Ben," I said.

"I was hoping for a redhead," Ben said.

"What do you say?"

"All right, all right," Ben said. "Give her the ten percent."

"Have we got a deal?" I asked her.

"We've got a deal," she said, and grinned.

Powdered sugar was clinging to her lips.

We had budgeted ourselves very carefully because it simply wouldn't have paid to undertake the project if it was going to come to too much of a weekly investment for the three of us individually. You have to remember that whereas this dream of ours had been taking shape over a long period of time, during which we'd had many meetings and discussions, we nevertheless knew very little about the movie business, and were a little bit afraid we wouldn't be able to make the thing work. Ben, for example, though he had naturally taken a lot of photographs in his lifetime, both still and motion picture, made his *real* living as an accountant, and naturally had a lot to learn. Solly worked as a short-order cook in a delicatessen downtown, and had written his beautiful screenplay at night and on Sundays. And I personally was a lingerie salesman for Benjamin Brothers Apparel, but this doesn't necessarily mean I did not have a feel for directing; I have always been very good with people, there are those who say I am maybe *too* sensitive when it comes to personal relationships.

What I'm trying to explain is that the project was a risky one for three amateurs, and we all knew it would require a great deal of concentration and energy to bring it off and make our dream come true. And also, it couldn't cost us too much because then the economics of it would have been self-defeating, if you know what I mean. We were paying the girl fifty dollars a week, and we were planning to pay her leading man twenty-five dollars a week, and also we had rented a big empty loft for *another* fifty dollars a week, which came to a bottom line cost of positively one hundred and twenty-five dollars a week, which was maybe not expensive for what we had in mind, but which was a considerable sum for us to be splitting three ways. If you figure it out, it came to almost forty-two dollars a week for each of us. And if the girl didn't work out, we would have lost our initial hundred-dollar advance, which was supposed to cover the first two weeks of shooting the scenes with her leading man.

The leading man we found was Harry.

Knowing what I now know, I wish we had never laid eyes on him. In fact, knowing what I now know, I wish Harry had got hit by a bus on the first day of shooting. Or even the second day. Or a falling safe from a high building. Or a catastrophe in the subway. Harry was a dope. He wasn't even good-looking, but that was okay because we didn't want her leading man to be too good-looking as that would run contrary to the intent of Solly's script when it got to the play-within-a-play sections which were actually the major sections of the movie. Harry was working daytimes as an insurance adjuster, and he was reluctant to accept our offer at first because he was very conscientious about his job, and he didn't want to get to work tired in the morning. I should tell you at this point, though I hold no hard feelings, that it was *Ben* who brought that dope Harry around. They had gone to high school together, and Ben remembered him from the locker room as somebody who was not too spectacularly built, which was also in keeping with the tone and the intent of Solly's beautiful screenplay.

Anyway, we told Harry that our shooting schedule, as far as it concerned him, would be from eight p.m. to midnight, and then he could go home and get a good night's rest before he went to his job at the insurance company. We told him that twenty-five dollars a week was really just a token payment, but the work was not exactly disagreeable, and besides we were willing to pay him five percent of the profits once the picture broke even and we were all on the way to becoming millionaires. We did this because we felt certain he would begin talking to the girl later on when they became acquainted, and we didn't want any jealousy on the set about who was getting a percentage and who wasn't. It was offering him the percentage that did the trick. Up to then, he was only mildly interested; we had shown him pictures of the girl—fully clothed, of course—which Ben had taken the minute we signed her, and though she was very nicely shaped, in fact very marvelously shaped, she wasn't too beautiful in the face, though she did have a nice innocent and sophisticated look about her. Harry wasn't too sure he wanted to make love to her in front of a camera. He said he had gone out with much prettier girls in his lifetime, which frankly I found hard to believe when you consider this was Harry the dope talking. But when we offered the five percent, he all at once decided that maybe it would be all right for him to lower his standards just this once, provided it really wouldn't take more of his time than from eight to midnight. We told him that as the shooting went on, he would be required to perform even less and less, and he agreed to work for us. So there we were. We had our script, we had our leading players, we had this big old loft to shoot the movie in, and we had our dream.

So we began.

It was very difficult to explain Solly's script, especially to a pair of dopes like Harry and the girl. The first thing she wanted to know was what the CAST OF CHARACTERS page meant. That particular page was at the very beginning of the script, and it looked like this:

```
CAST OF CHARACTERS
(In Order of Appearance)
THE GIRL
THE LEADING MAN
THE WRITER
THE CAMERAMAN
THE DIRECTOR
```

Solly explained to her that the movie utilized a play-within-a-play technique, which these days was very popular and chic, not to mention tasteful. He also explained that the movie was *about* a movie. That is to say, we were really making two movies here, one of them the movie we were making and the other one a movie about the movie we were making. The girl immediately complained that we hired her to make only *one* movie, and now we were telling her she had to act in *two* movies. It took us an hour and a half of valuable time to explain that it was really only *one* movie, and if she just trusted our taste and our judgment she would see that it worked as art and also as a delicate probing of the sexual impulses, dreams, and realizations of all human beings. She listened carefully to everything we said, and then she thought it over, and then she said, "Still, if it's *two* movies, I want a bigger percentage."

So we upped her percentage to fifteen points, and since Harry was standing there listening to all this, we were forced to raise *his* percentage to ten, which meant that together they were into the movie for twenty-five points. This didn't bother us. We just wanted to get the thing going. But now that the girl had fifteen percent of the picture, she began immediately behaving like a star. First she wanted to know what kind of camera Ben had there on the tripod.

"That is an eight-millimeter camera," Ben told her. "We will have the film blown up later. It's cheaper to do it this way than to shoot in thirty-five from the beginning. It's the stock that costs a lot of money, you see."

"What do you mean 'stock'?" she said.

"The raw stock. The film."

"Is this picture in color?" she said.

"Yes, of course," Ben said.

"Because I look very good in color," she said.

"Oh, yes, everything will be in color," he said. He turned to me, and said, "I'm ready to roll whenever you are."

"What about the lights?" the girl asked. "Are we just going to shoot with just the lights that are here?"

"I'm using very fast film," Ben said. "We don't need any special lighting. Also, it will make the picture look more natural this way."

"And where's my makeup man?" she said.

"We want you to look very natural," I said. "That was one of the things that first attracted us to you. The natural look you have."

"Well," she said, and thought this over.

Solly, who is normally a very patient man, said, "I don't want to butt in here on technical matters, but *time* is what costs money on a movie set. *Time* costs more money than film. And we have been here since eight o'clock tonight, and it is now almost ten, and we haven't shot a foot of film. If we're going to complete this thing in the time we have laid out for it, then if everybody is ready, I think we ought to start shooting the first scene."

"I was only worried about makeup," the girl said, "because I have a tiny little beauty spot on the underside of my left breast, and I wondered if you wanted to touch it up or anything."

"We'll see about that when we come to it," I said.

"Actually, the beauty spot will make you look even more natural," Solly said.

"We'll see when you take off your clothes," Ben said.

"Will I be taking off my clothes tonight?"

"Yes, in the first scene you take off your clothes," Solly said.

"Because I feel a little funny about taking off my clothes in a room full of men, in front of a camera."

"Well, there's only us," I said.

"Still."

"And remember that millions and *millions* of people will be seeing you naked when this picture is released. And we'll all make millions and millions of dollars," I added.

"Yes," she said, "but still."

"I wish we could begin," Solly said.

"Are you ready?" I asked her.

"I guess so," she said, "but if I seem a little embarrassed at first, I hope that'll be all right."

"That's perfect for the part," Solly said. "Don't worry about it."

"Am I supposed to wear just my own clothes?" the girl said.

"Yes, that's part of it too," I said. "We want this to be as natural as we can make it, without a lot of fancy costumes and such."

"I thought I'd have maybe a special wardrobe."

"Well," I said, "we've picked out some very beautiful and tasteful lingerie for you to wear later on in the picture, and also some attractive costumes with leather and buckles and such, that will set you off to fine advantage, but that's later. In the beginning scenes, in these opening scenes where you apply for a job in the film, we want you to look as natural as possible."

"If I'd known you wanted me to look so natural, I wouldn't have worn a bra," she said.

"No, the bra is good," I said. "For some strange reason, men enjoy seeing a girl in her underwear, the bra will be fine."

"Well, okay," she said. "But it isn't even my *best* bra."

"I'm sure it'll be fine," I said.

"Well, okay," she said.

"Are we ready to begin," I said. "Harry? Are you ready?"

"I'm ready," Harry said, "though if there's any sex stuff in these opening scenes, I don't know if I'm ready for *that*."

"Let me explain the scene to you, okay?" I said.

"I mean, a person can't just perform on *cue*, you know what I mean?" Harry said.

"Yes, I know just what you mean," the girl said, and smiled at him. "I'll tell you the truth, I'm very excited about this being the first day of shooting and all—the first *night* of shooting, I should say—but I'm not excited *that* way, I mean I'm not too terribly physically or sexually excited at this given moment. Are you?"

"No," he said, "I'm not excited at all. In fact, I'm not even excited about it being the first night of shooting. I had a terrible day today, this man came in with his car almost totalled, and he insisted . . ."

"Could we please begin?" Solly said. "Please?"

"People?" I said. "Are we ready?"

"Ready," Ben said.

"Ready," the girl said.

"Sure," Harry said, and shrugged.

I explained the first scene to them. In this scene, the girl is supposed to come up to the loft and audition for the three producers of the film, who are also serving respectively as script writer, cameraman, and director. They have arranged for the girl to meet her leading man, and in a tasteful and artistic setting, they ask that she take off her clothes so that they can judge whether or not she will be physically suited to the role.

"Well, I'm certainly *physically* suited," the girl said. "Otherwise you wouldn't have hired me, would you?"

"Yes," I explained. "Of *course* you are, but that's in real life, and this is in the movie. In the movie, the producers aren't sure yet, which is why they ask you to take off your clothes."

"Well, are these producers blind or something? I mean, anybody can *see* I'm physically suited, even with my clothes *on*."

"There's a reason for this," I said, "because for some strange reason, men like to see a girl taking off her clothes."

"You mean this is like a sort of strip tease, is that it?" she asked.

"Yes, sort of. But tasteful. We don't want to get into any sex scenes right off, you see."

"Thank God," she said. "I really don't think I'm up to anything like that tonight. Are you, Harry?"

"No," he said, "I'm definitely not."

"Okay then," I said, "what you do is come into the loft, and ask if this is where we're casting this movie, and we'll answer you but nobody will see us, the camera will just be on you. And we'll introduce you to Harry and then ask if you would mind taking off your clothes, and you should take them off slowly and shyly, and that'll be the scene. Later on, we may ask you to kiss Harry or something mild like that, neither of you will have to do anything you don't really *feel* like doing tonight. We'll just play it slow and easy, we want to do a sensitive job here, and your personal feelings are very much in our minds."

"Well, okay," the girl said.

"Is something wrong?" I said.

"Well, before I take off my clothes, I want you to know the contract is binding, no matter what. I'm getting fifty dollars a week, and fifteen percent of the profits, and that's that."

"Of course," I said. "That's our agreement."

"Okay," she said. "In which case, I want you to know I'm not a natural blonde."

"That's all right," I said. "Quiet on the set, please."

I won't bore you with all the details of that first night's shooting, or even of the progress we made during the next two weeks. I will say that Solly had been absolutely right about the girl. She had looked spectacular when she was wearing clothes, but she looked positively fantastically unbelievable when she took them off. Also, when she got over her shyness and embarrassment, she really did a good job with the sex scenes she performed on camera with Harry. I guess this was because Solly had written such a good script, spare and neat and what I guess you could call lean. He very much had in mind the feelings of the actors, and wanted each of the sex scenes to appear spontaneous, instead of like some of these scenes you see in cheap porn flicks, where you just *know* the actors are being told what to do each and every minute. Solly's script made it all seem very natural and very beautiful and also, I might say in compliment, very artistic; I always give credit where credit is due. For example, in the scenes we shot that first week, where the girl gets the part and then starts to become acquainted with the leading man—who was Harry the dope—Solly didn't do what a lot of script writers do, he didn't clutter up the page with a lot of unnecessary directions. A sample of his writing from one of the early scenes will explain to you what I mean.

```
34 THE LOFT—INT—NIGHT
The Girl is becoming acquainted with
the Leading Man.
They do sexual intercourse together.
```

During all of these scenes, Ben, Solly, and I were sort of what you might call off-stage actors, or, since this was a movie we were making, I guess you would have called us off-*camera* actors. That is to say, we were in the script even during those first two weeks of shooting, but all you did was hear our voices. And though you never actually *saw* any of us, you knew there was a director there, and a cameraman, and a writer, which was the beauty part of the script, the play-within-a-play aspect. It wasn't until *after* those two weeks of shooting that any of us would appear on camera as real live actors, which was what the script called for because, you see, there was supposed to be intensely personal human relationships developed between the girl and the people making the movie—the movie itself was supposed to become an artistic microcosm of life itself, if you know what I mean. In other words, the girl was supposed to perform with her leading man only during the early parts of the movie, and then become gradually involved with the people working with her, and do on camera with them what she had earlier been doing with him, but more. I know that sounds complicated, but it was in Solly's script, and when we explained it to the girl, she said, "I don't understand. Does this mean I have to do this with Solly in front of the camera?"

"Not Solly *himself,*" I said. "The writer of the movie."

"Solly *is* the writer of the movie," she said.

"In real *life,* he's the writer of the movie," I said. "But in the movie, he's only *pretending* to be the writer of the movie."

"And we're supposed to do it here? In the loft?"

"Yes. The loft is where we're shooting the movie, and what happens is that during the coffee break, The Girl gets involved with The Writer, and this leads to a beautiful sex experience for both of them."

"But Solly is *bald,*" she said.

"My dear," I said, "you'd be surprised how many bald men go to see pornographic movies. There are at least millions and millions of them."

"If we could afford an actor to play the part," Solly said, "we'd hire him in a minute. But that would only cut into our profits."

"I didn't mean to hurt your feelings, Solly," the girl said. "It's just I have never balled a bald man in my life."

"There is always a first time," Solly said.

This was at one a.m. in the morning at the start of the third week's shooting. Ben had told the girl he needed to reload the camera, and he was in the bathroom now, with the light out. We had sent Harry home at midnight. He had gone reluctantly, it seemed to me, but I didn't yet suspect anything was developing between him and the girl. All I knew was that he had done his job very realistically during those first two weeks, and we were ready to phase him out since his services were not too strenuously required during the remaining eighteen weeks of shooting. In fact, as I explained to the girl, she was supposed to become more and more involved with the people making the film, and less and less involved with her leading man, until the very end of the picture when she got married.

"Married?" she said. "To who?"

"To Harry. We have a nice little scene where you get married at the end. But that's after you have sort of experienced all different kinds of sexual experience and gratification with the various men working on this film, which experience provides the bedrock of a good marital relationship later on."

"You mean, sort of, I learn different things from them, and this prepares me for being like a good wife to Harry later on, is that it?"

"That's it *exactly*," I said.

"That's beautiful," she said, and she began to weep.

Ben came out of the bathroom, camera in hand. "All loaded," he said, "and ready to shoot." He looked at the girl. "Is something wrong?" he asked.

"Everything's fine," I said. "Solly, are you ready?"

"Ready," Solly said, and began taking off his clothes.

We worked very hard during those next few weeks, both on camera and off. Now that we were really *into* the movie, so to speak, the hours got longer; we would start work at eight and sometimes not finish till three or four in the morning. You have to remember that we were all holding daytime jobs, and I mention this only to explain our dedication to the project. And besides, this was still costing each of us close to forty-two dollars a week because, since we were gentlemen, we agreed to continue paying Harry his twenty-five a week even though his services would not be required on the picture again till we came to the very end of it. We explained to the girl that the end might be some time away, since whereas she was doing an excellent job and we were all very pleased with her (including *Ben,* who had preferred a redhead for the part), we were nonetheless not getting *exactly* the kind of professional footage we wanted, and this might require shooting a great many scenes over again, maybe even three and four times. So this would probably take us past the twenty weeks we were hoping for.

The girl said this was okay with her, she was as interested in doing as artistic a job as the rest of us, but it would help if she understood a lot of the words in the script, like sometimes Solly's descriptions were very artistic but a little difficult to understand. We asked her to point out a specific instance in the script, and she said, "Well, like this one."

```
174 THE LOFT—INT—NIGHT
The Girl is clad in leather straps.
She does fellatio on The Cameraman.
```

"I just don't know what he means by 'clad in leather straps,' " the girl said.

"We'll show you the costume when we get to it," I said.

"And also," she said, "it would help if I could see some of the scenes we already shot, so that I could know what I was doing right or doing wrong."

"That's very bad for an actress," I said. "It only makes her self-conscious. Just take our word that you look beautiful and entirely convincing. I think I can say, in fact, that even in those scenes where Solly or I were handling the camera while Ben was working with you, even *those* scenes came out beautiful."

"Even the close-ups?"

"The close-ups are particularly beautiful."

"Well, okay," she said. "But this scene we're supposed to shoot tonight, the one where I'm supposed to be between you and Solly?"

"Between The Director and The Writer, you mean."

"Yeah, you and Solly," she said. "I want you to know that I can't even draw a straight *line* with my left hand. So I don't know how I'm supposed to do this both together. I might get mixed up."

"Just do your best," I said. "Believe me, you're everything we hoped for. You're making our dream come true."

"Well, thanks," she said, and lowered her eyes. "And I want *you* fellows to know something, too. And that is that I think you really are trying hard here not to make a cheap or dirty picture. I think it's marvellous the way you pay so much attention to detail and want to get things absolutely right. I really do hope we make lots of money on it, but that's not the important thing. The important thing is that I got a chance to work with professional people who really *care*. That, to me, is very very important, and I just wanted to thank you."

And that was when Harry the dope stepped in and ruined the entire thing.

He called me at Benjamin Brothers Apparel, and left a message that I was to return his call right away. When I got back off the road, it must have been three or four o'clock in the afternoon. I called him up, and he said he wanted to meet me for a drink before we began shooting that night. I thought for a minute that maybe Ben had forgotten to send him his twenty-five dollar check, and I asked Harry if that was the problem, but he said, "No, no, I got the check, it's something else." So I agreed to meet him at a bar near the loft, though to tell the truth I wasn't too anxious to talk to him. We were supposed to shoot a very delicate scene that night in which The Director and The Girl experiment with a great many interesting and artistic approaches to exploring personalities through sexual experience, and I wanted to prepare myself for it by taking a little nap before I reported for work.

Harry was already sitting at a table when I came in. I walked over, pulled out a chair and sat down. He stared at me for a long time, the dope.

"I can guess what the problem is," I said. "You're wondering when you'll be back in the movie again. Well, I'm happy to tell you it's going along splendidly, and it'll seem like no time at all till we shoot that big wedding scene."

I smiled at him. He was still staring at me.

"That's not what I want to talk about," he said.

"What do you want to talk about?"

"There is no film in the camera," he said.

"What?"

"There has *never* been any film in the camera."

"That's ridiculous," I said. "Who told you that?"

"I found out for myself."

"How did you find out?" I said. "And besides, it's a lie."

"It's not a lie," Harry said. "Do you remember going out for hamburgers last night at two in the morning? Do you remember that?"

"I remember it."

"I sneaked into the loft."

"You *didn't* sneak into the loft. We locked the door behind us."

"I went up the fire escape and in through the window. There was no film in that camera."

"That's because we were finished for the night. Ben had already unloaded."

"You were not finished for the night. You came back to the loft at precisely three-ten a.m."

"At which time Ben probably *re*loaded the camera."

"There was no film any place in the loft. I looked all over the loft. There was no film. None. Now I understand why Ben always went into the bathroom to reload. You are *not* shooting a movie there," Harry said.

"Of *course* we're shooting a movie."

"You are paying a girl fifty dollars a week so that the three of you can indulge whatever bizarre sexual fantasies you have, sometimes seven and eight hours a night, every day of the week including Saturdays and Sundays."

"We are doing nothing of the sort."

"That's *just* what you're doing," Harry said. "You are treating that girl like a common streetwalker, except that you'd have to pay a streetwalker more than you're paying her. It's obscene," Harry said.

"Harry," I said, "don't be a dope."

"I am not a dope," he said, "I happen to be a very highly regarded insurance adjuster. And anyway, I wanted to see you today only to tell you it's finished."

"What's finished?"

"The picture's finished, the whole set-up is finished. I've already discussed it with her, and she's quitting. In fact, she's *already* quit."

"You've discussed it with the girl?"

"I've been seeing her regularly. I've been seeing her every day. She told me what was going on, and that was when I got suspicious and decided to check up."

"Harry," I said, "don't be a dope. If that's what you suspect . . . if what you suspect is that the three of us figured out a scheme to get a little sexual pleasure at a minimal weekly cost . . . if that's what you suspect, which is a lie, we'll be happy to cut you in on the deal, we'll put you back in the picture starting tonight. I'll ask Solly to rewrite the script so that there's a great deal of action between The Girl and The Leading Man, we'll do that right away, if that's what you suspect, though of course it's a lie."

"I love her," Harry said.

"You what?"

"I love her. I've asked her to marry me."

"Harry," I said, "that's in the *movie!*"

"It's in real life, too," he said. "She's going to marry me, we're leaving this city as soon as you and I are finished with our talk here. You just try to go anywhere near her, or telephone her, or *anything,* and I'll call the police. I'm sure what you did here was illegal. You signed a contract with her, and also with me, and we're supposed to get a percentage of the profits on this movie you were making without any goddamn *film* in the camera!"

"Harry," I said, "you can't fault us for a small oversight like forgetting to put film in the camera."

He hit me in the nose then, and broke it.

I will never forgive Harry. Never. I don't mean about the nose because to tell the truth my nose was never such a prize to begin with, and besides, they taped it up nice, and the bones knitted, though a little crooked. I am talking about the way he ruined our dream. Solly tells me the best laid plans, and all that, but it doesn't make me feel any better. And Ben has been going around town telling anybody who'll listen that the idea was his to begin with, which it wasn't, and anyway that's not the point. The point is he's killing any chance we might possibly have of finding ourselves *another* girl, and making *her* a star, too, when if only he'd shut up . . .

Ah, what the hell.

That's show biz.

The Prisoner

They were telling the same tired jokes in the squadroom when Randolph came in with his prisoner.

Outside the grilled windows, October lay like a copper coin, and the sun struck only glancing blows at the pavement. The season had changed, but the jokes had not, and the climate inside the squadroom was one of stale cigarette smoke and male perspiration. For a tired moment, Randolph had the feeling that the room was suspended in time, unchanging, unmoving and that he would see the same faces and hear the same jokes until he was an old, old man.

He had led the girl up the precinct steps, past the hanging green globes, past the desk in the entrance corridor, nodding perfunctorily at the desk sergeant. He had walked beneath the white sign with its black-lettered DETECTIVE DIVISION and its pointing hand, and then had climbed the steps to the second floor of the building, never once looking back at the girl, knowing that in her terror and uncertainty she was following him. When he reached the slatted rail divider, which separated the corridor from the detective squadroom, he heard Burroughs telling his old joke, and perhaps it was the joke which caused him to turn harshly to the girl.

"Sit down," he said. "On that bench!"

The girl winced at the sound of his voice. She was a thin girl wearing a straight skirt and a faded green cardigan. Her hair was a bleached blonde, the roots growing in brown. She had wide blue eyes, and they served as the focal point of an otherwise uninteresting face. She had slashed lipstick across her mouth in a wide, garish red smear. She flinched when Randolph spoke, and then she backed away from him and went to sit on the wooden bench in the corridor, opposite the men's room.

Randolph glanced at her briefly, the way he would look at a bulletin board notice about the Policeman's Ball. Then he pushed through the rail divider and walked directly to Burroughs' desk.

"Any calls?" he asked.

"Oh, hi, Frank," Burroughs said. "No calls. You're interrupting a joke."

"I'm sure it's hilarious."

"Well, I think it's pretty funny," Burroughs said defensively.

"I thought it was pretty funny, too," Randolph said, "for the first hundred times."

He stood over Burroughs' desk, a tall man with close-cropped brown hair and lustreless brown eyes. His nose had been broken once in a street fight, and together with the hard, unyielding line of his mouth, it gave his face an over-all look of meanness. He knew he was intimidating Burroughs, but he didn't much give a damn. He almost wished that Burroughs would really take offense and come out of the chair fighting. There was nothing he'd have liked better than to knock Burroughs on his ass.

"You don't like the jokes, you don't have to listen," Burroughs said, but his voice lacked conviction.

"Thank you. I won't."

From a typewriter at the next desk Dave Fields looked up. Fields was a big cop with shrewd blue eyes and a friendly smile. The smile belied the fact that he could be the toughest cop in the precinct when he wanted to.

"What's eating you, Frank?" he asked, smiling.

"Nothing. What's eating you?"

Fields continued smiling. "You looking for a fight?" he asked.

Randolph studied him. He had seen Fields in action, and he was not particularly anxious to provoke him. He wanted to smile back and say something like, "Ah, the hell with it. I'm just down in the dumps"—anything to let Fields know he had no real quarrel with him. But something else inside him took over, something that had not been a part of him long ago.

He held Fields' eyes with his own. "Any time you're ready for one," he said, and there was no smile on his mouth.

"He's got the crud," Fields said. "Every month or so, the bulls in this precinct get the crud. It's from dealing with criminal types."

He recognized Fields' maneuver and was grateful for it. Fields was smoothing it over. Fields didn't want trouble, and so he was joking his way out of it now, handling it as it should have been handled. But whereas he realized Fields was being the bigger of the two men, he was still immensely satisfied that he had not backed down. Yet his satisfaction rankled.

"I'll give you some advice," Fields said. "You want some advice, Frank? Free?"

"Go ahead," Randolph said.

"Don't let it get you. The trouble with being a cop in a precinct like this one is that you begin to imagine everybody in the world is crooked. That just ain't so."

"No, huh?"

"Believe me, Frank, it ain't."

"Thanks," Randolph said. "I've been a cop in this precinct for eight years now. I don't need advice on how to be a cop in this precinct."

"I'm not giving you that kind of advice. I'm telling you how to be a *man* when you leave this precinct."

For a moment, Randolph was silent. Then he said, "I haven't had any complaints."

"Frank," Fields said softly, "your best friends won't tell you."

"Then they're not my best . . ."

"All right, get in there!" a voice in the corridor shouted.

Randolph turned. He saw Boglio first, and then he saw the man with Boglio. The man was small and thin with a narrow moustache. He had brown eyes and lank brown hair, and he wet his moustache nervously with his tongue.

"Over there!" Boglio shouted. "Against the wall!"

"What've you got, Rudy?" Randolph asked.

"I got a punk," Boglio said. He turned to the man and bellowed, "You hear me? Get the hell over against that wall!"

"What'd he do?" Fields asked.

Boglio didn't answer. He shoved out at the man, slamming him against the wall alongside the filing cabinets. "What's your name?" he shouted.

"Arthur," the man said.

"Arthur *what?*"

"Arthur Semmers."

"You drunk, Semmers?"

"No."

"Are you high?"

"What?"

"Are you on junk?"

"What's—I don't understand what you mean."

"Narcotics. Answer me, Semmers."

"Narcotics? Me? No, I ain't never touched it, I swear."

"I'm gonna ask you some questions, Semmers," Boglio said. "You want to get this, Frank?"

"I've got a prisoner outside," Randolph said.

"The little girl on the bench?" Boglio asked. His eyes locked with Randolph's for a moment. "That can wait. This is business."

"Okay," Randolph said. He took a pad from his back pocket and sat in a straight-backed chair near where Semmers stood crouched against the wall.

"Name's Arthur Semmers," Boglio said. "You got that, Frank?"

"Spell it," Randolph said.

"S-E-M-M-E-R-S," Semmers said.

"How old are you, Semmers?" Boglio asked.

"Thirty-one."

"Born in this country?"

"Sure. Hey, what do you take me for, a greenhorn? Sure, I was born right here."

"Where do you live?"

"Eighteen-twelve South Fourth."

"You getting this, Frank?"

"I'm getting it," Randolph said.

"All right, Semmers, tell me about it."

"What do you want to know?"

"I want to know why you cut up that kid."

"I didn't cut up nobody."

"Semmers, let's get something straight. You're in a squad room now, you dig me? You ain't out in the street where we play the game by your rules. This is *my* ball park, Semmers. You don't play the game my way, and you're gonna wind up with the bat rammed down your throat."

"I still didn't cut up nobody."

"Okay, Semmers," Boglio said. "Let's start it this way. Were you on Ashley Avenue, or weren't you?"

"Sure, I was. There's a law against being on Ashley Avenue?"

"Were you in an alleyway near number four sixty-seven Ashley?"

"Yeah."

"Semmers, there was a sixteen-year-old kid in that alleyway, too. He was stabbed four times, and we already took him to the hospital, and that kid's liable to die. You know what homicide is, Semmers?"

"That's when somebody gets killed."

"You know what Homicide cops are like?"

"No. What?"

"You'd be laying on the floor almost dead by now if you was up at Homicide. Just thank God you're here, Semmers, and don't try my patience."

"I never seen no kid in the alley. I never cut up nobody."

Without warning, Boglio drew back his fist and smashed it into Semmers' face. Semmers lurched back against the wall, bounced off it like a handball, and then clasped his shattered lip with his hand.

"Why'd you—"

"Shut up!" Boglio yelled.

From where he sat, Randolph could see the blood spurting from Semmers' mouth. Dispassionately, he watched.

"Tell me about the kid," Boglio said.

"There ain't nothing to—"

Again, Boglio hit him, harder this time.

"Tell me about the kid," he repeated.

"I—"

The fist lashed out again. Randolph watched.

"You going to need me any more?" he asked Boglio.

"No," Boglio said, drawing back his fist.

From across the room, Fields said, "For Christ's sake, lay off, Rudy. You want to kill the poor bastard?"

"I don't like punks," Boglio said. He turned again to the bloody figure against the wall.

Randolph rose, ripped the pages of notes from the black book, and put them on Boglio's desk. He was going through the gate in the railing when Fields stopped him.

"How does it feel?" Fields asked.

"What do you mean?"

"Being an accomplice."

"I don't know what you're talking about," Randolph said.

"Don't you?"

"No."

"You beginning to think the way Boglio does? About punks, I mean?"

"My thoughts are my business, Dave," Randolph said. "Keep out of them."

"Boglio's thoughts are his business, too."

"He's questioning a punk who knifed somebody. What the hell do you want him to do?"

"He's questioning a human being who maybe did and maybe didn't knife somebody."

"What's the matter, Dave? You in love with this precinct?"

"I think it stinks," Fields said. "I think it's a big, stinking prison."

"All right. So do I."

"But for Christ's sake, Frank, learn who the prisoners are! Don't become—"

"I can take care of myself," Randolph said.

Fields sighed. "What are your plans for the little girl outside?"

"She's trash," Randolph said.

"So?"

"So what do you want? Go back to the D.D. report you were typing, Dave. I'll handle my own prisoners."

"Sure," Fields said, and turned and walked to his desk.

Randolph watched his retreating back. Casually, he lighted a cigarette and then walked out into the corridor. The girl looked up as he approached. Her eyes looked very blue in the dimness of the corridor. Very blue and very frightened.

"What's your name?" Randolph asked.

"Betty," the girl said.

"You're in trouble, Betty," Randolph said flatly.

"I . . . I know."

"How old are you, Betty?"

"Twenty-four."

"You look younger."

The girl hesitated. "That's . . . that's because I'm so skinny," she said.

"You're not that skinny," Randolph said harshly. "Don't play the poor little slum kid with me."

"I wasn't playing anything," Betty said. "I *am* skinny. I know I am. It's nothing to be ashamed of."

Her voice was very soft, the voice of a young girl, a frightened young girl. He looked at her, and he told himself, *She's a tramp*, and his mind clicked shut like a trap.

"Lots of girls are skinny," Betty said. "I know lots of girls who—"

"Let's lay off the skinny routine," Randolph said drily. "We already made that point." He paused. "You're twenty-four, huh?"

"Yes." She nodded and a quiet smile formed on her painted mouth. "How old are you?"

"I'm thirty-two," Randolph said before he could catch himself, and then he dropped his cigarette angrily to the floor and stepped on it. "You mind if I ask the questions?"

"I was only curious. You seem . . . never mind."

"What do I seem?"

"Nothing."

"All right, let's get down to business. How long have you been a hooker?"

The girl looked at him blankly. "What?"

"Don't you hear good?"

"Yes, but what does hooker mean?"

Randolph sighed heavily. "Honey," he said, "the sooner we drop the wide-eyed innocence, the better off we'll both be."

"But I don't—"

"A hooker is a prostitute!" Randolph said, his voice rising. "Now come off it!"

"Oh," the girl said.

"Oh," Randolph repeated sarcastically. "Now how long?"

"This . . . this was my first time."

"Sure."

"Really," she said eagerly. "I'd . . . I'd never gone out looking for . . . for men before. This was my first time."

"And you picked me, huh?" Randolph asked, unbelievingly. "Well, honey, you picked the wrong man for your first one."

"I didn't know you were a cop."

"Now you know."

"Yes. Now I know."

"And you also know you're in pretty big trouble."

"Yes," the girl said.

"Good," Randolph answered, grinning.

Actually, the girl wasn't in as much trouble as she imagined herself to be—and Randolph knew it. She had indeed stopped him on the street and asked, "Want some fun, mister?" and Randolph had immediately put the collar on her. But in the city for which Randolph worked, it would have been next to impossible to make a prostitution charge stick. Randolph conceivably had a Dis Cond case, but disorderly conduct was a dime-a-dozen misdemeanor and was hardly worth bothering with in a precinct where felonies ran wild. So Randolph knew all this, and he had known it when he collared the girl, and he sat now with a grin on his face and watched her, pleased by her troubled expression, pleased with the way her hands fluttered aimlessly in her lap.

"You can get out of it," he said softly.

"How?" the girl asked eagerly.

His voice dropped to a whisper. "If you know the right cop," he said.

The girl stared at him blankly for a moment. "I haven't any money," she said at last. "I . . . I wouldn't have done this if I had money."

"There are other ways," Randolph said.

"Oh." She stared at him and then nodded slightly. "I see."

"Well?"

"Yes," she said, still nodding. "All right. Whatever you say."

"Let's go," Randolph said.

He walked briskly to the railing and leaned on it. To no one in particular, he said, "I'll be back in an hour or so." Before he turned, he noticed the curiously sour expression on Dave Fields' face. Briskly, he walked to the girl. "Come on," he said.

They went down the steps to the ground floor. At the desk, a patrolman was booking a seventeen-year-old kid who was bleeding from a large cut behind his ear. The blood had trailed down his neck and stained his tee-shirt a bright red. The girl gasped when she saw the boy, and then turned quickly away, heading for the steps.

"If he's the one they're booking," Randolph said, "I hate to think what the other guy must look like."

The girl didn't answer. She began walking quickly, and Randolph fell in beside her. "Where to?" he asked.

"My place," she said. An undisguised coldness had crept into her voice.

"Don't take this so big," he said. "It's part of a working day."

"I didn't know that," the girl said.

"Well, now you do."

They walked in silence. Around them, the concrete fingers of the city poked at the October sky. The fingers were black with the soot of decades, grimy fingers covered with waste and not with the honest dirt of labor. The streets crawled with humanity. Old men and young men, kids playing stickball, kids chalking up the sidewalks, women with shopping bags, the honest citizens of the precinct—and the others. In the ten minutes it took them to walk from the precinct to the girl's apartment, Randolph saw fourteen junkies in the streets. Some of those junkies would be mugging before the day ended. Some would be shoplifting and committing burglaries. All would be blind by nightfall.

He saw the bright green and yellow silk jackets of a teenage gang known as "The Marauders," and he knew that the appearance of a blue and gold jacket in their territory would bring on a street bop and broken ribs and bloody heads.

He saw the hookers and the pimps and the sneak thieves and the muggers and the ex-cons and the kids holding J. D. cards and the drunks and the fences and the peddlers of hot goods—he saw them all, and they surrounded him with a feeling of filth, a feeling he wanted desperately to search out and crush because somewhere in the filth he had lost himself.

Somewhere, long ago, a young patrolman had cracked a liquor store holdup, and the patrolman had been promoted to Detective/Third Grade, and the patrolman's name was Frank Randolph. And somewhere back there, the patrolman Frank Randolph had ceased to exist, and the detective Frank Randolph had inhabited the shell of his body. The eyes had turned hard, and the fists had turned quick, and the step had turned cautious because there was danger in these streets, and the danger awakened every animal instinct within a man, reduced him to a beast stalking blood in the narrow, dark passages of the jungle. There was hatred within the muscular body of Frank Randolph, a hatred bred of dealing with tigers, a hatred which excluded the timid antelopes who also lived in the forest. And so he walked with a young, thin girl, walked toward her apartment where he would use his shield as a wedge to enter her bed and her body. He had begun using his shield a long time ago. He was as much an addict to his shield as the junkies in the streets were addicts to the white god.

The tenement stood in a row of somber-faced buildings, buildings that solemnly mourned the loss of their latter-day splendor. The fire escapes fronting each building were hung with the trappings of life: blankets, potted plants, pillows, empty beer cans, ash trays, guitars. Autumn had come late this year, lingering over the slow death of a hot summer, and the cliff dwellers had taken to their slum terraces, the iron-barred rectangles that gave them a piece of sky and a breath of air.

"This is it," she said.

He followed her up the stoop. A woman was sitting on the steps, knitting. She glanced up at him as he passed, sensing immediately, with the instinct of self-preservation, that he was a cop. He could almost feel her shrinking away from him, and his own instinct asked the question, "What's she done to be afraid of?"

Garbage cans were stacked in the hallway. The refuse had been collected earlier that day, but the cans were never washed and they filled the air with the stink of waste. There was a naked light bulb hanging in the entrance foyer, but it would not be turned on until dusk.

The girl climbed the steps ahead of him. He walked behind her; her legs were remarkably good for a girl so thin. They climbed steadily. There were voices behind the doors. He heard the voices in the medley of sound, and he reflected on the doors he had broken, a quick flatfooted kick against the lock to spring it, since he'd been a detective. Rarely had he knocked on a door. Rarely had he given the occupant a chance to unlatch it. The kick was quicker, and it precluded the possibility of a door being opened to reveal a hostile gun inside.

"It's on the third floor," the girl said.

"All right," he answered, and he kept following her, watching her legs.

"Be careful, there's a broken bottle."

He skirted the shards of brown glass, smelling the whiskey fumes as he passed the alcohol-soaked wood. The girl stopped at a door at the end of the hall. She unlocked it and waited for him to enter. When they were both inside, she put the police lock in place, leaning the heavy, unbending steel bar against the door, hooking it securely into the steel plate embedded in the floor, so that it formed a formidable triangle against which entrance was impossible.

The kitchen was small but clean. A round table sat in the center of the room, and a bowl was on the table. A single apple rested in the bowl. The girl went to the window and lifted the shade. Light, but not sunlight, entered the room. It was a pale light that bounced from the brick walls of the tenement not four feet away, leaping the airshaft between the buildings. The girl turned.

"I . . . I don't know what to do," she said. "I've never done this before."

"No?" he said, and there was a trace of sarcasm in his voice.

"No. Could . . . could we talk a little?"

"What about?"

"I don't know. Anything." The room grew silent. Patiently, Randolph waited.

"I'm . . . I'm sorry the place isn't nicer," the girl said.

"It'll do."

"I meant—" She shrugged.

"What?"

"I don't know. A girl likes to think—" She stopped, shrugging again. "Would you like a beer or something? I think we have some cold in the frigidaire."

"No, thanks," Randolph said. He grinned. "We're not allowed to drink on duty."

The girl missed his humor. She nodded and then sat opposite him at the table. Silence crowded the room again.

"Have you been a cop long?" the girl asked.

"Eight years."

"It must be terrible. I mean, being a cop in this neighborhood."

For a moment, Randolph was surprised. He looked at the girl curiously and said, "What do you mean?"

"All the . . . all the dirt here," she said.

"It . . ." He paused, studying her. "You get used to it."

"I'll never get used to it," she said.

She seemed about to cry. For a panicky instant, he wanted to bolt from the room. He sat undecided at the table, and then he heard himself saying, "This isn't so bad. This is a nice apartment."

"You don't really mean that," she said.

"No," he answered honestly. "I don't."

The girl seemed to want to tell him about the apartment. Words were perched on the edge of her tongue, torrents of words, it seemed, but when she spoke she only said, "I haven't got my own room."

"That's all right," he said. "We can use . . ." And then he stopped his tongue because he sensed the girl had meant something entirely different, and the sudden insight surprised him and frightened him a little.

"Where do you live?" she asked.

"In a hotel," he said.

"That must be nice."

He wanted to say, "No, it's very lonely." Instead, he said, "Yeah, it's all right."

"I've never been to a hotel. Do people wait on you?"

"This is an apartment hotel. It's a little different."

"Oh."

She sat at the table, and he watched her, and suddenly she was trembling.

"What's the matter?" he asked.

"I'm scared," she said.

"Why?"

"Because of . . . of what I almost did. What I almost became."

"What do you mean?"

"I'm glad you arrested me," she said. "I'm glad I got caught the first time. I don't want to be—"

She began crying. Randolph watched her, and he felt inordinately big, sitting across from her, awkwardly immense.

"Look," he said, "what do you want to bawl for?"

"I . . . I can't help it."

"Well, cut it out!" he said harshly.

"I'm sorry." She turned and took a dish towel from the sink, daubed at her eyes with it. "I'm sorry. Let's . . . let's do it."

"Is this really your first time?" he asked suspiciously.

"Yes."

"What made you . . . well . . . I don't understand."

"I got tired," she said. "I got so damned tired. I don't want to fight any more."

"Fight what?"

"Fight getting dirty. I'm tired of fighting." She sighed wearily and held out her hand. "Come," she said.

She stood stock-still, her hand extended, her shoulders back.

"Come," she repeated.

There was a strength in the rigidity of her body and the erectness of her head. In the narrow stillness of her thin body, there was a strength and he recognized the strength because he had once possessed it. He rose, puzzled, and he reached out for her hand, and he knew that if he took her hand, if he allowed this girl to lead him into the other room, he would destroy her as surely as he had once destroyed himself. He knew this, and somehow it was very important to him that she be saved, that somewhere in the prison of the precinct, somewhere in this giant, dim, dank prison there should be someone who was not a prisoner. And he knew with sudden painful clarity why there were potted plants on the barred fire escapes of the tenements.

He pulled back his hand.

"Keep it," he said harshly, swiftly.

"What?"

"Keep it," he said, and he knew she misunderstood what he was asking her to keep, but he did not explain. He turned and walked from the room, and down the steps past the stacked garbage cans in the hallway and then out into the street.

He walked briskly in the afternoon sunshine. He saw the pushers and the pimps and the prostitutes and the junkies and the fences and the drunks and the muggers.

And when he got back to the precinct, he nodded perfunctorily at the desk sergeant and then climbed the stairs to the Detective Division.

Dave Fields met him just inside the slatted rail divider. Their eyes met, locked.

"How'd you make out?" Fields asked.

Unwaveringly, unhesitatingly, Randolph replied, "Fine. The best I've ever had," and Fields turned away when he added, "Any coffee brewing in the Clerical Office?"

Every Morning

He sang softly to himself as he worked on the long white beach. He could see the pleasure craft scooting over the deep blue waters, could see the cottony clouds moving leisurely across the wide expanse of sky. There was a mild breeze in the air, and it touched the woolly skullcap that was his hair, caressed his brown skin. He worked with a long rake, pulling at the tangled sea vegetation that the norther had tossed onto the sand. The sun was strong, and the sound of the sea was good, and he was almost happy as he worked.

He watched the muscles ripple on his long brown arms as he pulled at the rake. She would not like it if the beach were dirty. She liked the beach to be sparkling white and clean . . . the way her skin was.

"Jonas!"

He heard the call, and turned toward the big house. He felt the same panic he'd felt a hundred times before. He could feel the trembling start in his hands, and he turned back to the rake, wanting to stall as long as he could, hoping she would not call again, but knowing she would.

"Jonas! Jo-naaaas!"

The call came from the second floor of the house, and he knew it came from her bedroom, and he knew she was just rising, and he knew exactly what would happen if he went up there. He hated what was about to happen, but at the same time it excited him. He clutched the rake more tightly, telling himself he would not answer her call, lying to himself because he knew he would go if she called one more time.

"Jonas! Where the devil are you?"

"Coming, Mrs. Hicks," he shouted.

He sighed deeply and put down the rake. He climbed the concrete steps leading from the beach, and then he walked past the barbecue pit and the beach house, moving under the Australian pines that lined the beach. The pine needles were soft under his feet, and though he knew the pines were planted to form a covering over the sand, to stop sand from being tracked into the house, he still enjoyed the soft feel under his shoes. For an instant, he wished he were barefoot, and then scolded himself for having a thought that was strictly "native."

He shook his head and climbed the steps to the screened back porch of the house. The hibiscus climbed the screen in a wild array of color, pinks and reds and purples. The smaller bougainvillea reached up for the sun where it splashed down through the pines. He closed the door behind him and walked through the dim cool interior of the house, starting up the steps to her bedroom.

When he reached her door, he paused outside, and then he knocked discreetly.

"Is that you, Jonas?"

"Yes, Mrs. Hicks."

"Well, come in."

He opened the door and stepped into the bedroom. She was

sitting in bed, the sheet reaching to her waist. Her long blonde hair spilled over her shoulders, trailing down her back. She wore a white nylon gown, and he could see the mounds of her breasts beneath the gown, could see the erect rosebuds of her nipples. Hastily, he lowered his eyes.

"Good morning, Jonas," she said.

"Good morning, Mrs. Hicks."

"My, it's a beautiful morning, isn't it?"

"Yes, Mrs. Hicks."

"Where were you when I called, Jonas?"

"On the beach, Mrs. Hicks."

"Swimming, Jonas?" She lifted one eyebrow archly, and a tiny smile curled her mouth.

"Oh, no, Mrs. Hicks. I was raking up the . . ."

"Haven't you ever felt like taking a swim at that beach, Jonas?"

He did not answer. He stared at his shoes, and he felt his hands clench at his sides.

"Jonas?"

"Yes, Mrs. Hicks?"

"Haven't you ever felt like taking a swim at that beach?"

"There's lots of public places to swim, Mrs. Hicks."

"Yes." The smile expanded. Her green eyes were smiling now, too. She sat in bed like a slender cat licking her chops. "That's what I like about Nassau. There are lots of places to swim." She continued smiling for a moment, and then she sat up straighter, as if she were ready for business now.

"Well," she said, "what shall we have for breakfast? Has the cook come in, Jonas?"

"Yes, Mrs. Hicks."

"Eggs, I think. Coddled. And some toast and marmalade.

And a little juice." He made a movement toward the door, and she stopped him with a wave of her hand. "Oh, there's no rush, Jonas. Stay. I want you to help me."

He swallowed, and he put his hands behind his back to hide the trembling. "Yes . . . Mrs. Hicks."

She threw back the sheet, and he saw her long legs beneath the hem of the short nightgown. She reached for her slippers on the floor near her bed, squirmed her feet into them, and then stood up. Luxuriantly, she stretched her arms over her head and yawned. The nightgown tightened across her chest, listing as she raised her arms, showing more of the long curve of her legs. She walked to the window and threw open the blinds, and the sun splashed through the gown, and he saw the full outline of her body, and he thought: *Every morning, every morning the same thing.*

He could feel the sweat beading his brow, and he wanted to get out of that room, wanted to get far away from her and her body, wanted to escape this labyrinth that led to one exit alone.

"Ahhhhhhhhh." She let out her breath and then walked across the room to her dressing table. She sat and crossed her legs. "Do you like working for me?" she asked.

"Yes, Mrs. Hicks," he said quickly.

"You don't really, though, do you?"

"I like it, Mrs. Hicks," he said.

"I like you to work for me, Jonas. I wouldn't have you leave for anything in the world. You know that, don't you, Jonas?"

"Yes, Mrs. Hicks."

There has to be a way out, he thought. *There has to be some way. A way other than the one . . . the one . . .*

"Have you ever thought of quitting this job, Jonas?"

"No, Mrs. Hicks," he lied.

"That's sensible, you know. Not quitting, I mean. It wouldn't be wise for you to quit, would it, Jonas? Aside from the salary, I mean, which is rather handsome, wouldn't you say, Jonas?"

"It's a handsome salary," he said.

"Yes. But aside from that, aside from losing the salary if you quit. I wouldn't like you to quit, Jonas. I would let Mr. Hicks know of my displeasure, and my husband is really quite a powerful man, you know that, don't you?"

"Yes, Mrs. Hicks."

"It might be difficult for you to get work afterwards, I mean if you ever decided to leave me. Heaven knows, there's not much work for Bahamians as it is. And Mr. Hicks is quite powerful, knowing the Governor and all, isn't that right, Jonas?"

When he did not answer, she giggled suddenly.

"Oh, we're being silly. You like the job, and I like you, so why should we talk of leaving?" She paused. "Has my husband gone to the club?"

"Yes, Mrs. Hicks."

"Good," she said. "Come do my hair, Jonas."

"I . . ."

"Come do my hair," she said slowly and firmly.

"Y . . . yes, Mrs. Hicks."

She held out the brush to him, and he took it and then placed himself behind her chair. He could see her face in the mirror of the dressing table, could see the clean sweep of her throat, and beneath that the first rise of her breasts where the neck of the gown ended. She tilted her head back and her eyes met his in the mirror.

"Stroke evenly now, Jonas. And gently. Remember. Gently."

He began stroking her hair. He watched her face as he stroked, not wanting to watch it, but knowing that he was inside the trap now, and knowing that he had to watch her face, had to watch her lips part as he stroked, had to watch the narrowing of those green eyes. Every morning, every morning, the same thing, every morning driving him out of his mind with her body and her glances, always daring him, always challenging him, and always reminding him that it could not be. He stroked, and her breath came faster in her throat, and he watched the animal pleasure on her face as the brush bristles searched her scalp.

And as he stroked, he thought again of the only way out, and he wondered if he had the courage to do it, wondered if he could ever muster the courage to stop all this, stop it finally and irrevocably. She counted softly as he stroked, and her voice was a whisper, and he continued to think of what he must do to end it, and he felt the great fear within him, but he knew he could not take much more of this, not every morning, and he knew he could not leave the job because she would make sure there would never be work for him again.

But even knowing all this, the way out was a drastic one, and he wondered what it would be like without her hair to brush every morning, without the sight of her body, without the soft caress of her voice.

Death, he thought.

Death.

"That's enough, Jonas," she said.

He handed her the brush. "I'll tell the cook to . . ."

"No, stay."

He looked at her curiously. She always dismissed him after the brushing. Her eyes always turned cold and forbidding then, as if she had had her day's sport and was then ready to end the farce . . . until the next morning.

"I think something bit me yesterday. An insect, I think," she said. "I wonder if you'd mind looking. You natives . . . what I mean, you'd probably be familiar with it."

She stood up and walked toward him, and then she began unbuttoning the yoke neck of her gown. He watched her in panic, not knowing whether to flee or stand, knowing only that he would have to carry out his plan after this, knowing that she would go further and further unless it were ended, and knowing that only he could end it, in the only possible way open for him.

He watched her take the hem of her gown in her fingers and pull it up over her waist. He saw the clean whiteness of her skin, and then she pulled the gown up over her back, turning, her breasts still covered, bending.

"In the center of my back, Jonas, do you see it?"

She came closer to him, and he was wet with perspiration now. He stared at her back, the fullness of her buttocks, the impression of her spine against her flesh.

"There's . . . there's nothing, Mrs. Hicks." he said. "Nothing."

She dropped the gown abruptly, and then turned to face him, the smile on her mouth again, the yoke of the gown open so that he could see her breasts plainly.

"Nothing?" she asked, smiling. "You saw nothing, Jonas?"

"Nothing, Mrs. Hicks," he said, and he turned and left her, still smiling, her hands on her hips.

He slit his wrists with a razor blade the next morning. He watched the blood stain the sand on the beach he'd always kept so clean, and he felt a strange inner peace possess him as the life drained out of him.

The native police did not ask many questions when they arrived, and Mrs. Hicks did not offer to show them her torn and shredded nightgown, or the purple bruises on her breasts and thighs.

She hired a new caretaker that afternoon.

One Down

She leaned back against the cushions of the bed, and there was that lazy, contented smile on her face as she took a drag on her cigarette. The smoke spiralled around her face, and she closed her eyes sleepily. I remembered how I had once liked that sleepy look of hers. I did not like it now.

"It's good when you're home, Ben," she said.

"Uh-huh," I murmured. I took a cigarette from the box on the night table, lighted it, and blew out a stream of smoke.

"Yes, yes, it's really good." She drew on her cigarette, and I watched the heave of her breasts, somehow no longer terribly interested.

"I hate your job," she said suddenly.

"Do you?"

"Yes," she said, pouting. "It's like a . . . a wall between us. When you're gone, I sit here and just curse your job and pray that you'll be home again soon. I hate it, Ben. I really do."

"Well," I said drily, "we have to eat, you know."

"Couldn't you get another job?" she asked. It was only about the hundredth time she'd asked that same question.

"I suppose," I said wearily.

"Then why don't you?" She sat up suddenly. "Why don't you, Ben?"

"I like traveling," I said. I was so tired of this, so damned tired of the same thing every time I was here. All I could think of now was what I had to do. I wanted to do it and get it over with.

She grinned coyly. "Do you miss me when you're on the road?"

"Sure," I said.

She cupped her hands behind my neck and trailed her lips across my jaw line. I felt nothing.

"Very much?"

She kissed my ear, shivered a little, and came closer to me.

"Yes, I miss you very much," I said.

She drew away from me suddenly. "Do you like the house, Ben? I did just what you said. I moved out of the apartment as soon as I got your letter. You should have told me sooner, Ben. I had no idea you didn't like the city."

"The neighbors were too snoopy," I said. "This is better. Out in the country like this."

"But it's so lonely. I've been here a week already, and I don't know a soul yet." She giggled. "There's hardly a soul *to* know."

"Good," I said.

"Good?" Her face grew puzzled. "What do you mean, Ben?"

"Adele," I told her, "you talk too much."

I pulled her face to mine and clamped my mouth onto hers, just to shut her up. She brought her arms up around my neck immediately, tightening them there, bringing her body close to mine. I tried to move her away from me gently, but my arms were full of her, and her lips were moist and eager. Her eyes closed tightly, and I sighed inwardly and listened to the lonely chirp of the crickets outside the window.

"Do you love me?" she asked later.

"Yes."

"Really, Ben? Really and truly?"

"Really and truly."

"How much do you love me?"

"A whole lot, Adele."

"But do you . . . where are you going, Ben?"

"Something I want to get from my jacket."

"Oh, all right." She stopped talking, thinking for a moment. "Ben, if you had to do it all over again, would you marry me? Would you still choose me as your wife?"

"Of course." I walked to the closet and opened the door. I knew just where I'd left it. In the righthand jacket pocket.

"What is it you're getting, Ben? A present?" She sat up against the pillows again. "Is it a present for me?"

"In a way," I said. I closed my fist around it and turned abruptly. Her eyes opened wide.

"Ben! A gun. What . . . what are you doing with a gun?"

I didn't answer. I grinned, and she saw something in my eyes, and her mouth went slack.

"Ben, no!" she said.

"Yes, Adele."

"Ben, I'm your wife. Ben, you're joking. Tell me you're joking."

"No, Adele, I'm quite serious."

She swung her legs over the side of the bed, the covers snatching at the thin material of her gown, pulling it over her thighs.

"Ben, why? Why are you . . . Ben, please. Please!"

She was cringing against the wall now, her eyes saucered with fear.

I raised the gun.

"Ben!"

I fired twice, and both bullets caught her over her heart.

I watched the blood appear on the front of her gown, like red mud slung at a clean, white wall. She toppled forward suddenly, her eyes blank. I put the gun away, dressed, and packed my suitcase.

It took me two days to get there. I opened the screen door and walked into the kitchen. There was the smell of meat and potatoes frying, a smell I had come to dislike intensely. The radio was blaring, the way it always was when I arrived. I grimaced.

"Anybody home?" I called.

"Ben?" Her voice was surprised, anxious. "Is that you, Ben?"

"Hello, Betty," I said tonelessly. She rushed to the front door and threw herself into my arms. Her hair was in curlers, and she smelled of frying fat.

"Ben, Ben darling, you're back. Oh Ben, how I missed you."

"Did you?"

"Ben, let me look at you." She held me away from her and then lifted her face and took my mouth hungrily. I could still smell the frying fat aroma.

I pushed her away from me gently. "Hey," I said, "cut it out. Way you're behaving, people would never guess we've been married for three years already."

She sighed deeply. "You know, Ben," she said, "I hate your job."

Kiss Me, Dudley

She was cleaning fish by the kitchen sink when I climbed through the window, my .45 in my hand. She wore a low-cut apron, shadowed near the frilly top. When she saw me, her eyes went wide, and her lips parted, moist and full. I walked to the sink, and I picked up the fish by the tail, and I batted her over the eye with it.

"Darling," she murmured.

I gave her another shot with the fish, this time right over her nose. She came into my arms, and there was ecstasy in her eyes, and her breath rushed against my throat. I shoved her away, and I swatted her full on the mouth. She shivered and came to me again. I held her close, and there was the odor of fish and seaweed about her. I inhaled deeply, savoring the taste. My father had been a sea captain.

"They're outside," I said, "all of them. And they're all after me. The whole stinking, dirty, rotten, crawling, filthy, obscene, disgusting mess of them. Me. Dudley Sledge. They've all got guns in their maggoty fists, and murder in their grimy eyes."

"They're rats," she said.

"And all because of you. They want me because I'm help-
ing you."

"There's the money, too," she reminded me.

"Money?" I asked. "You think money means anything to them?
You think they came all the way from Washington Heights for a
lousy ten million bucks? Don't make me laugh." I laughed.

"What are we going to do, Dudley?"

"Do? Do? I'm going to go out there and cut them down like
the unholy rats they are. When I get done, there'll be twenty-six
less rats in the world, and the streets will be a cleaner place for our
kids to play in."

"Oh, Dudley," she said.

"But first . . ."

The pulse in her throat began beating wildly. There was a
hungry animal look in her eyes. She sucked in a deep breath and
ran her hands over her hips, smoothing the apron. I went to her,
and I cupped her chin in the palm of my left hand.

"Baby," I said.

Then I drew back my right fist and hit her on the mouth. She
fell back against the sink, and I followed with a quick chop to the
gut, and a fast uppercut to the jaw. She went down on the floor
and she rolled around in the fish scales, and I thought of my sea
captain father, and my mother who was a nice little lass from New
England. And then I didn't think of anything but the blonde in my
arms, and the .45 in my fist, and the twenty-six men outside, and
the four shares of Consolidated I'd bought that afternoon, and the
bet I'd made on the fight with One-Lamp Louie, and the defective brake lining on my Olds, and the bottle of rye in the bottom
drawer of my file cabinet back at Dudley Sledge, Investigations.

I enjoyed it.

She had come to me less than a week ago.

Giselle, my pretty red-headed secretary, had swivelled into the office and said, "Dud, there's a woman to see you."

"Another one?" I asked.

"She looks distraught."

"Show her in."

She walked into the office then, and my whole life changed. I took one look at the blonde hair piled high on her head. My eyes dropped to the clean sweep of her throat, to the figure filling out the green silk dress. When she lifted her green eyes to meet mine, I almost drowned in their fathomless depths. I gripped the desk top and asked, "Yes?"

"Mr. Sledge?"

"Yes."

"My name is Melinda Jones," she said.

"Yes, Miss Jones."

"Oh, please call me Agnes."

"Agnes?"

"Yes. All my friends call me Agnes. I . . . I was hoping we could be friends."

"What's your problem, Agnes?" I asked.

"My husband."

"He's giving you trouble?"

"Well, yes, in a way."

"Stepping out on you?"

"Well, no."

"What then?"

"Well, he's dead."

I sighed in relief. "Good," I said. "What's the problem?"

"He left me ten million dollars. Some of his friends think the money belongs to them. It's not fair, really. Just because they were in on the bank job Percy . . ."

"Percy?"

"My husband. Percy *did* kill the bank guards, and it was he who crashed through the road block, injuring twelve policemen. The money *was* rightfully his."

"Of course," I said. "No doubt about it. And these scum want it?"

"Yes. Oh, Mr. Sledge, I need help so desperately. Please say you'll help me. Please, please. I beg you. I'll do anything, anything."

"Anything?"

Her eyes narrowed, and she wet her lips with a sharp, pink tongue. Her voice dropped to a husky whisper. "Anything," she said.

I belted her over the left eye.

That was the beginning, and now they were all outside, all twenty-six of them, waiting to close in, waiting to drop down like the venomous vultures they were. But they hadn't counted on the .45 in my fist, and they hadn't counted on the slow anger that had been building up inside me, boiling over like a black brew, filling my mind, filling my body, poisoning my liver and my bile, quickening my heart, putting a throb in my appendix, tightening the pectoral muscles on my chest, girding my loins. They hadn't counted on the kill lust that raged through my veins. They hadn't counted on the hammer that kept pounding one word over and over again in my skull: kill, kill, *kill!*

They were all outside waiting, and I had to get them. We were inside, and they knew it, so I did the only thing any sensible person would have done under the circumstances.

I set fire to the house.

I piled rags and empty crates and furniture and fish in the basement, and then I soaked them with gasoline. I touched a match, and the flames leaped up, lapping at the wooden cross-beams, eating away at the undersides of the first-floor boards.

Melinda was close to me. I cupped her chin in one hand, and then tapped her lightly with the .45, just bruising her. We listened to the flames crackling in the basement, and I whispered, "That fish smells good."

And then all hell broke loose, just the way I had planned it. They stormed the house, twenty-six strong. I threw open the front door and I stood there with the .45 in my mitt, and I shouted, "Come on, you rats. Come and get it!"

Three men appeared on the walk and I fired low, and I fired fast. The first man took two in the stomach, and he bent over and died. The second man took two in the stomach, and he bent over and died, too. I hit the third man in the chest, and I swore as he died peacefully.

"Agnes," I yelled, "there's a submachine gun in the closet. Get it! And bring the hand grenades and the mortar shells."

"Yes, Dud," she murmured.

I kept firing. Three down, four down, five down. I reloaded, and they kept coming up the walk and I kept cutting them down. And then Melinda came back with the ammunition. I gathered up a batch of hand grenades, stuck four of them in my mouth and pulled the pins. I grabbed two in each hand and lobbed them out on the walk and six more of the rats were blown to their reward.

I watched the bodies come down to the pavement, and I took a quick count of arms and legs. It had been seven of the rats.

"Seven and five is thirteen," I told Melinda. "That leaves eleven more."

Melinda did some quick arithmetic. "Twelve more," she said.

I cut loose with the sub-machine gun. Kill, *kill*, my brain screamed. I swung it back and forth over the lawn, and they dropped like flies. Fourteen, fifteen, sixteen. Nine more to go. Seventeen, eighteen, and they kept dying, and the blood ran red on the grass, and the flames licked at my back. They all ran for cover, and there was nothing to cut down, so I concentrated on a clump of weeds near the barn, shooting fast bursts into it. Pretty soon there was no more weeds, and the barn was a skeleton against the deepening dusk. I grabbed a mortar and tossed it into the yard, just for kicks. Pretty soon, there was no more barn.

Behind me, I heard Melinda scream. I whirled. Her clothes were aflame, and I seized her roughly and threw her to the floor. I almost lost my mind, and I almost forgot all about the nine guys still out there. I tore myself away from her, and I ran into the yard with two mortar shells in my mouth, the sub-machine gun in my right hand, and the .45 in my left. I shook my head, and the mortar shells flew, and three more of the rats were dead and gone. I fired a burst with the machine gun, and another two dropped. There were four or five left now, and I picked them off one by one with the .45. The yard ran red with blood, and the bodies lay like twisted sticks. I sighed heavily and walked back to the house— because the worst part still lay ahead of me.

I found her in the bedroom.

She had taken a quick sponge bath, and her body gleamed like dull ivory in the gathering darkness.

"All right, Agnes," I said. "It's all over."

"What do you mean, Dud?"

"The whole mess, Agnes. Everything, from start to finish. A big hoax. A big plot to sucker Dudley Sledge. Well, no one suckers Sledge. No one."

"I don't know what you mean, Dud."

"You don't know, huh? You don't know what I mean? I mean the phony story about the bank job, and the ten million dollars your husband left you."

"He did leave it to me, Dudley."

"No, Agnes. That was all a lie. Every bit of it. I'm only sorry I had to kill twenty-six bird-watchers before I realized the truth."

"You're wrong, Dudley," she said. "Dead wrong."

"No, baby. I'm right, and that's the pity of it because I love you, and I know what I have to do now."

"Dudley . . ." she started.

"No, Agnes. Don't try to sway me. I know you stole that ten million from the Washington Heights Bird Watchers Society. You invented that other story because you wanted someone with a gun, someone who would keep them away from you. Well, twenty-six people have paid . . . and now one more has to pay."

She clipped two earrings to her delicate ears, snapped a bracelet onto her wrist, dabbed some lipstick onto her wide mouth. She was fully dressed now, dressed the way she'd been the first time in my office, the first time I'd slugged her, the time I knew I was hopelessly in love with her.

She took a step toward me, and I raised the .45.

"Kiss me, Dudley," she said.

I kissed her, all right. I shot her right in the stomach.

She fell to the floor, a look of incredible ecstasy in her eyes, and when I turned around I realized she wasn't reaching for the mortar shell on the table behind me. Nor was she reaching for the submachine gun that rested in the corner near the table. She was reaching for the ten million bucks.

There were tears in my eyes. "I guess that's the least I can do for you, Agnes," I said. "It was what you wanted, even in death."

So I took the ten million bucks, and I bought a case of Irish whiskey.

Chinese Puzzle

The girl slumped at the desk just inside the entrance doorway of the small office. The phone lay uncradled, just the way she'd dropped it. An open pad of telephone numbers rested just beyond reach of her lifeless left hand.

The legend on the frosted glass door read *Gotham Lobster Company*. The same legend was repeated on the long row of windows facing Columbus Avenue, and the sun glared hotly through those windows, casting the name of the company onto the wooden floor in shadowed black.

Mr. Godrow, President of Gotham Lobster, stood before those windows now. He was a big man with rounded shoulders and a heavy paunch. He wore a gray linen jacket over his suit pants, and the pocket of the jacket was stitched with the word *Gotham*. He tried to keep his meaty hands from fluttering, but he wasn't good at pretending. The hands wandered restlessly, and then exploded in a gesture of impatience.

"Well, aren't you going to *do* something?" he demanded.

"We just got here, Mr. Godrow," I said. "Give us a little . . ."

"The police are supposed to be so good," he said petulantly.

"This girl drops dead in my office and all you do is stand around and look. Is this supposed to be a sightseeing tour?"

I didn't answer him. I looked at Donny, and Donny looked back at me, and then we turned our attention to the dead girl. Her left arm was stretched out across the top of the small desk, and her body was arched crookedly, with her head resting on the arm. Long black hair spilled over her face, but it could not hide the contorted, hideously locked grin on her mouth. She wore a tight silk dress, slit on either side in the Oriental fashion, buttoned to the throat. The dress had pulled back over a portion of her right thigh, revealing a roll-gartered stocking. The tight line of her panties was clearly visible through the thin silk of her dress. The dead girl was Chinese, but her lips and face were blue.

"Suppose you tell us what happened, Mr. Godrow," I said.

"Freddie can tell you," Godrow answered. "Freddie was sitting closer to her."

"Who's Freddie?"

"My boy," Godrow said.

"Your son?"

"No, I haven't any children. My boy. He works for me."

"Where is he now, sir?"

"I sent him down for some coffee. After I called you." Godrow paused, and then reluctantly said, "I didn't think you'd get here so quickly."

"Score one for the Police Department," Donny murmured.

"Well, you fill us in until he gets back, will you?" I said.

"All right," Godrow answered. He said everything grudgingly, as if he resented our presence in his office, as if this whole business of dead bodies lying around should never have been allowed to happen in his office. "What do you want to know?"

"What did the girl do here?" Donny asked.

"She made telephone calls."

"Is that all?"

"Yes. Freddie does that, too, but he also runs the addressing machine. Freddie . . ."

"Maybe you'd better explain your operation a little," I said.

"I sell lobsters," Godrow said.

"From this office?" Donny asked skeptically.

"We take the orders from this office." Godrow explained, warming up a little. It was amazing the way they always warmed up when they began discussing their work. "My plant is in Booth-bay Harbor, Maine."

"I see."

"We take the orders here, and then the lobsters are shipped down from Maine, alive of course."

"I like lobsters," Donny said. "Especially lobster tails."

"Those are not lobsters," Godrow said indignantly. "Those are crawfish. African rock lobster. There's a big difference."

"Who do you sell to, Mr. Godrow?" I asked.

"Restaurants. That's why Mary worked for me."

"Is that the girl's name? Mary?"

"Yes, Mary Chang. You see, we do a lot of business with Chinese restaurants. Lobster Cantonese, you know, like that. They buy the Jumbos usually, in half-barrel quantities for the most part. They're good steady customers."

"And Miss Chang called these Chinese restaurants, is that right?"

"Yes. I found it more effective that way. She spoke several Chinese dialects, and she inspired confidence, I suppose. At any rate, she got me more orders than any Occidental who ever held the job."

"And Freddie? What does he do?"

"He calls the American restaurants. We call them every morning. Not all of them each morning, of course, but those we feel are ready to reorder. We give them quotations, and we hope they'll place orders. We try to keep our quotes low. For example, our Jumbos today were going for . . ."

"How much did Miss Chang receive for her duties, Mr. Godrow?"

"She got a good salary."

"How much?"

"Why? What difference does it make?"

"It might be important, Mr. Godrow. How much?"

"A hundred and twenty-five a week, plus a dollar commission on each barrel order from a new customer." Godrow paused. "Those are good wages, Mr. . . ."

"Parker, Detective Ralph Parker."

"Those are good wages, Mr. Parker." He paused again. "Much more than my competitors are paying."

"I wouldn't know about that, Mr. Godrow, but I'll take your word for it. Now . . ."

A shadow fell across the floor, and Godrow looked up and said, "Ah, Freddie, it's about time."

I turned to the door, expecting to find a sixteen-year-old kid maybe. Freddie was not sixteen, nor was he twenty-six. He was closer to thirty-six, and he was a thin man with sparse hair and a narrow mouth. He wore a rumpled tweed suit and a stained knitted tie.

"This is my boy," Godrow said. "Freddie, this is Detective Parker and . . ."

"Katz," Donny said. "Donald Katz."

"How do you do?" Freddie said.

"Since you're here," I said, "suppose you tell us what happened this morning, Freddie."

"Mr. Godrow's coffee . . ." Freddie started apologetically.

"Yes, yes, my coffee," Godrow said. Freddie brought it to his desk, put it down, and then fished into his pocket for some silver which he deposited alongside the paper container. Godrow counted the change meticulously, and then took the lid from the container and dropped in one lump of sugar. He opened his top drawer and put the remaining lump of sugar into a small jar there.

"What happened this morning, Freddie?" I asked.

"Well, I got in at about nine, or a little before," he said.

"Were you here then, Mr. Godrow?"

"No. I didn't come in until nine-thirty or so."

"I see. Go on, Freddie."

"Mary . . . Miss Chang was here. I said good morning to her, and then we got down to work."

"I like my people to start work right away," Godrow said. "No nonsense."

"Was Miss Chang all right when you came in, Freddie?"

"Yes. Well, that is . . . she was complaining of a stiff neck, and she seemed to be very jumpy, but she started making her phone calls, so I guess she was all right."

"Was she drinking anything?"

"Sir?"

"Was she drinking anything?"

"No, sir."

"Did she drink anything all the while you were here?"

"No, sir. I didn't see her, at least."

"I see." I looked around the office and said, "Three phones here, is that right?"

"Yes," Godrow answered. "One extension for each of us. You

know how they work. You push a button on the face of the instrument, and that's the line you're on. We can all talk simultaneously that way, on different lines."

"I know how it works," I said. "What happened then, Freddie?"

"We kept calling, that's all. Mr. Godrow came in about nine-thirty, like he said, and we kept on calling while he changed to his office jacket."

"I like to wear this jacket in the office," Godrow explained. "Makes me feel as if I'm ready for the day's work, you know."

"Also saves wear and tear on your suit jacket," Donny said.

Godrow seemed about to say something, but I beat him to the punch. "Did you notice anything unusual about Miss Chang's behavior, Mr. Godrow?"

"Well, yes, as a matter of fact. As Freddie told you, she was quite jumpy. I dropped a book at one point, and she almost leaped out of her chair."

"Did *you* see her drink anything?"

"No."

"All right, Freddie, what happened after Mr. Godrow came in?"

"Well, Mary started making another phone call. This was at about nine-thirty-five. She was behaving very peculiarly by this time. She was twitching and well . . . she was having . . . well, like spasms. I asked her if she was all right, and she flinched when I spoke, and then she went right on with her call. I remember the time because I started a call at about the same time. You see, we have to get our orders in the morning if Boothbay is to deliver the next morning. That means we're racing against the clock, sort of, so you learn to keep your eyes on it. Well, I picked up my phone and started dialing, and then Mary started talking Chinese to someone on her phone. She sits at the desk right next to mine, you see, and I hear everything she says."

"Do you know who she was calling?"

"No. She always dials . . . dialed . . . the numbers and then started talking right off in Chinese. She called all the Chinese restau . . ."

"Yes, I know. Go on."

"Well, she was talking on her phone, and I was talking on mine, and all of a sudden she said in English, 'No, why?' "

"She said this in English?"

"Yes."

"Did you hear this, Mr. Godrow?"

"No. My desk is rather far away, over here near the windows. But I heard what she said next. I couldn't miss hearing that. She yelled it out loud."

"What was that, sir?"

"She said 'Kill me? No! No!' "

"What happened then?"

"Well," Freddie said, "I was still on the phone. I looked up, and I didn't know *what* was going on. Mary started to shove her chair back, and then she began . . . shaking all over . . . like . . . like . . ."

"The girl had a convulsion," Godrow put in. "If I'd known she was predisposed toward . . ."

"Did she pass out?"

"Yes," Freddie said.

"What did you do then?"

"I didn't know what to do."

"Why didn't you call a doctor?"

"Well, we did, after the second convulsion."

"When was that?"

"About . . . oh I don't know . . . ten, fifteen minutes later. I really don't know."

"And when the doctor came, what did he say?"

"Well, he didn't come," Freddie said apologetically.

"Why not? I thought you called him."

"The girl died after the second convulsion," Godrow said. "Good Lord, man, she turned blue! Why should I pay a doctor for a visit when the girl was dead? I cancelled the call."

"I see."

"It's obvious she was predisposed toward convulsions, and whoever spoke to her on the phone frightened her, bringing one on," Godrow said. "He obviously told her he was going to kill her or something."

"This is all very obvious, is it, Mr. Godrow?" I asked.

"Well, of course. You can see the girl is blue. What else . . ."

"Lots of things," I said. "Lots of things could have caused her coloration. But only one thing would put that grin on her face."

"What's that?" Godrow asked.

"Strychnine poisoning," I said.

When we got back to the squadroom, I put a call through to Mike Reilly. The coroner had already confirmed my suspicions, but I wanted the official autopsy report on it. Mike picked up the phone on the third ring and said, "Reilly here."

"This is Ralph," I said. "What've you got on the Chinese girl?"

"Oh. Like you figured, Ralph. It's strychnine, all right."

"No question?"

"None at all. She sure took enough of the stuff. Any witnesses around when she went under?"

"Yes, two."

"She complain of a stiff neck, twitching, spasms?"

"Yes."

"Convulsions?"

"Yes."

"Sure, that's all strychnine. Yeah, Ralph. And her jaws locked the way they were, that grin. And the cyanotic coloring of lips and face. Oh, no question. Hell, I could have diagnosed this without making a test."

"What else did you find, Mike?"

"She didn't have a very big breakfast, Ralph. Coffee and an English muffin."

"Have any idea when she got the strychnine?"

"Hard to say. Around breakfast, I suppose. You're gonna have a tough nut with strychnine, Ralph."

"How so?"

"Tracing it, I mean. Hell, Ralph, they sell it by the can. For getting rid of animal pests."

"Yeah. Well, thanks, Mike."

"No trouble at all. Drop in anytime."

He hung up, and I turned to Donny who had already started on a cup of coffee.

"Strychnine, all right."

"What'd you expect?" he said. "Malted milk?"

"So where now?"

"Got a check on the contents of the girl's purse from the lab. Nothing important. Lipstick. Some change. Five-dollar bill, and three singles. Theatre stubs."

"For where?"

"Chinese theatre in Chinatown."

"Anything else?"

"Letter to a sister in Hong Kong."

"In Chinese?"

"Yes."

"And?"

"That's it. Oh yes, a program card. She was a transfer student at Columbia. Went there nights."

"So what do you figure, Donny?"

"I figure some bastard slipped the strychnine to her this morning before she came to work. Maybe a lover, how do I know? She called him later to say hello. She talks Chinese on the phone, so who can tell whether she's calling a restaurant or her uncle in Singapore? The guy all at once says, 'You know why you're feeling so punk, honey?' So she *is* feeling punk. She's got a stiff neck, and her reflexes are hypersensitive, and she's beginning to shake a little. She forgets she's supposed to be talking to a Chinese restaurant owner. She drops the pose for a minute and says 'No, why?' in English. The boyfriend on the other end says, 'Here's why, honey. I gave you a dose of strychnine when I saw you this morning. It's going to kill you in about zero minutes flat.' The kid jumps up and screams 'Kill me? No! No!' Curtain. The poison's already hit her."

"Sounds good," I said. "Except for one thing?"

"Yeah?"

"Would the poisoner take a chance like that? Tipping her off on the phone?"

"Why not? He probably knew how long it would take for the poison to kill her."

"But why would she call him?"

"Assuming it was him. How do I know? Maybe she didn't call anybody special. Maybe the joker works at one of the Chinese restaurants she always called. Maybe she met him every morning for chop suey, and then he went his way and she went hers. Or maybe she called . . . Ralph, she could have called anyone."

"No. Someone who spoke Chinese. She spoke Chinese to the party in the beginning."

"Lots of Chinese in this city, Ralph."

"Why don't we start with the restaurants? This book was open on her desk. Two pages showing. She could have been talking to someone at any one of the restaurants listed on those pages—assuming she opened the book to refer to a number. If she called a sweetheart, we're up the creek."

"Not necessarily," Donny said. "It'll just take longer, that's all."

There were a lot of Chinese restaurants listed on those two pages. They were not listed in any geographical order. Apparently, Mary Chang knew the best times to call each of the owners, and she'd listed the restaurant numbers in a system all her own. So where the first number on the list was in Chinatown, the second was up on Fordham Road in the Bronx. We had a typist rearrange the list according to location, and then we asked the skipper for two extra men to help with the legwork. He gave us Belloni and Hicks, yanking them off a case that was ready for the D.A. anyway. Since they were our guests, so to speak, we gave them the easy half of the list, the portion in Chinatown where all the restaurants were clustered together and there wouldn't be as much hoofing to do. Donny and I took the half that covered Upper Manhattan and the Bronx.

A Chinese restaurant in the early afternoon is something like a bar at that time. There are few diners. Everyone looks bleary-eyed. The dim lights somehow clash with the bright sunshine outside. It's like stepping out of reality into something unreal and vague. Besides, a lot of the doors were locked solid, and when a man can't speak English it's a little difficult to make him understand what a police shield means.

It took a lot of time. We pounded on the door first, and then we talked to whoever's face appeared behind the plate glass. We showed shields, we gestured, we waited for someone who spoke English. When the doors opened, we told them who we were and what we wanted. There was distrust, a natural distrust of cops, and another natural distrust of Westerners.

"Did Gotham Lobster call you this morning?"

"No."

"When did Gotham call you?"

"Yes'day. We take one ba'l. One ba'l small."

"Who did you speak to at Gotham?"

"Ma'y Chang."

And on to the next place, and the same round of questions, and always no luck, always no call from Gotham or Mary Chang. And then we hit a place on the Grand Concourse where the waiter opened the door promptly. We told him what we wanted, and he hurried off to the back of the restaurant while we waited by the cash register. A young Chinese in an immaculate blue suit came out to us in about five minutes. He smiled and shook hands and then said, "I'm David Loo. My father owns the restaurant. May I help you?"

He was a good-looking boy of about twenty, I would say. He spoke English without a trace of singsong. He was wearing a white button-down shirt with a blue-and-silver striped silk tie. A small Drama Masks tie-clasp held the tie to the shirt.

"I'm Detective Parker, and this is my partner, Detective Katz. Do you know Mary Chang?"

"Chang? Mary Chang? Why, no, I . . . oh, do you mean the girl who calls from Gotham Lobster?"

"Yes, that's her. Do you know her?"

"Oh yes, certainly."

"When did you see her last?"

"See her?" David Loo smiled. "I'm afraid I've never seen her.

I spoke to her on the phone occasionally, but that was the extent of our relationship."

"I see. When did you speak to her last?"

"This morning."

"What time was this?"

"Oh, I don't know. Early this morning."

"Can you try to pinpoint the time?"

David Loo shrugged. "Nine, nine-fifteen, nine-thirty. I really don't know." He paused. "Has Miss Chang done something?"

"Can you give us a closer time than that, Mr. Loo? Mary Chang was poisoned this morning, and it might be . . ."

"Poisoned? My God!"

"Yes. So you see, any help you can give us would be appreciated."

"Yes, yes, I can understand that. Well, let me see. I came to the restaurant at about . . . nine-ten it was, I suppose. So she couldn't have called at nine, could she?" David Loo smiled graciously, as if he were immensely enjoying this game of murder. "I had some coffee, and I listened to the radio back in the kitchen, and . . ." Loo snapped his fingers. "Of course," he said. "She called right after that."

"Right after what?"

"Well, I listen to music a lot, and WNEW is a good station for music."

"Go on."

"Well, they have a newsbreak every hour on the half-hour. I remember the news coming on at nine-thirty, and then as the newscaster signed off, the phone rang. That must have been at nine-thirty-five. The news takes five minutes, you see. As a matter of fact, I always resent that intrusion on the music. If a person likes music, it seems unfair . . ."

"And the phone rang at nine-thirty-five, is that right?"

"Yes, sir, I'm positive."

"Who answered the phone?"

"I did. I'd finished my coffee."

"Was it Mary Chang calling?"

"Yes."

"What did she say?"

"She said, 'Gotham Lobster, good morning.' I said good morning back to her—she's always very pleasant on the phone—and . . ."

"Wasn't she pleasant *off* the phone?"

"Well, I wouldn't know. I only spoke to her on the phone."

"Go on."

"She gave me a quotation then and asked if I'd like some nice lobster."

"Was this in Chinese?"

"Yes. I don't know why she spoke Chinese. Perhaps she thought I was the chef."

"What did you do then?"

"I asked her to hold on, and then I went to find the chef. I asked the chef if he needed any lobster, and he said we should take a half-barrel. So I went back to the phone. But Miss Chang was gone by that time." Loo shrugged. "We had to order our lobsters from another outfit. Shame, too, because Gotham has some good stuff."

"Did you speak to her in English at all?"

"No. All Chinese."

"I see. Is that customary? I mean, do you usually check with the chef after she gives her quotation?"

"Yes, of course. The chef is the only one who'd know. Sometimes, of course, the chef himself answers the phone. But if he doesn't, we always leave the phone to check with him."

"And you didn't speak to her in English at all?"

"No, sir."

"And you didn't know her, other than through these phone conversations?"

"No, sir."

"Ever have breakfast with her?" Donny asked.

"Sir?"

"Did you ever . . ."

"No, of course not. I told you I didn't know her personally."

"All right, Mr. Loo, thank you very much. We may be back."

"Please feel free to return," he said a little coldly.

We left the restaurant, and outside Donny said, "So?"

"So now we know who she was speaking to. What do you think of him?"

"Educated guy. Could conceivably run in the same circles as a Columbia student. And if he *did* poison her this morning and then tell her about it on the phone, it's a cinch he'd lie his god-damn head off."

"Sure. Let's check Miss Chang's residence. Someone there might know whether or not Loo knew her better than he says he did."

Mary Chang, when she was alive, lived at International House near the Columbia campus, on Riverside Drive. Her room-mate was a girl named Frieda who was a transfer student from Vienna. The girl was shocked to learn of Miss Chang's death. She actually wept for several moments, and then she pulled herself together when we started questioning her.

"Did she have any boyfriends?"

"Yes. A few."

"Do you know any of their names?"

"I know *all* of their names. She always talked about them."

"Would you let us have them, please?"

Frieda reeled off a list of names, and Donny and I listened. Then Donny asked, "A David Loo? Did he ever come around?"

"No, I don't think so. She never mentioned a David Loo."

"Never talked about him at all?"

"No."

"That list you gave us—all Chinese names. Did she ever date any American boys?"

"No. Mary was funny that way. She didn't like to go out with Americans. I mean, she liked the country and all, but I guess she figured there was no future in dating Occidentals." Frieda paused. "She was a pretty girl, Mary, and a very happy one, always laughing, always full of life. A lot of American boys figured her for . . . an easy mark, I suppose. She . . . sensed this. She wouldn't date any of them."

"Did they ask her?"

"Oh, yes, all the time. She was always very angry when an American asked her for a date. It was sort of an insult to her. She . . . she knew what they wanted."

"Where'd she eat breakfast?"

"Breakfast?"

"Yes. Where'd she eat? Who'd she eat with?"

"I don't know. I don't remember ever seeing her eat breakfast."

"She didn't eat breakfast?"

"I don't think so. We always left here together in the morning. I have a job, too, you see. I work at Lord and Taylor's. I'm . . ."

"Yes, you left here together?"

"To take the subway. She never stopped to eat."

"Coffee?" I asked. "An English muffin? Something?"

"No, not when I was with her."

"I see. What subway did you take?"

"The Broadway line."

"Where did she get off?"

"At 72nd Street."

"What time did she get off the subway usually?"

"At about nine, or maybe a few minutes before. Yes, just about nine."

"But she didn't stop for breakfast."

"No. Mary was very slim, very well-built. I don't think she ate breakfast in the morning."

"She ate breakfast *this* morning," I said. "Thank you, Miss. Come on, Donny."

There was an Automat on West 72nd Street, a few doors from Broadway. Mary Chang wouldn't have gone to the Automat because Mary Chang had to be at work at nine, and she got off the train at nine. We walked down the street, all the way up to the building that housed the offices of Gotham Lobster, close to Columbus Avenue. There was a luncheonette on the ground floor of that building. Donny and I went inside and took seats at the counter, and then we ordered coffee.

When our coffee came, we showed the counter man our buzzers. He got scared all at once.

"Just a few questions," we told him.

"Sure, sure," he said. He gulped. "I don't know why . . ."

"You know any of the people who work in this building?"

"Sure, most of 'em. But . . ."

"Did you know Mary Chang?"

He seemed immensely relieved. "Oh, her. There's some trouble with her, ain't there? She got shot, or stabbed, or something, didn't she?"

"Did you know her?"

"I seen her around, yeah. Quite a piece, you know? With them tight silk dresses, slit up there on the side." He smiled. "You ever seen her? Man, I go for them Chinese broads."

"Did she ever eat here?"

"No."

"Breakfast?"

"No."

"She never stopped here in the morning for coffee?"

"No, why should she do that?"

"I don't know. You tell me."

"Well, what I mean, he always comes down for the coffee, you know."

I felt Donny tense beside me.

"Who?" I asked. "Who came down for the coffee?"

"Why, Freddie. From the lobster joint. Every morning like clockwork, before he went upstairs. Two coffees, one heavy on the sugar. That Chinese broad liked it sweet. Also a jelly doughnut and a toasted English. Sure, every morning."

"You're sure about this?"

"Oh yes, sure. The boss didn't know nothing about it, you know. Mr. Godrow. He don't go for that junk. They always had their coffee before he come in in the morning."

"Thanks," I said. "Did Freddie come down for the coffee this morning?"

"Sure, every morning."

We left the luncheonette and went upstairs. Freddie was working the addressing machine when we came in. The machine made a hell of a clatter as the metal address plates fed through it.

We said hello to Mr. Godrow and then walked right to the machine. Freddie fed postcards and the address plates banged onto the cards and then dropped into the tray below.

"We've got an idea, Freddie," I said.

He didn't look up. He kept feeding postcards into the machine. The cards read MAINE LIVE LOBSTERS AT FANTASTIC PRICES!

"We figure a guy who kept asking Mary Chang out, Freddie. A guy who constantly got refused."

Freddie said nothing.

"You ever ask her out, Freddie?"

"Yes," he said under the roar of the machine.

"We figure she drove the guy nuts, sitting there in her tight dresses, drinking coffee with him, being friendly, but never anything more, never what he wanted. We figured he got sore at all the Chinese boys who could date her just because they were Chinese. We figure he decided to do something about it. Want to hear more, Freddie?"

"What is this?" Godrow asked. "This is a place of business, you know. Those cards have to . . ."

"You went down for your customary coffee this morning, Freddie."

"Coffee?" Godrow asked. "What coffee? Have you been . . ."

"Only this time you dumped strychnine into Mary Chang's. She took her coffee very sweet, and that probably helped to hide the bitter taste. Or maybe you made some comment about the coffee being very bitter this morning, anything to hide the fact that you were poisoning her."

"No . . ." Freddie said.

"She drank her coffee and ate her English muffin, and then— the way you did every morning—you gathered up the cups and the napkins and the crumbs and whatever, and you rushed out with them before Mr. Godrow arrived. Only this time, you were disposing of evidence. Where'd you take them? The garbage cans on Columbus Avenue? Do they collect the garbage early, Freddie?"

"I . . . I . . ."

"You knew the symptoms. You watched, and when you thought the time was ripe, you couldn't resist boasting about what you'd done. Mary was making a call. You also knew how these calls worked because you made them yourself. There was usually a pause in the conversation while someone checked with the chef. You waited for that pause, and then you asked Mary if she knew why she was feeling so ill. You asked her because you weren't making a call, Freddie, you were plugged in on her extension, listening to her conversation. She recognized your voice, and so she answered you in English. You told her then, and she jumped up, but it was too late, the convulsion came. Am I right, Freddie?"

Freddie nodded.

"You'd better come with us," I said.

"I . . . I still have to stamp the quotations on these," Freddie said.

"Mr. Godrow will get along without you, Freddie," I said. "He'll get himself a new boy."

"I . . . I'm sorry," Freddie said.

"This is terrible," Godrow said.

"Think how Mary Chang must have felt," I told him, and we left.

The Interview

Sir, *ever since the Sardinian accident, you have refused to grant any interviews . . .*

    I had no desire to join the circus.

Yet you are not normally a man who shuns publicity.

Not normally, no. The matter on Sardinia, however, was blown up out of all proportion, and I saw no reason for adding fuel to the fire. I am a creator of motion pictures, *not* of sensational news stories for the press.

There are some "creators of motion pictures" who might have welcomed the sort of publicity the Sardinian . . .

Not I.

Yet you will admit the accident helped the gross of the film.

I am not responsible for the morbid curiosity of the American public.

Were you responsible for what happened in Sardinia?

On Sardinia. It's an island.

On Sardinia, if you will.

I was responsible only for directing a motion picture. Whatever else happened, happened.

You were there when it happened, however . . .

I was there.

So certainly . . .

I choose not to discuss it.

The actors and technicians present at the time have had a great deal to say about the accident. Isn't there anything you'd like to refute or amend? Wouldn't you like to set the record straight?

The record is the film. My films are my record. Everything else is meaningless. Actors are beasts of burden and technicians are domestic servants, and refuting or amending anything either might care to utter would be a senseless waste of time.

Would you like to elaborate on that?

On what?

On the notion that actors . . .

It is not a notion, it is a simple fact. I have never met an intelligent actor. Well, let me correct that. I enjoyed working with only one actor in my entire career, and I still have a great deal of respect for him—or at least as much respect as I can possibly muster for anyone who pursues a profession that requires him to apply makeup to his face.

Did you use this actor in the picture you filmed on Sardinia?

No.

Why not? Given your respect for him . . .

I had no desire to donate fifty percent of the gross to his already swollen bank account.

Is that what he asked for?

At the time. It may have gone up to seventy-five percent by now, I'm sure I don't know. I have no intention of ever giving a ploughhorse or a team of oxen fifty percent of the gross of a motion picture *I* created.

If we understand you correctly . . .

You probably don't.

Why do you say that?

Only because I have never been quoted accurately in any publication, and I have no reason to believe your magazine will prove to be an exception.

Then why did you agree to the interview?

Because I would like to discuss my new project. I have a meeting tonight with a New York playwright who will be delivering the final draft of a screenplay upon which we have labored long and hard. I have every expectation that it will now meet my requirements. In which case, looking ahead to the future, this interview should appear in print shortly before the film is completed and ready for release. At least, I hope the timetable works out that way.

May we know who the playwright is?

I thought you were here to talk to *me*.

Well, yes, but . . .

It has been my observation that when Otto Preminger or Alfred Hitchcock or David Lean or even some of the fancy young *nouvelle vague* people give interviews, they rarely talk about anyone but themselves. That may be the one good notion any of them has ever contributed to the industry.

You sound as if you don't admire too many directors.

I admire some.

Would you care to name them?

I have admiration for Griffith, DeMille, Eisenstein, several others.

Why these men in particular?

They're all dead.

Are there no living directors you admire?

None.

None? It seems odd that a man known for his generosity would be so chary with praise for other acknowledged film artists.

Yes.

Yes, what?

Yes, it would seem odd, a distinct contradiction of personality. The fact remains that I consider every living director a threat, a challenge, and a competitor. There are only so many motion picture screens in the world, and there are thousands of films competing to fill those screens. If the latest Hitchcock thriller has them standing on line outside Radio City, the chances are they *won't* be standing on line outside *my* film up the street. The theory that an outstanding box-office hit helps *all* movies is sheer rubbish. The outstanding hit helps only itself. The other films suffer because no one wants to see them, they want to see only the big one, the champion, the one that has the line outside on the sidewalk. I try to make certain that all of my films generate the kind of excitement necessary to sustain a line on the sidewalk. And I resent the success of any film but my own.

Yet you have had some notable failures.

Failures are never notable. Besides, I do not consider any of my films failures.

Are we talking now about artistic failures or box-office failures?

I have never made an artistic failure. Some of my films were mildly disappointing at the box office. But not very many of them.

When the Sardinian film was ready to open last June . . .

July. It opened on the Fourth of July.

Yes, but before it opened, when . . .

That would have been June, yes. July is normally preceded by June.

There was speculation that the studio would not permit its showing.

Rubbish.

The rumors were unfounded? That the studio would suppress the film?

The film opened, didn't it? And was a tremendous success, I might add.

Some observers maintain that the success of the film was due only to the publicity given the Sardinian accident. Would you agree to that?

I'll ask *you* a question, young man. Suppose the accident on Sardinia had been related to a film called *The Beach Girl Meets Hell's Angels,* or some such piece of trash? Do you think the attendant publicity would have insured the success of *that* film?

Perhaps not. But given your name and the stellar quality of . . .

You can stop after my name. Stars have nothing to do with any of my pictures. I could put a trained seal in one of my films, and people would come to see it. I could put *you* in a film, and people would come to see it.

Don't you believe that films are a collaborative effort?

Certainly not. I tell the script writer what I want, and he writes it. I tell the set designer what to give me, and he gives it to me. I tell the cameraman where to aim his camera and what lens to use. I tell the actors where to move and how to speak their lines. Does that sound collaborative to you? Besides, I resent the word "effort."

Why?

Because the word implies endeavor without success. You've tried to do something and you've failed. None of my films are "efforts." The word "effort" is like the word "ambitious." They both spell failure. Haven't you seen book jackets that proudly announce "This is So-and-So's most ambitious effort to date." What does that mean to you? To me, it means the poor bastard has set his sights too high. And failed.

Are you afraid of failure?

I cannot abide it.

Do you believe the Sardinian film was a success? Artistically?

I told you earlier . . .

Yes, but many critics felt the editing of the film was erratic. That the sequences filmed before the drowning were inserted piecemeal into . . .

To begin with, whenever critics begin talking about editing or camera angles or dolly shots or anything technical, I instantly fall asleep. They haven't the faintest notion of what film-making is all about, and their pretentious chatter about the art may impress maiden ladies in Flushing Meadows, but it quite leaves me cold. In reality, *none* of them know what's going on either behind the camera or up there on the screen. Do you know what a film critic's sole requirement is? That he has seen a lot of movies, period. To my way of thinking, *that* qualifies him as an expert on popcorn, not on celluloid.

In any event, you were rather limited, were you not, in editing the final portion of the film?

Limited in what way?

In terms of the footage you needed to make the film a complete entity?

The film *was* a complete entity. Obviously, I could not include footage that did not exist. The girl drowned. That was a simple fact. We did not shoot the remainder of the film as originally planned, we *could* not. But the necessary script revisions were made on the spot—or rather in Rome. I flew to Rome to consult with an Italian screenwriter, who did the work I required.

He did not receive credit on the film.

He *asked* that his name be removed from the picture. I acceded to his wishes.

But not without a struggle.

There was no struggle.

It was reported that you struck him.

Nonsense.

On the Via Veneto.

The most violent thing I've ever done on the Via Veneto was to sip a Campari-soda outside Doney's.

Yet the newspapers . . .

The Roman press is notoriously inaccurate. In fact, there isn't a single good newspaper in all Italy.

But, sir, there was some dispute with the screen writer, wasn't there? Surely, the stories about it couldn't all have been . . .

We had some words.

About what?

Oh my, we *must* pursue this deadly dull rot, mustn't we? All right, all right. It was *his* allegation that when he accepted the job, he had no idea the publicity surrounding the girl's death would achieve such hideous proportions. He claimed he did not wish his good Italian name—the little opportunist had written only one film prior to my hiring him, and that an Italian Western starring a second-rate American television actor—did not wish his name associated with a project that had even a *cloud* of suspicion hanging over it. Those were his exact words. Actually, quite the opposite was true. Which is why I resisted his idiotic ploy.

Quite the opposite? What do you mean?

Rather than trying to *avoid* the unfortunate publicity, I felt he was trying to capitalize on it. His move was really completely transparent, the pathetic little bastard. I finally let him have his way. I should have thought he'd be proud to have his name on one of my pictures. As an illuminating sidelight, I might add he did *not* return the five-thousand dollars a week I'd paid for the typing he did. Apparently, my *money* did not have a similar "cloud of suspicion" hanging over it.

"Typing," did you say?

Typing. The ideas for changing the script to accommodate the . . . to allow for a more plausible resolution were all mine.

A resolution to accommodate the drowning?

To explain the absence of the girl in the remainder of the film. I'm reluctant to discuss this, because it has a ghoulish quality I frankly find distasteful. The girl *did,* after all, drown; she *did* die. But that was a simple fact, and we must not lose sight of another simple fact. However cold-blooded this may sound, and I am well aware that it may be an unpopular observation, there had already been an expenditure of three million dollars on that film. Now I'm sure you know that leading players *have* taken ill, *have* suffered heart attacks, *have* died during the filming of other pictures. To my knowledge, such events have never caused a picture to halt production, and neither do I know of a single instance in which a film was entirely scrapped, solely because of the death of one of the leading players. Yet this was the very pressure being brought to bear on me immediately following the drowning, and indeed up to the time of the film's release.

Then the studio did *try to suppress the film?*

Well . . . at first, they only wanted to stop production. I refused. Later, when they saw the rough cut—this was when all the publicity had reached its peak—they sent in a team of strong-armed Executive Producers, and Production Chiefs, and what-have-you, all know-nothings with windy titles, who asked me to suppress the film. I told them exactly where to go. And then later on, when the film had been edited and scored, the same thing happened. I finally threatened suit. My contract called for a large percentage of the gross of that film, and I had no intention of allowing it to crumble unseen in the can.

You did not feel it was a breach of good taste to exhibit the film?

Certainly not. The girl met with an accident. The accident was no one's fault. She drowned. If a stunt man had died riding a horse over a cliff, would there have been all that brouhaha about releasing the film? I should say not.

But you must agree the circumstances surrounding the drowning . . .

The drowning was entirely accidental. We were shooting in shallow water.

The reports on the depth of the water vary from ten feet to forty feet. Neither of which might be considered shallow.

The water was no higher than her waist. And she was a tall girl. Five feet seven, I believe. Or eight. I'm not sure which.

Then how did she drown, sir?

I have no idea.

You were there, were you not?

I was on the camera barge, yes.

Then what happened?

I suppose we must set this to rest once and for all, mustn't we? I would much rather discuss the present and/or the future, but apparently we cannot do that until we've dealt *ad nausem* with the past.

As you wish, sir.

I wish the accident had never happened, sir, that is what *I* wish. I also wish I would not be pestered interminably about it. The Italian inquest determined that the drowning was entirely accidental. What was good enough for the Italian courts is damn well good enough for me. But there is no satisfying the American appetite for scandal, is there? Behind each accident or incident, however innocuous, however innocent, the American public *must* insist upon a plot, a conspiracy, a cabal. Nothing is permitted to be exactly what it appears to be. Mystery, intrigue must surround everything. Nonsense. Do you think any of us *wanted* that girl to drown? I've already told you how much money we'd spent on the picture before the accident. I would estimate now that the delay in completion, the cost of revisions, the necessity for bringing in a second girl to resolve the love story added at least a million dollars to the proposed budget. No one wanted the drowning. If for business reasons *alone,* no one wanted it.

Yet it happened.

It happened.

How?

The exact sequence of events is still unclear to me.

Your assistant director . . .

Yes.

Testified at the inquest . . .

Yes, yes.

That the girl pleaded not to go into the water.

The water was unusually cold that morning. There was nothing we could do about *that.* It was a simple fact. The light was perfect, we had our set-up, and we were prepared to shoot. Actors are like children, you know. If I had allowed her to balk at entering the water, the next thing I knew she'd have balked at walking across a lawn.

The writer of the original screenplay claims that the scene you were shooting that morning . . .

Where the girl swims in to the dock? What about it?

He claims he did not write that scene. He claims it was not in the original script.

Well, let him take that up with the Writers Guild.

Was it in the original script?

I have no idea. If there were no innovations during the shooting of a film . . . really, does anyone expect me to follow a script precisely? What then is my function as director? To shout "Louder" or "Softer" to an actor? Let the writers direct their own scripts, in that case. I assure you they would not get very far.

Was *the scene an innovation? The scene in the water?*

It might have been. I can't recall. If it was not in the original shooting script, as our Hollywood hack claims, then I suppose it *was* an innovation. By definition, yes, it would have been an innovation, isn't that so?

When was it added to the script?

I don't recall. I will sometimes get ideas for scenes the night before I shoot them. In which case, I will call in the technicians involved, and describe the set-up I will need the next day, and I will have it in the morning. If there is additional dialogue involved, I'll see to it that the actors and the script girl have the necessary pages, and I'll ask the actors to study them overnight. If there is no additional dialogue..

Was there any dialogue in this scene?

No. The girl was merely required to swim in to the dock from a speedboat.

What do you do in such a case? In an added scene where there's no dialogue?

Oh, I'll usually take the actor aside and sketch in the scene for him. The gist of it. This was a particularly simple scene. She had only to dive over the side of the boat and swim in to the dock.

In shallow water?

Well, not so shallow that she was in any danger of hitting the bottom, if that's what you mean.

Then perhaps the estimates of the water's depth . . .

The water's depth was no problem for anyone who knew how to swim.

Did the girl know how to swim?

Of course she did. You certainly don't think I'd have allowed her to play a scene in water . . .

I merely wondered if she was a good swimmer or . . .

Adequate. She was neither Eleanor Holm nor Esther Williams, but the part didn't call for an Olympic champion, you know. She was an adequate swimmer.

When did you explain the gist of the scene to her?

That morning, I believe. If memory serves me . . . yes, I believe the idea came to me the night before, and I called in the people involved and told them what I would need the following morning. Which is when I explained the scene to her. At least, that's usually the way it works; I assume it worked the same way concerning this particular scene.

You explained that she would have to dive over the side of the boat and swim in to the dock?

Which is all she had to do.

Did she agree to do this?

Why, of course. She was an inexperienced little thing, this was her first film. Of course, she agreed. There was never any question of her *not* agreeing. She'd been modeling miniskirts or what-have-you for a teenage fashion magazine when I discovered her. This was an enormous opportunity for her, this film. Look at the people I surrounded her with! Do you know what we had to pay her leading man? Never mind. It still irritates me.

Is it true he threatened to walk off the picture after the girl drowned?

He has said so in countless publications across the length and breadth of the world. I'm surprised he hasn't erected a billboard on the moon. But I imagine he's petitioning NASA for the privilege this very moment.

But did *he threaten to walk off?*

He did. I could not allow it, of course. Neither would his contract allow it. An actor will sometimes be deluded into believing he is something more than a beast of the field. Even with today's largely independent production structure, the studio serves as a powerful steam roller flattening out life's annoying little bumps for any second-rate bit player who's ever seen his own huge face grinning down idiotically from a screen. The *real* head sometimes gets as big as the fantasy head up there. Walk off the picture? I'd have sued his socks from under him.

Why did he threaten to walk off?

We'd had difficulty from the start. I think he was searching for an excuse, and seized upon the girl's drowning as a ripe opportunity.

What sort of difficulty?

I do not believe I need comment on the reputation of the gentleman involved. It has been adequately publicized, even in the most austere family publications.

Is it true, then, that a romance was developing between him and the girl?

I have never yet worked on a film in which a romance did not develop between the girl and her leading man. That is a simple fact of motion picture production.

Was it a simple fact of this *motion picture?*

Unfortunately, yes.

Why do you say "unfortunately?"

The girl had a brilliant career ahead of her. I hated to see her in a position that . . . I hated to see her in such a vulnerable position.

Vulnerable?

The Italian press would have enjoyed nothing better than to link her romantically with someone of his reputation. I warned her against this repeatedly. We'd spent quite a lot of money grooming this girl, you know. Stardom may happen overnight, but it takes many *days* of preparation for that overnight event.

Did she heed your warnings?

She was very young.

Does that mean to say . . . ?

Nineteen, very young.

There were, of course, news stories of a developing romance between them. Despite your efforts.

Yes, despite them. Well.

Yes?

The young are susceptible. And yet, I warned her. Until the very end, I warned her. The night before she drowned, there was a large party at the hotel, given in my honor. We had seen the rushes on the shooting we'd done the day before, and we were all quite pleased, and I, of course, was more than ever certain that the girl was going to be a tremendous smash. That I had found someone, developed someone, who would most certainly become one of the screen's enduring personalities. No question about it. She had . . . she had a luminous quality that . . . it's impossible to explain this to a layman. There are people, however, who are bland, colorless, insipid, until you photograph them. And suddenly, the screen is illuminated with a life force that is positively blinding. She had that quality. And so I told her again, that night of the party, I took her aside, and we were drinking quietly, and I reminded her of what she had been, an unknown model for a juvenile fashion magazine, and of what she would most certainly become once this film was released, and I begged her not to throw this away on a silly flirtation with her leading man, a man of his reputation. The press was there, you know, this was quite an occasion—I had met the host on the Riviera, oh years, ago, when I was doing another film, and this was something of a reunion. Well. Well, I suppose none of it matters quite, does it? She's dead. She drowned the next day.

What happened? At the party?

They managed to get some photographs of her. There is a long covered walk at the hotel, leading to the tower apartments that overlook the dock. The *papparazzi* got some pictures of the two of them in a somewhat, shall we say, compromising attitude. I tried to get the cameras, I struggled with one of the photographers . . .

Were these the photographs that were later published? After the accident?

Yes, yes. I knew even then, of course. When I failed to get those cameras, I knew her career was ruined. I knew that everything I'd done, all the careful work, the preparation—and all for *her,* you know, all to make the girl a *star,* a person in her own right—all of it was wasted. I took her to her room. I scolded her severely, and reminded her that makeup call was for six a.m.

What happened the next morning?

She came out to the barge at eight o'clock, made up and in costume. She was wearing a bikini, with a robe over it. It was quite a chilly day.

Was she behaving strangely?

Strangely? I don't know what you mean. She seemed thoroughly chastised, as well she might have. She sat alone and talked to no one. But aside from that, she seemed perfectly all right.

No animosity between you?

No, no. A bit of alienation perhaps. I had, after all, been furious with her the night before and had soundly reprimanded her. But I *am* a professional, you know, and I *did* have a scene to shoot. As I recall, I was quite courteous and friendly. When I saw she was chilled, in fact, I offered her my thermos.

Your thermos?

Yes. Tea. A thermos of tea. I like my tea strong, almost to the point of bitterness. On location, I can never get anyone to brew it to my taste, and so I do it myself, carry the thermos with me. That's what I offered to her. The thermos of tea I had brewed in my room before going out to the barge.

And did she accept it?

Gratefully. She was shivering. There was quite a sharp wind, the beginning of the mistral, I would imagine. She sat drinking the tea while I explained the scene to her. We were alone in the stern, everyone else was up forward, bustling about, getting ready for the shot.

Did she mention anything about the night before?

Not a word. Nor did I expect her to. She only complained that the tea was too bitter. I saw to it that she drank every drop.

Why?

Why? I've already told you. It was uncommonly cold that day. I didn't want to risk her coming down with anything.

Sir . . . was there any other *reason for offering her the tea? For making certain that she drank every drop?*

What do you mean?

I'm only reiterating now what some of the people on the barge have already said.

Yes, and what's that?

That the girl was drunk when she reported for work, that you tried to sober her up, and that she was still drunk when she went into the water.

Nonsense. No one drinks on my sets. Even if I'd worked with W. C. Fields, I would not have permitted him to drink. And I respected him highly. For an actor, he was a sensitive and decent man.

Yet rumors persist that the girl was drunk when she climbed from the camera barge into the speedboat.

She was cold sober. I would just love to know how such rumors start. The girl finished her tea and was sitting *alone* with me for more than three hours. We were having some color difficulty with the speedboat, I didn't like the way the green bow was registering, and I asked that it be repainted. As a result, preparation for the shot took longer than we'd expected. I was afraid it might cloud up and we'd have to move indoors to the cover set. The point is, however, that in all that time not a single soul came anywhere near us. So how in God's name would anyone know whether the girl was drunk or not? Which she wasn't, I can definitely assure you.

They say, sir . . .

They, they, who the hell are *they*?

The others on the barge. They say that when she went forward to climb down into the speedboat, she seemed unsure of her footing. They say she appeared glassy-eyed . . .

Rubbish.

. . . that when she asked if the shooting might be postponed . . .

All rubbish.

. . . her voice was weak, somehow without force.

I can tell you definitely and without reservation, and I can tell you as the single human being who was with that girl from the moment she stepped onto the barge until the moment she climbed into the speedboat some three and a half-hours later, that she was at all times alert, responsive, and in complete control of her faculties. She did not want to go into the water because it was cold. But that was a simple fact, and I could not control the temperature of the ocean or the air. Nor could I reasonably postpone shooting when we were in danger of losing our light, and when we finally had everything including the damn speedboat ready to roll.

So she went into the water. As instructed.

Yes. She was supposed to swim a short distance underwater,

and then surface. That was the way I'd planned the scene. She went into the water, the cameras were rolling, we . . . none of us quite realized at first that she was taking an uncommonly long time to surface. By the time it dawned upon us, it was too late. *He,* of course, immediately jumped into the water after her . . .

He?

Her leading man, his heroic move, his hairy-chested *star* gesture. She was dead when he reached her.

What caused her to drown? A cramp? Undertow? What?

I haven't the foggiest idea. Accidents happen. What more can I say? This was a particularly unfortunate one, and I regret it. But the past is the past, and if one continues to dwell upon it, one can easily lose sight of the present. I tend not to ruminate. Rumination is only stagnation. I plan ahead, and in that way the future never comes as a shock. It's comforting to know, for example, that by the time this appears in print, I will be editing and scoring a film I have not yet begun to shoot. There is verity and substance to routine that varies only slightly. It provides a reality that is all too often lacking in the motion picture industry.

This new film, sir . . .

I thought you'd never ask.

What is it about?

I never discuss the plot or theme of a movie. If I were able to do justice to a story by capsulizing it into three or four paragraphs, why would I then have to spend long months filming it? The synopsis, as such, was invented by Hollywood executives who need so-called "story analysts" to provide simple translations because they themselves are incapable of reading anything more difficult than "Run, Spot, Run."

What can you tell us about your new film, sir?

I can tell you that it is set in Yugoslavia, and that I will take full cinematic advantage of the rugged coastal terrain there. I can tell you that it is a love story of unsurpassing beauty, and that I have found an unusually talented girl to play the lead. She has never made a film before, she was working with a little theatre group on La Cienega when I discovered her, quite by chance. A friend of mine asked me to look in on an original the group was doing, thought there might be film possibilities in it, and so forth. The play was a hopeless botch, but the girl was a revelation. I had her tested immediately, and the results were staggering. What happens before the cameras is all that matters, you know, which is why some of our important stage personalities have never been able to make a successful transition to films. This girl has a vibrancy that causes one to forget completely that there are mechanical appliances such as projectors or screens involved. It is incredible, it is almost uncanny. It is as though her life force transcends the medium itself, sidesteps it so to speak; she achieves direct uninvolved communication at a response level I would never have thought existed. I've been working with her for, oh, easily six months now, and she's remarkably receptive, a rare combination of intelligence and incandescent beauty. I would be foolish to make any sort of prediction about the future, considering the present climate of Hollywood, and the uncertain footing of the entire industry. But if this girl continues to listen and to learn, if she is willing to work as hard in the months ahead as she has already worked, then given the proper vehicle and the proper guidance—both of which I fully intend to supply—I cannot but foresee a brilliant career for her.

Is there anything you would care to say, sir, about the future of the industry in general?

I never deal in generalities, only specifics. I feel that so long as there are men dedicated to the art of making good motion pictures—and I'm not talking now about pornography posing as art, or pathological disorders posing as humor—as long as there are men willing to make the sacrifices necessary to bring quality films to the public, the industry will survive. I intend to survive along with it. In fact, to be more specific, I intend to endure.

Thank you, sir.

Accident Report

There was a blanket thrown over the patrolman by the time we got there. The ambulance was waiting, and a white-clad intern was standing near the step of the ambulance, puffing on a cigarette.

He looked up as I walked over to him, and then flicked his cigarette away.

"Detective Jonas," I said.

"How do you do?" the intern answered. "Dr. Mallaby."

"What's the story?"

"Broken neck. It must have been a big car. His chest is caved in where he was first hit. I figure he was knocked down, and then run over. The bumper probably broke his neck. That's the cause of death, anyway."

Andy Larson walked over to where we were standing. He shook his head and said, "A real bloody one, Mike."

"Yeah." I turned to the intern. "When was he hit?"

"Hard to say. No more than a half-hour ago, I'd guess offhand. An autopsy will tell."

"That checks, Mike," Andy said. "Patrolman on the beat called it in about twenty-five minutes ago."

"A big car, huh?"

"I'd say so," the intern answered.

"I wonder how many big cars there are in this city?"

Andy nodded. "You can cart him away, Doc," he said. "The boys are through with their pictures."

The intern fired another cigarette, and we watched while he and an attendant put the dead patrolman on a stretcher and then into the ambulance. The intern and the attendant climbed aboard, and the ambulance pulled off down the street. They didn't use the siren. There was no rush now.

A cop gets it, and you say, "Well, gee, that's tough. But that was his trade." Sure. Except that being a cop doesn't mean you don't have a wife, and maybe a few kids. It doesn't hurt any less, being a cop. You're just as dead.

I went over the accident report with Andy.

ACCIDENT NUMBER: *463-A*
SURNAME: *BENSON*
FIRST NAME AND INITIALS: *James C.*
PRECINCT NUMBER: *32*   AIDED NUMBER: *67-4*
ADDRESS: *1812 Crescent Avenue*
SEX: *M*   AGE: *28*

My eyes skipped down the length of the card, noting the date, time, place of occurrence.

NATURE OF ILLNESS OR INJURY: *Hit and run*
FATAL SERIOUS SLIGHT UNKNOWN

I kept reading, down to the circled items on the card that told me the body had been taken to the morgue and claimed already.

The rest would have been routine in any other case, but it was slightly ironic here.

TRAFFIC CONTROLLED BY OFFICER? *Yes*
NAME: *Ptrlmn James C. Benson* **SHIELD NUMBER:** *3685*
TRAFFIC CONTROLLED BY LIGHTS? *Yes*

I read the rest of the technical information about the direction of the traffic moving on the lights, the police action taken, the city involved, and then flipped the card over. Under NAMES AND ADDRESSES OF WITNESSES (IF NONE, SO STATE) the single word *None* was scribbled. The officer who'd reported the hit and run was Patrolman P. Margolis. He'd been making the rounds, stopped for his usual afternoon chat with Benson, and had found the traffic cop dead in the gutter. There were skid marks on the asphalt street, but there hadn't been a soul in sight.

"How do you figure it, Andy?" I asked.

"A few ideas."

"Let's hear them."

"The guy may have done something wrong. Benson may have hailed him for something entirely different. The guy panicked and cut him down."

"Something wrong like what?"

"Who knows? Hot furs in the trunk. Dead man in the back seat. You know."

"And you figure Benson hailed him because he was speeding, or his windshield wiper was crooked? Something like that?"

"Yeah, you know."

"I don't buy it, Andy."

"Well, I got another idea."

"What's that? Drunk?"

Andy nodded.

"That's what I was thinking. Where do we start?"

"I've already had a check put in on stolen cars, and the lab boys are going over the skid marks. Why don't we go back and see if we can scare up any witnesses?"

I picked my jacket off the back of the chair, buttoned it on, and then adjusted my shoulder holster. "Come on."

The scene of the accident was at the intersection of two narrow streets. There was a two-family stucco house on one corner, and empty lots on the other three corners. It was a quiet intersection, and the only reason it warranted a light was the high school two blocks away. A traffic cop was used to supplement the light in the morning and afternoon when the kids were going to and coming from school. Benson had been hit about ten minutes before classes broke. It was a shame, because a bunch of homebound kids might have saved his life—or at least provided some witnesses.

"There's not much choice," Andy said.

I looked at the stucco house. "No, I guess not. Let's go."

We climbed the flat, brick steps at the front of the house, and Andy pushed the bell button. We waited for a few moments, and then the door opened a crack, and a voice asked, "Yes?"

I flashed my buzzer. "Police officers," I said. "We'd like to ask a few questions."

The door stayed closed, with the voice coming from behind the small crack. "What about?"

"Accident here yesterday. Won't you open the door?"

The door swung wide, and a thin young kid in his undershirt peered out at us. His brows pulled together in a hostile frown. "You got a search warrant?" he asked.

"What have you got to hide, sonny?" Andy asked.

"Nothing. I just don't like cops barging in like storm troopers."

"Nobody's barging in on you," Andy said. "We want to ask a few questions, that's all."

"All right, what do you want?"

"Were you home this afternoon?" I said.

"Yeah."

"All afternoon?"

"Yeah."

"You hear any noise out here in the street?"

"What kind of noise?"

"You tell me."

"I didn't hear any noise."

"A car skidding, maybe? Something like that?"

"No."

"Did you *see* anything unusual?"

"I didn't see anything. You're here about the cop who was run over, ain't you?"

"That's right, son."

"Well, I didn't see anything."

"You live here alone?"

"No. With my mother."

"Where is she?"

"She ain't feeling too good. That's why I've been staying home from school. She's been sick in bed. She didn't hear anything, either. She's in a fog."

"Have you had the doctor?"

"Yeah, she'll be all right."

"Where's your mother's room?"

"In the back of the house. She couldn't have seen anything out here even if she was able to. You're barking up the wrong tree."

"How long you been out of school, son?"

"Why?"

"How long?"

"A month."

"Your mother been sick that long?"

"Yeah."

"How old are you?"

"Fifteen."

"You better get back to school," Andy said. "Tell the city about your mother, and they'll do something for her. You hear that?"

"I hear it."

"We'll send someone around to check tomorrow. Remember that, sonny."

"I'll remember it," the kid said, a surly look on his face.

"Anybody else live here with you?"

"Yeah. My dog. You want to ask him some questions, maybe?"

"That'll be all, son," I said. "Thanks."

"For what?" the kid asked, and slammed the door.

"Lousy little snot-nose," Andy said.

There were thirty-nine cars stolen in New York City that day. Of the bigger cars, two were Buicks, four were Chryslers, and one was a Cadillac. One of the Chryslers was stolen from a neighborhood about two miles from the scene of the accident.

"How about that?" Andy asked.

"How about it?"

"The guy stole the buggy and when Benson hailed him, he knew he was in hot water. He cut him down."

"*If* Benson hailed him."

"Maybe Benson only stuck up his hand to stop traffic. The guy misunderstood, and crashed through."

"We'll see," I said.

We checked with the owner of the Chrysler. She was a fluttery woman who was obviously impressed with the fact that two policemen were calling on her personally about her missing car.

"Well, I never expected such quick action," she said. "I mean, *really.*"

"The car was a Chrysler, ma'm?" I asked.

"Oh, yes," she said, nodding her head emphatically. "We've never owned anything *but* a Chrysler."

"What year, ma'm?"

"I gave all this information on the phone," she said.

"I know, ma'm. We're just checking it again."

"It's brand new."

"The color?"

"Blue. A sort of robin's egg blue, do you know? I told that to the man who answered the phone."

"Licence number?"

"Oh, again? Well, just a moment." She stood up and walked to the kitchen, returning with her purse. She fished into the purse, came up with a wallet, and then rummaged through that for her registration. "Here it is," she said.

"What, ma'm?"

"77T8458."

Andy looked up. "That's a Nassau County plate, ma'am."

"Yes. Yes, I know."

"In the Bronx? How come?"

"Well . . . oh, you'll think this is silly."

"Let's hear it, ma'm."

"Well, a Long Island plate is so much more impressive. I mean . . . well, we plan on moving there soon, anyway."

"And you went all the way to Nassau to get a plate?"

"Yes."

Andy coughed politely. "Well, maybe that'll make it easier."

"Do you think you'll find the car?"

"We certainly hope so, ma'm."

We found the car that afternoon. It was parked on a side street in Brooklyn. It was in perfect condition, no damage to the front end, no blood anywhere on the grille or bumper. The lab checked the tires against the skid marks. Negative. This, coupled with the fact that the murder car would undoubtedly have sustained damages after such a violent smash, told us we'd drawn a blank. We returned the car to the owner.

She was very happy.

By the end of the week, we'd recovered all but one of the stolen cars. None of them checked with what we had. The only missing car was the Cadillac. It had been swiped from a parking lot in Queens, with the thief presenting the attendant with a ticket for the car. The M.O. sounded professional, whereas the car kill looked like a fool stunt. When another Caddy was stolen from a lot in Jamaica, with the thief using the same *modus operandi,* we figured it for a ring, and left it to the Automobile Squad.

In the meantime, we'd begun checking all auto body and fender repair shops in the city. We had just about ruled out a stolen car by this time, and if the car was privately owned, the person who'd run down Benson would undoubtedly try to have the damage to his car repaired.

The lab had reported finding glass slivers from a sealed beam imbedded in Benson's shirt, together with chips of black paint. From the position of the skid marks, they estimated that he'd been hit by the right side of the car, and they figured the broken light would be on that side, together with the heaviest damage to the grille.

Because Andy still clung to the theory that the driver had been involved in something fishy just before he hit Benson, we checked with the local precinct squads for any possibly related robberies or burglaries, and we also checked with the Safe, Loft and Truck Squad. There'd been a grocery store holdup in the neighborhood vicinity on the day of the hit and run, but the thief had already been apprehended, and he was driving an old Ford. Both headlights were intact, and any damage to the grille had been sustained years ago.

We continued to check on repair shops.

When the Complaint Report came in, we leaped on it at once. We glossed over the usual garbage in the heading, and skipped down to the DETAILS:

Telephone message from one Mrs. James Dailey, owner and resident of private dwelling at 2389 Barnes Avenue. Dispatched Radio Motor Patrol No 761. Mrs. Dailey returned from two-week vacation to find picket fence around house smashed in on Northwest corner. Tire marks in bed of irises in front yard indicate heavy automobile or light truck responsible for damage. Black paint discovered on damaged pickets. Good tire marks in wet mud of iris bed, casts made. Tire size 7.69-15-4-ply. Estimated weight 28 pounds. Further investigation of tread marks disclosed tire to be Sears, Roebuck and Company, registered trademark Allstate Tires. Catalogue number 95K01227K. Case still active pending receipt of reports and further investigation.

"You can damn well *bet* it's still active," Andy said. "This may be it, Mike."

"Maybe," I said.

It wasn't. The tire was a very popular seller, and the mail order house sold thousands of them every year, both through the mails and over the counter. It was impossible to check over-the-counter sales, and a check of mail-order receipts revealed that no purchases had been made within a two-mile radius of the hit and run. We extended the radius, checked on all the purchasers, and found no suspicious-looking automobiles, although all the cars were big ones. There was one black car in the batch—and there wasn't a scratch on it.

But Mrs. Dailey's house was about ten blocks from the scene of the killing, and that was too close for coincidence. We checked out a car and drove over.

She was a woman in her late thirties, and she greeted us at the door in a loose housecoat, her hair up in curlers.

"Police officers," I said.

Her hand went to her hair, and she said, "Oh, my goodness." She fretted a little more about her appearance, belted the house-coat tighter around her waist, and then said, "Come in, come in."

We questioned her a little about the fence and the iris bed, got substantially what was in the Complaint Report, and then went out to look at the damage. She stayed in the house, and when she joined us later, she was wearing tight black slacks and a chartreuse sweater. She'd also tied a scarf around her hair, hiding the curlers.

The house was situated on a corner, with a side street intersecting Barnes Avenue, and then a gravel road cutting into another intersection. The tire marks seemed to indicate the car had come down the gravel road, and then backed up the side street, knocking over the picket fence when it did. It all pointed to a drunken driver.

"How does it look?" she asked.

"We're working on it," Andy said. "Any of your neighbors witness this?"

"No. I asked around. No one saw the car. They heard the crash, came out and saw the damaged fence, but the car had gone already."

"Was anything missing from your house or yard?"

"No. It was locked up tight. We were on vacation, you know."

"What kind of car does your husband drive, ma'm?"

"An Olds. Why?"

"Just wondering."

"Let's amble up the street, Mike," Andy said. "Thank you very much, ma'm."

We got into the car, and Mrs. Dailey watched us go, striking a pretty pose in the doorway of her house. I looked back and saw her wave at one of her neighbors, and then she went inside.

"Where to?" I asked Andy.

"There's a service station at the end of that gravel road, on the intersection. If the car came up that road, maybe he stopped at the station for gas. We've got nothing to lose."

We had nothing to gain, either. They gassed up a hundred big black cars every day. They didn't remember anything that looked out of line. We thanked them, and stopped at the nearest diner for some coffee. The coffee was hot, but the case sure as hell wasn't.

It griped us. It really griped us.

Some son of a bitch had a black car stashed away in his garage. The car had a damaged front end, and it may still have had blood stains on it. If he'd been a drunken driver, he'd sure as hell sobered up fast enough—and long enough to realize he had to keep that car out of sight. We mulled it over, and we squatted on it, and we were going over all the angles again when the phone rang.

I picked it up. "Jonas here."

"Mike, this is Charlie on the desk. I was going to turn this over to Complaint, but I thought you might like to sit in on it."

"Tie in with the Benson kill?"

"Maybe."

"I'll be right down." I hung up quickly. "Come on, Andy."

We went downstairs to the desk, and Charlie introduced us to a Mr. George Sullivan and his daughter Grace, a young kid of about sixteen. We took them into an empty office, leaving Charlie at the desk.

"What is it, Mr. Sullivan?" I asked.

"I want better protection," he said.

"Of what, sir?"

"My child. Grace here. All the kids at the high school, in fact."

"What happened, sir?"

"You tell him, Grace."

The kid was a pretty blonde, fresh and clean-looking in a sweater and skirt. She wet her lips and said, "Daddy, can't . . ."

"Go on, Grace, it's for your own good."

"What is it, Miss?" Andy asked gently.

"Well . . ."

"Go on, Grace. Just the way you told it to me. Go on."

"Well, it was last week. I . . ."

"Where was this, Miss?"

"Outside the high school. I cut my last period, a study hour. I wanted to do some shopping downtown, and anyway a study hour is nowhere. You know, they're not so strict if you cut one."

"Yes, Miss."

"I got out early, about a half-hour before most of the kids start home. I was crossing the street when this car came around the corner. I got onto the sidewalk, and the car slowed down and started following me."

"What kind of a car, Miss?"

"A big, black one."

"Did you notice the year and make?"

"No. I'm not so good at cars."

"All right, what happened?"

"Well, the man driving kept following me, and I started walking faster, and he kept the car even with me all the time. He leaned over toward the window near the curb and said, 'Come on, sweetheart, let's go for a ride.' " She paused. "Daddy, do I have to . . ."

She swallowed hard, and then stared down at her loafers.

"I didn't answer him. I kept walking, and he pulled up about ten feet ahead of me, and sat waiting there. When I came up alongside the car, he opened the door and got out. He . . . he . . . made a grab for me and . . . and I screamed."

"What happened then?"

"He got scared. He jumped into the car and pulled away from the curb. He was going very fast. I stopped screaming after he'd gone because . . . because I didn't want to attract any attention."

"When was this, Miss?"

"Last week."

"What day?"

"It was Wednesday," Mr. Sullivan put in. "She came home looking like hell, and I asked her what was wrong, and she said nothing. I didn't get the story out of her until today."

"You should have reported this earlier, Miss," Andy said.

"I . . . I was too embarrassed."

"Did you notice the license plate on the car?"

"Yes."

"Did you get the number?"

"No. It was a funny plate."

"How do you mean funny?"

"It was a New York plate, but it had a lot of lettering on it."

"A lot of lettering? Was it a suburban plate? Was the car a station wagon?"

"No, it wasn't."

"A delivery truck?"

"No, it was a regular car. A new one."

"A new car," I repeated.

"Are you going to do something about this?" Mr. Sullivan asked.

"We're going to try, sir. Did you get a good look at the man, Miss?"

"Yes. He was old. And fat. He wore a brown suit."

"How old would you say, Miss?"

"At least forty."

Mr. Sullivan smiled, and then the smile dropped from his face. "There should be a cop around there. There definitely should be."

"Would you be able to identify the man if we showed him to you?"

"Yes, but . . . do I have to? I mean, I don't want any trouble. I don't want the other kids to find out."

"No one will find out, Miss."

"This wouldn't have happened if there was a cop around," Mr. Sullivan said.

"There was a cop," I told him. "He's dead."

When they left, we got some coffee and mulled it over a bit more.

"A new car," Andy said.

"With a funny plate. What the hell did she mean by a funny plate?"

"On a new car."

I stood up suddenly.

"What?" Andy said.

"A new car, Andy. A funny plate. A New York plate with lettering on it. For Christ's sake, it was a *dealer's* plate!"

Andy snapped his fingers. "Sure. That explains how he kept the car hidden so well. It's probably on some goddamn garage floor, hidden behind the other cars in the showroom."

"Let's go, Andy," I said.

It wasn't difficult. It's tough to get a dealer's franchise, and there aren't very many dealers in any specific neighborhood. We tried two, and we hit the jackpot on the third try.

We spotted the car in one corner of the big garage. We walked over to it, and there was a mechanic in grease-stained overalls working on the right headlight.

"Police," I told him. "What's wrong there?"

He continued working, apparently used to periodic checks from the Automobile Squad. "Sealed beam is broken. Just replacing it."

"What happened to the grille?"

"Oh, a small accident. Damn shame, too. A new car."

Andy walked around to the back and saw the paint scratches on the trunk. He nodded when he came around to me again.

"Back's all scratched, too," he said to the mechanic.

"Yeah, this goddamn car's been a jinx ever since we got it in."

"How so?"

"Got a headache with this one. The day we took it out for a test, the fool driver ran it into a ditch. Sliced hell out of both rear tires, and we had to replace them. All this in the first week we had this pig."

"Did you replace with Allstate?" I asked.

The mechanic looked up in surprise. "Why, yeah. How'd you know?"

"Where's your boss?" Andy asked.

"In the front office." The mechanic got up. "Hey, what's this all about?"

"Nothing that concerns you, Mac. Fix your car."

We went to the front office, a small cubicle that held two desks and two leather customer chairs. A stout man was sitting at one desk, a telephone to his ear. I estimated his age at about forty-two, forty-three.

He looked up and smiled when we came in, nodded at us, and then continued talking.

"Yes . . . well, okay, if you say so. Well look, Sam, I can't sell cars if I haven't got them . . . You just do your best, that's all. Okay, fine." He hung up without saying goodbye, got out of his chair and walked over to us.

"Can I help you gentlemen?"

"Yes," Andy said. "We're interested in a car. Are you the owner of this place?"

"I am."

"With whom are we doing business?"

"Fred Whitaker," he said. "Did you have any particular car in mind?"

"Yes. The black Buick on the floor."

"A beautiful car," Whitaker said, smiling.

"The one with the smashed grille and headlight," I added.

The smile froze on his face, and he went white. "Wh . . . what?"

"Did you smash that car up?"

Whitaker swallowed hard. "No . . . no. One of my mechanics did it."

"Who?"

"I've . . . I've fired him. He . . ."

"We can check this, Whitaker."

"Are . . . are you policemen?"

"We are. Come on, let's have it all. We've got a girl to identify you."

Whitaker's face crumbled. "I . . . I guess that's best, isn't it?"

"It's best," Andy said.

"I didn't mean to run him down. But the girl screamed, you know, and I thought he'd heard it. He stuck up his hand, and I . . . I got scared, I suppose, and there was no one around, so I . . . I knocked him . . . I knocked him down. Is he all right? I mean . . ."

"He's dead," I said.

"Dead?" Whitaker's eyes went wide. "Dead . . ."

"Was it you who smashed that picket fence?" Andy asked.

Whitaker was still dazed.

"Wh . . . what?" he said.

"The picket fence. On Barnes."

"Oh. Yes, yes. That was afterwards. I was still scared. I . . . I made a wrong turn, and I saw a police car, and I wanted to get away fast. I . . . I backed into the fence."

"Why'd you bother that little girl, Whitaker?"

He collapsed into a chair. "I don't know," he said. "I don't know."

"You're in a jam," Andy said. "You'd better come along with us."

"Yes, yes." He stood up, took his hat from a rack in the corner, and then started for the door. At the door, he stopped and said, "I'd better tell my mechanics. I'd better tell them I'll be gone for the day."

I looked at Whitaker, and I thought of Benson. My eyes met Andy's, and I put it into words for both of us.

"You'll be gone a lot longer than that, Whitaker."

Hot Cars

Because there was less of a risk involved, *that's* why.

I'll tell you something, John, I'd appreciate it if for once you let me get a word in edgewise here, instead of all the time interrupting. I been in this crumby cell with you for two months already, and the way the thing reads I'll be in here for at least another three years, figuring on parole. But every time I try to explain the whole *beauty* part of the deal, you stick your nose in and tell me if it was such a beauty I wouldn't be doing a stretch for grand larceny right this very minute. While at the same time *you* keep telling *me* you're the world's best pickpocket, and I have always had the decency never to even suggest that if you were such a good pickpocket what are *you* doing in here? So, if you can just for once keep your mouth shut and let me tell the whole thing before lights-out, I would sincerely appreciate it, because otherwise you're a nice cellmate, though you snore and pick your teeth.

The way we done it, there was never no risk involved, that was the beauty part. We didn't have to stand out there on the street practically naked and force the side flap, and then hook the door latch with a wire hanger, and unlock it, and then open the hood and cross the wires, all of which takes a lot of time even if you are an experienced person. There is the danger there of some eager-beaver cop coming up and saying, "Hey, what are you doing there?" and maybe shooting you in the leg or something. I know a car man in Frisco who got shot not in the leg but also where it hurts a lot.

So what we done is we looked through the classified ads, you understand me, John? Like in this newspaper here, and stop picking your teeth, that's a disgusting habit. Like right here, I'll read this thing out loud to you so you can get an idea how we set up the marks, and spitting out little pieces of meat like that, what the hell's the matter with you, John? This here is a typical ad we would circle with a red pencil and then give the guy a call. I'll read it to you.

CADILLAC ELDORADO CONV 1971
Firemist green with white vinyl top & inter.
AM/FM stereo tape deck, air cond, 6-way seat,
monitor lights, dr locks, 1 owner. $3300 firm.

And then the phone number, and all that crap where you should contact the person who is selling the car. I'm only giving you this as an example, John, because actually we tried to get cars that had a bigger demand, like right now a used Mercedes 280SL is very big because they ain't making them no more, and the model they're putting out costs something like fourteen grand, so there's a very big market for the old model, you follow me? You broke your friggin' toothpick. But like let's say this is the car we decide to heist, so what we done is Clara would call the person—she ain't been to see me, she ain't sent not even a postcard, I wonder what's the matter with that dame? She was one of the best in the business,

I got to tell you, John, the tale she gave that man on the phone was unbelievable, she'll probably come next visiting day, I hope.

She would call the number in the ad, and she would start the conversation by saying, for example, if it was this particular car in this ad here, she would say, "Are you the person advertising the Cadillac Eldorado convertible 1971?" she would say.

And he would say, "Yes, I am."

And then it would go like this:

"This is Mrs. Abigail Hendricks, what color is the car?"

She would use different names each time, of course, her real name is Clara Parsons. I think. At least, that is the name she told me was her real name. But for the sake of example, let's say this time she'd be using the name Abigail Hendricks. John, you can hurt your teeth using a paper clip that way. And the guy who was trying to sell his car would say, "Yes, I am the person advertising the Cadillac Eldorado convertible 1971."

"What color is the car?" the conversation would go.

"It's firemist green with a white vinyl top and interior."

"Oh, that's good," Clara would say. "What's firemist green?"

"A sort of off-green."

"It's not like a bright Kelly green, is it?"

"Oh no. No, not at all."

"I've always wanted a Cadillac," Clara would say. Or a Mercedes or a Lincoln Continental or a T-Bird, or whatever car was in the ad, you follow? "I used to have a Buick, I sold it last month. But in my secret heart I've always wanted a Cadillac. This is a convertible, isn't it?"

"Yes. Oh, yes."

"I've always wanted a Cadillac convertible. How many miles are on it?"

"40,000. More or less."

"Is it in good condition?"

"Excellent condition. It is in excellent condition."

"It wasn't in any accidents or anything, was it?"

"No, no. Never."

"And the interior is in good condition, too?"

"Perfect condition."

What's happening, John, is that the mark is trying to sell *her,* you understand? He don't know yet that we are going to heist his Caddy, he's got no idea we are setting him up. He just listens to the tale, and tries his best to get Clara to *buy* the goddamn car.

"And it's thirty-three hundred dollars, is that right?"

"That's all."

"That sounds a little high. Is that just the asking price? What I mean is are you willing to come down a little?"

"That's the firm price."

"I'm a widow, you see. Excuse me one minute, could you? I think I hear one of the children."

That was where she'd put down the phone, and go to the refrigerator and get herself a bottle of beer or something, or come over to where I was sitting and give me a little kiss, I wonder why she ain't written, well, she'll probably show up next week and surprise me. So she'd let him wait on the phone for just a little bit, and then she'd go back and pick up the receiver again and say to him. "I'm sorry I took so long. I live in this big old house in Larchmont, Andrea's room is all the way down the hall. I have three children, two boys and a girl, it isn't easy raising a family all alone, believe me. My husband passed away last June, you see."

"I'm sorry to hear that."

"Well, I'm just getting over it, actually. Do you think it's frivolous of me to want a Cadillac?"

"No, a Cadillac is a very fine motor car."

"It's just, you know, I think I've been in mourning long enough, don't you? Do you know what color my Buick was, the one that I sold?"

"What color?"

"Black. It was a '72 Skylark wagon, are you familiar with that particular automobile?"

"I can't say I'm too familiar with it."

"I got twenty-five hundred dollars for it, which is how I happen to have the money to buy another car. That Buick always reminded me of a hearse, and now that I'm finally getting over my husband's passing away, I think I ought to have something more light-hearted, don't you think? Firemist green. That sounds very light-hearted."

"It is. It's a very light-hearted motor car."

"Do you think I should come see it?"

"That's entirely up to you, Mrs. Hendricks. I have several people coming to see it tomorrow, so I can't guarantee . . ."

"Oh, please don't sell it till I've at least had a chance to *look* at it. Where are you located, exactly?"

Let's say the guy lives on Seventy-eighth and Central Park West, or wherever. So he'll tell Clara, "I'm on Seventy-eighth and Central Park West."

"In the city, is that?"

"Yes, in the city."

"Because I live in Larchmont, you see,"

We didn't live in Larchmont, I hope you understand that. John, you listening to me, or what? I can't tell if you're listening when you got your eyes closed like that. Where we really lived was in a hotel on Forty-seventh Street just east of Broadway, that was where we made our headquarters in New York. But Clara keeps mentioning that she lives in Larchmont because she wants to give this picture of a respectable widow living in a big old house she probably inherited when her old man kicked off, and she's raising three adorable little kids, and she's got this nice check deposited for twenty-five hundred, so it's reasonable she could have scraped up another eight-hundred someplace, right? Just nod, John. That way I'll know you're not asleep.

Anyway, she goes on about how much she's always wanted a firemist green Caddy, and she asks if any tapes go along with the AM/FM stereo deck, her favorites are Mantovani and Frank Sinatra, though she loves other recording artists, too, and then finally she says, "What time do you go to bed?"

"Well, after the Eleven O'Clock news, usually."

"Because I have this friend who's a mechanic," she says, "he knows cars inside out and backwards, and if I can get hold of him, I thought maybe I could come look at the car tonight. How long will it take me to get there from Larchmont?"

"A half-hour," he says. "Forty minutes? Something like that."

"Can I call you back in five minutes?" Clara says. "I just want to see if my friend is free. If he is, we'll come right down."

"Certainly."

"Now don't sell it in the next five minutes, okay?"

"I promise I won't sell it in the next five minutes."

"I'll get right back to you."

So that's when she hangs up, and comes over to me and sits on my lap or something, and I put my hand up under her skirt or something—you realize I haven't seen her in two months? Well, maybe she went to visit her mother in Tallahassee who is sickly. Then she calls back the guy and tells him she can't get ahold of her mechanic friend, but she doesn't want to lose the car, so she will come down to see it anyway if she can get somebody to drive her into the city. And if the car is as nice as she's sure it's going to be, she'll give the guy a deposit check right on the spot, and tomorrow when the bank opens, she'll go get him a certified check for the balance. So the guy hangs up, and since we are only ten minutes or so away from where he lives, we usually make love or something to kill the time, and then we hop into the little Volkswagen and drive up there and start the real pitch.

Now this is where I have to tell you what *really* happened the last time we pulled this, though it was a freak occurrence and has nothing to do with the beautiful way everything was working before then. We had heisted a total of seven cars in as many states, though of course when they caught me I only admitted to the one I was driving. What happened was that we went through that whole routine with a man who had a 1968 tobacco-brown Mercedes-Benz 280SL with genuine beige leather interior, air-conditioned, two tops, fully-loaded, it was a nice car, I could have got rid of it in New Jersey in thirty seconds flat. The beauty part, you see, is that any of these cars we heisted would not officially become *hot* cars till the next morning, by which time the serial numbers would be filled off the engine, and the car repainted, and new plates put on it. In other words, by the time the mark realized his goddamn car had actually been stolen, we already had at least a ten-hour lead on the cops, by which time the car was already being driven out to Texas or someplace. That was the way it usually worked, you'll understand what I mean in a minute if you can stop scratching your ass for a minute.

So the night I got busted, we drove over to see this guy who had advertised the Benz. This was after Clara had gave him the whole pitch on the phone about always wanting to have a Benz with two tops, and all that crap, and about not being able to get ahold of her mechanic friend, but not wanting to lose the car, and so on. So we meet the guy at a garage in the Bronx, it's underneath a two-story clapboard house, he's got the Benz locked in this two-car garage, there's a big padlock on the door. He turns on this little overhead light bulb, and Clara looks over the car and I look at my watch and tell her, "Abigail, I'm sorry I have to go, but I'll be late for work."

"But how will I get back to Larchmont?" she says. We have already established on the phone that she will have to find somebody to drive her to where the car is, you see, and I am the somebody she found to drive her, but I have to get to work now because I'm a respectable hard-working person who is just doing Abigail Hendricks a favor. I am dressed respectable, you know, I am wearing a suit and a tie, and I explain to the mark that I am a bank guard, and that I have to relieve the other guard at midnight, and it is almost that time now. We used the bank guard routine because it made me sound like an upholder of law and order. It always worked perfect. So Clara is worrying now about how she is going to get home to Larchmont, and I tell her that maybe I can let her have the Volks, if she promises to pick me up at the bank tomorrow morning at nine o'clock sharp which is what time I go off, and usually I am very sleepy by then. I also tell her to be very careful with the car since it is practically in mint condition though it is a 1963 model, and it is here that we establish Clara has never had an accident in the fifteen years she's been driving. I have to tell you that Clara *looks* as if she's never had an accident. She is wearing a brown suit, and her hair is pulled back in a bun, and she is wearing little gold-rimmed eyeglasses, and she looks like her own maiden aunt who lives next door to her mother in Tallahassee. So I give her the keys, and she asks me how I will get down to the bank, and I tell her it's okay I'll catch a taxi, and then I leave her with the mark, and I know in about an hour or so I am going to have myself a nice 1968 Mercedes-Benz 280SL to drive over to

New Jersey and sell on the spot to this man who will file off the serial numbers and paint it red or whatever.

So Clara goes to work on the mark.

She tells him she just adores this car, this is the car she's been looking for all her life, and it is certainly the frivolous kind of car that will help her get over her recent bereavement, a year is a long enough time to be mourning a husband, doesn't the mark think so? Yes, the mark thinks so. But she's worried, you see, about whether the car is in good running condition, she just wishes her mechanic friend had been able to come down there to the Bronx with her, would it be all right if she drove it around the block a few times, just to see if it worked and all? So the mark and her get in the car, and she drives it around the block three or four times, and then they come back to the garage, and she says, "Well, it *seems* to be all right, but I'm just not sure."

"Well," he says, "why don't you come back tomorrow with your mechanic friend?" It is now almost midnight, and the guy wants to go to bed, right? He can't stand there all night trying to convince this nice lady she should buy his car.

"Yes, but by that time you might have sold the car," Clara says.

"That's a possibility," he says.

"I just love the car."

"Yeah, well," he says, "what can I tell you, lady?"

"Oh, I don't *care*," she says, "I'll buy it!" She gives a nervous little giggle which is supposed to convince the mark she's never made such a big business decision in her life. And then she says, "I *still* wish my mechanic friend could look it over, though."

"Well, then, come back tomorrow," the mark says.

Now this is the moment of truth. This is when the mark can get away completely, wriggle off the hook, this is where Clara can blow the whole thing if she's not careful, and if she's not a very good actress, which of course she is. You have to remember that before this night, we had successfully swiped a total of seven cars in seven states, without running the risk of getting shot at in the street by some cop anxious for a promotion.

"I'll tell you what I'll do," she says, "I'll leave you a deposit, would that be all right? That way you can hold the car for me, and when I get a chance to have my mechanic friend look it over, we'll close the deal. Would that be all right?"

"That will be fine," the mark says, "but it has to be a non-returnable deposit."

"Oh," Clara says.

"Because otherwise your mechanic friend could look over the car and decide he doesn't like the way it rattles or something, not that it rattles, but you know what I mean."

"Yes, I see," Clara says. "Well, how much of a deposit do you want?"

"The car is selling for forty-five hundred dollars," he says. "That's what I put in the ad, that's a fair price for this car."

"Oh, yes, it *is,* I'm not arguing about the price."

"So if you let me have a check for, say, fifteen hundred, I'll hold the car for you till your mechanic friend takes a look at it."

"Well, fifteen hundred sounds like a lot," Clara says, "especially if my friend should find something wrong with the car, and I lose the whole thing."

"That's true," the mark says, "how does a thousand sound?"

"Well, I suppose," Clara says, and thinks about it for another minute, and then takes out her checkbook and writes the guy a phony check for a thousand, signing the name Abigail Hendricks, which is the name on the checking account we have opened in Larchmont with a minimum deposit of two hundred dollars. There is not a bank in the entire United States that will ask you for identification when you are opening a checking account. All they care to see is the long green, and you can tell them you are Adolph Hitler, and they will say, "Very good, Mr. Hitler, did you want the checks in green, yellow, pink, or blue?"

So Clara hangs the paper on the guy, and they shake on the deal, and then she starts worrying out loud. The trouble is that her mechanic friend goes to work at eight in the morning, and he doesn't quit till five, and by the time they got down here it'd be maybe six-thirty, and besides he's usually tired after a long day's work, and maybe wouldn't want to come down here at all, it'd be so much easier if she could take the car up to him. Still worrying out loud, still trying to figure this out, she says that maybe, if this is all right, maybe she could come down for the car in the morning, and drive it up to the garage where her friend works, and have him look at it there. Then, if everything was all right, she'd come down with a certified check which she'd have to get from the bank before three o'clock when it closed. But no, that wouldn't be so good because that would mean she'd have to make the trip in, and then drive back to Larchmont, and then drive the car back to the Bronx again, whereas she has a better idea.

Since she has to come to the city anyway tomorrow morning, to pick up her bank guard friend who was kind enough to drive her in, if she could take the Benz home with her *tonight,* she would have her mechanic friend look at it first thing in the morning, and then she could drive it back down with a certified check in her hand, no later than ten a.m., and that would be that. In the meantime, if it was all right, and if the mark promised to take good care of it, she would leave her bank guard friend's Volkswagen in the garage there overnight. That would be some sort of security for the mark, although he already had her check for a thousand dollars, and she was sure his collision insurance covered anybody else driving his car, though she had never had an accident in her entire life.

It is at this point that the mark either says yes or no.

He has seen the lady, he has sized her up as a respectable widow with a bank guard friend and also a mechanic friend, he has her check for a thousand dollars in his hand, and he also has a 1963 Volkswagen in his garage, and nine times out of ten he will say, "Okay, lady, take the car home with you, but be back here with it tomorrow morning at ten o'clock the latest, with the certified check in your hand."

Then Clara gives the mark her phony address in Larchmont, and also her phony telephone number, and she tells him the mechanic's name is Curly Rogers or something, and he works for a Mobil station in town there, and that is where she'll be at eight o'clock on the dot tomorrow morning, after which, if everything is okay, she will go to the bank and get the certified check, and be back with it at ten. That's the way it usually works, unless the mark says no he will not under any circumstances allow anyone to take his car overnight, in which case nothing ventured nothing gained. But that is the way it worked seven times for us, and that is exactly the way it worked this time too. Clara shook hands with the mark, and gave him the keys to the Volkswagen, in case he had to move it or anything, like in case the garage caught on fire, and she drove off in the tobacco-brown 1968 Mercedes-Benz 280SL with the genuine beige leather interior, and she picked me up at the cafeteria where she knew I'd be waiting, and then I got behind the wheel of the car while she took a taxi to the hotel on West Forty-seventh.

I drove to New Jersey already counting the money in my head. The Benz was not yet hot, you understand that, John? The mark did not yet know it had been heisted, he did not yet know he was never going to see Abigail Hendricks again as long as he lived, he did not yet know the Volks in his garage had been stolen in Georgia a month ago, and painted blue instead of red, and fixed up with New York plates and a phony registration in the glove compartment, he did not even know that Clara's check was a phony. All he knew was that he had a deal almost in his pocket because the mechanic was sure as hell not going to find a thing wrong with this little beauty of a car.

John, that Benz was a little jewel, I have to tell you. I went over the Washington Bridge with it, and I could understand why that guy kept it padlocked in his garage, it was some sweet little automobile. I figured it was worth on the retail market at least what he had advertised it for, and I figured I could get fifteen hundred, maybe even two grand when I turned it over in New Jersey, and I was already counting that bread, I was already spending it with Clara in some fancy nightclub in Washington, D.C., which is where we intended to stop next; that is a nice city for heisting cars, Washington, D.C., but not Seattle, Washington. I was driving along at a nice respectable speed of thirty-five miles an hour because, whereas the car would not become hot till the next morning when the mark realized he was never going to see Clara nor the Benz again, I still did not want to take no chances on cops stopping me, the one thing I always try to avoid is traffic tickets of any kind.

When I heard the siren behind me, I was very much surprised.

I did not think it was me at first, but then I saw the red dome light blinking, and this cop's car was right alongside me and one of the cops was waving me over to the side of the road, so naturally I pulled over. They both had guns in their hands when they got out of the car.

"Hey, what is the trouble, officers?" I said.

"No trouble," one of them said. "Let's see your license and registration."

I showed them my license, and I fished around in the glove compartment for the registration, and I handed that to the cop who was doing all the talking while the other cop kept his gun pointed at my head and making me very nervous.

"Yeah, that's what I thought," the cop who was holding the registration said, and then he went back to the police car while the other cop kept holding the gun on me. I didn't understand what was happening. The car was not yet hot, and I had just shown them the real and legitimate registration for it. In the police car up ahead, I could see the first cop talking on the radio. The other cop still had his gun pointed at me.

Do you know what it was, John?

The friggin car was a stolen car! I don't mean me and Clara stealing it, I mean the *mark*. The mark had stolen that friggin Benz two weeks before from a dentist in Poughkeepsie and he hadn't so much as even changed the license plates, and he'd also had the nerve to advertise it for sale in the goddamn *New York Times!* Now that is what I call amateur night in Dixie. And also, John, when I tried to explain to the detectives who later questioned me that I had only borrowed the car from a friend in the Bronx, and I told them where the friggin mark lived, and they went there, it turned out he didn't live there at all, he was only renting the garage with the padlock on it from an old lady who was half-deaf and arthritic besides, and the name he had given her was probably a phony, and I guess he couldn't have cared less if Clara ran off with his friggin car because he already had her check for a thousand bucks, which he didn't know was phony, ahh, John, it was some mess, there ain't no justice.

So here I am doing time, and God knows where that friggin thief mark is, and also God knows where Clara is, though I'm sure she'll come see me next week, don't you think, John?

John?

Jesus, John, I *hate* it when you snore like that.

Eye Witness

He had seen a murder, and the sight had sunken into the brown pits that were his eyes. It had tightened the thin line of his mouth and given him a tic over his left cheekbone.

He sat now with his hat in his hands, his fingers nervously exploring the narrow brim. He was a thin man with a mustache that completely dominated the confined planes of his face.

He was dressed neatly, his trousers carefully raised in a crease-protecting lift that revealed taut socks and the brass clasp of one garter.

"That him?" I asked.

"That's him," Magruder said.

"And he saw the mugging?"

"He says he saw it. He won't talk to anyone but the lieutenant."

"None of us underlings will do, huh?"

Magruder shrugged. He'd been on the force for a long time now, and he was used to just about every type of taxpayer. I looked over to where the thin man sat on the bench against the wall.

"Well," I said, "let me see what I can get out of him."

Magruder cocked an eyebrow and asked, "You think maybe the Old Man *would* like to see him personally?"

"Maybe. If he's got something. If not, we'd be wasting his time. And especially on this case, I don't think . . ."

"Yeah," Magruder agreed.

I left Magruder and walked over to the little man. He looked up when I approached him, and then blinked.

"Mr. Struthers?"

"Yes," he said warily.

"I'm Detective Cappeli. My partner tells me you have some information about the . . ."

"You're not the lieutenant, are you?"

"No," I said, "but I'm working very closely with him on this case."

"I won't talk to anyone but the lieutenant," he said. His eyes met mine for an instant, and then turned away. He was not being stubborn, I decided. I hadn't seen stubbornness in his eyes. I'd seen fear.

"Why, Mr. Struthers?"

"Why? Why what? Why won't I tell my story to anyone else? Because I won't, that's why."

"Mr. Struthers, withholding evidence is a serious crime. It makes you an accessory after the fact. We'd hate to have to . . ."

"I'm not withholding anything. Get the lieutenant, and I'll tell you everything I saw. That's all, get the lieutenant."

I waited for a moment before trying again. "Are you familiar with the case at all, sir?"

Struthers considered his answer. "Just what I read in the papers. And what I saw."

"You know that it was Lieutenant Anderson's wife who was

mugged? That the mugger was after her purse and killed her without getting it?"

"Yes, I know that."

"Can you see then why we don't want to bring the lieutenant into this until it's absolutely necessary? So far, we've had ten people confessing to the crime, and eight people who claim to have seen the mugging and murder."

"I *did* see it," Struthers protested.

"I'm not saying you didn't, sir. But I'd like to be sure before I bring the lieutenant in on it."

"I just don't want any slip-ups," Struthers said. "I . . . I don't want him coming after me next."

"We'll offer you every possible protection, sir. The lieutenant, as you can well imagine, has a strong personal interest in this case. He'll certainly see that no harm comes to you."

Struthers looked around him suspiciously. "Well, do we have to talk here?"

"No, sir, you can come into my office."

He deliberated for another moment, and then said, "All right." He stood up abruptly, his fingers still roaming the hat brim. When we got to my office, I offered him a chair and a cigarette. He took the seat, but declined the smoke.

"Now then, what did you see?"

"I saw the mugger, the man who killed her." Struthers lowered his voice. "But he saw me, too. That's why I want to make absolutely certain that . . . that I won't get into any trouble over this."

"You won't, sir. I can assure you. Where did you see the killing?"

"On Third and Elm. Right near the old paint factory. I was on my way home from the movies."

"What did you see?"

"Well, the woman, Mrs. Anderson—I didn't know it was her at the time, of course—was standing on a corner waiting for the bus. I was walking down toward her. I walk that way often, especially coming home from the show. It was a nice night and . . ."

"What happened?"

"Well, it was dark, and I was walking pretty quiet, I guess. I wear gummies—gum sole shoes."

"Go on."

"The mugger came out of the shadows and grabbed Mrs. Anderson around the throat, from behind her. She threw up her arm, and her purse opened and everything inside fell on the sidewalk. Then he lifted his hand and brought it down, and she screamed, and he yelled, 'Quiet, you bitch!' He lifted his hand again and brought it down again, all the time yelling, 'Here, you bitch, here, here,' while he was stabbing her. He must have lifted the knife at least a dozen times."

"And you saw him? You saw his face?"

"Yes. She dropped to the ground, and he came running up the street toward me. I tried to get against the building, but I was too late. We stood face to face, and for a minute I thought he was going to kill me, too. But he gave a kind of a moan and ran up the street."

"Why didn't you come to the police at once?"

"I . . . I guess I was scared. Mister, I still *am*. You've got to promise me I won't get into any trouble. I'm a married man, and I got two kids. I can't afford to . . ."

"Could you pick him out of a lineup? We've already rounded up a lot of men, some with records as muggers. Could you pick the killer?"

"Yes. But not if he can see me. If he sees me, it's all off. I won't go through with it if he can see me."

"He won't see you, sir. We'll put you behind a screen."

"So long as he doesn't see me. He knows what I look like, too, and I got a family. I won't identify him if he knows I'm the one doing it."

"You've got nothing to worry about." I clicked down Magruder's toggle on the intercom, and when he answered, I said, "Looks like we've got something here, Mac. Get the boys ready for a run-through, will you?"

"Right. I'll buzz you."

We sat around and waited for Magruder to buzz.

"I won't do it unless I'm behind a screen," Struthers said.

"You'll have a one-way mirror, sir."

We'd waited for about five minutes when the door opened. A voice lined with anguish and fatigue said, "Mac tells me you've got a witness."

I turned from the window, ready to say, "Yes, sir," and Struthers turned to face the door at the same time.

His eyebrows lifted, and his eyes grew wide.

He stared at the figure in the doorway, and I watched both men as their eyes met and locked for an instant.

"No!" Struthers said suddenly. "I . . . I've changed my mind. I . . . I can't do it. I have to go. I have to go."

He slammed his hat onto his head and ran out quickly, almost before I'd gotten to my feet.

"Now what the hell got into him all of a sudden?" I asked.

Lieutenant Anderson shrugged wearily. "I don't know," he said. "I don't know."

Chalk

Her face was a piece of ugly pink chalk, and her eyes were two little brown mud puddles. Her eyes were mud puddles and they did not fit with the pink chalk. The chalk was ugly, and her eyes were mud puddles, and they made the chalk look uglier.

"Your eyes are mud puddles," I said, and she laughed.

I didn't like her to laugh. I was serious. She shouldn't have laughed when I told her something serious like that.

I hit the pink chalk with my fist but it didn't crumble. I wondered why it didn't crumble. I hit it again and water ran out of the mud puddles. I pushed my hand into one of the mud puddles and it turned all red, and it looked prettier with water coming out of it and red.

I tore the beads from her neck and threw them at the chalk. I felt her nails dig into my skin and I didn't like that. I twisted her arm and she struggled and pushed, and her body felt nice and soft up tight against mine. I wanted to squeeze her and when I began squeezing her she screamed, and the noise reminded me of the Third Avenue El when it stops going, and the noise reminded me of babies crying at night when I'm trying to sleep. So I hit her mouth to stop the noise but instead it got louder.

I ripped her dress in the front and I swore at her and told her to stop the noise, but she wouldn't stop so I kicked her in the leg and she fell. She looked soft and white on the floor. All except her face. It was still pink chalk.

Ugly pink chalk.

I stepped on it with all my might and the mud puddles closed and red came from her nose.

I stepped on her again and the pink chalk was getting red all over and it looked good and I kept stepping. And the red got thicker and redder, and then she started to twitch and jerk like as if she was sick and I bent down and asked, "Are you sick, Jeannie?"

She didn't answer except like a moan, and then she made a noise that sounded like the Third Avenue El again, and I had to hit her again to make her stop.

I kept punching her in the face and the noise stopped.

It was very quiet.

Her eyes weren't mud puddles. Why did I think they were mud puddles? They were two shiny glass marbles and they were looking right at me, only they couldn't see me because they were glass and you can't see out of glass.

The pink chalk was all red now except for white patches here and there. Her mouth was open but there was no noise.

Then I heard the ticking.

It was loud, like an ax splitting wood, and I was afraid it was going to wake her up and then she would make the noise all over again, and I would have to tell her to stop and hit her again. I did not want to hit her again because her eyes were only marbles and you can't see out of marbles, and her face was a pretty red and not made of chalk that would not crumble.

So I stepped on the ticking. I stepped on it twice so that I could be sure. Then I took off her clothes and she looked all red and white and quiet when I put her on the bed. I closed the light and then I left her to sleep. I felt sorry for her.

She couldn't see because her eyes were only marbles.

It was cold in the night. It shouldn't have been cold because the sky was an oil fire, all billowy and black. Why was it cold?

I saw a man coming and I stopped him because I wanted to know why it was so cold when the sky was burning up. He talked funny and he couldn't walk straight, and he said it was warm and I was crazy if I thought it was cold. I asked him if he was warm.

He said, "I am warm, and don't bother me because I feel wonderful and I don't want to lose this feeling."

I hit him and I took his coat because he was warm and he didn't need it if he was warm.

I ran fast down the street, and then I knew he was right. It *was* warm and I didn't need his coat so I went back to take it to him because he might be cold now. He wasn't there so I put the coat on the sidewalk in case he came back for it.

Then I ran down the street because it was nice and warm and it felt like springtime, and I wanted to run and leap. I got tired and I began to breathe hard so I sat down on the sidewalk. Then I was tired of sitting and I did not want to run anymore so I began looking at the windows but they were all dark. I did not like them to be dark because I liked to look at the things in the windows and if they were dark I couldn't see them.

Poor Jeannie. Her eyes were marbles and she could not see the things in the store windows. Why did God make my eyes out of white jelly and Jeannie's out of glass? I wondered how she knew me if she couldn't see me.

It was getting cold again and I swore at the man who had talked funny and couldn't walk straight. He had lied to me and made me feel warm when it was really cold all along. I lifted my hand up to the light in the street because it was yellow and warm, but I couldn't reach it and I was still cold.

Then, the wet fell out of the sky and I began to run so it wouldn't touch me. But it was all around me and the more I ran the more it fell. And the noise in the sky was like a dog growling under his teeth, and the lights that flashed were a pale, scary blue. I ran and ran and I was getting tired of running and the wet was making *me* wet, and the damp was creeping into my head and the dark was behind it the way the dark always was.

The damp pressed on the inside and it pushed outwards, and then the dark creeped up and I screamed, and it sounded like the Third Avenue El when it stops going, and I screamed again and it sounded like babies crying, and I punched myself in the face so I would stop the way Jeannie had. But I screamed again and the damp was all in and over my head. The dark was waiting, too.

I screamed because I didn't want the dark to come in, but I could see it was getting closer and I knew the way the damp always felt just before the dark came in. I hit my face again but the damp was heavy now and it was dripping inside my head and I knew the dark was coming and I ran away from it.

But it was there, and first it was gray like the ocean and then it got deeper like a dense fog and it turned black and blacker, and the dark came and I knew I was falling, and I couldn't stop because Jeannie's eyes were only marbles.

I am lying on a sidewalk in a strange street.

The sun is just rising and the bustle of the day has not yet begun. There is a severe pain in my head. I know I haven't been drinking, yet where did this terrible pain come from?

I rise and brush off my clothes.

It is then that I notice the blood on my hands and on my shoes. *Blood?*

Have I been fighting? No, no, I don't remember any fighting. I remember—I remember—calling on Jeannie.

She did not feel like going out, so we decided to sit at home and talk. She made coffee, and we were sitting and drinking and talking.

How do I come to be in this strange street? With blood on my body?

I begin to walk.

There are store windows with various forms of merchandise in them. There is a man's overcoat lying in the street, a ragged overcoat lying in a heap. I pass it rapidly.

It is starting to drizzle now. I walk faster. I must see Jeannie. Perhaps she can clear this up for me.

Anyway, the drizzle is turning into a heavy rain.

And I have never liked the darkness or dampness that come with a storm.

Still Life

It was two in the morning, raining to beat all hell outside, and it felt good to be sitting opposite Johnny Knowles sipping hot coffee. Johnny had his jacket off, with his sleeves rolled up and the .38 Police Special hanging in its shoulder holster. He had a deck of cards spread in front of him on the table, and he was looking for a black queen to put on his king of diamonds.

I was sitting there looking past Johnny at the rain streaming down the barred window. It had been a dull night, and I was half-dozing, the hot steam from the coffee cup haloing my head. When the phone began ringing, Johnny looked up from his Solitaire.

"I'll get it," I said.

I put down the cup, swung my legs out from under the table and picked up the receiver.

"Hannigan," I said.

Johnny was watching me now.

"Yep," I said. "I've got it, Barney. Right away."

I hung up and Johnny looked at me quizzically.

"Young girl," I said. "Gun Hill Road and Bronxwood Avenue. Looks bad, Johnny."

Johnny stood up quickly and began shrugging into his jacket. "Some guy found her lying on the sidewalk."

"Hurt bad?" Johnny asked.

"The guy who called in thinks she's dead."

We checked out a car and headed for Gun Hill Road. Johnny was silent as he drove, and I listened to the swick-swack of the windshield wipers, staring through the rain-streaked glass at the glistening wet asphalt outside. When we turned off White Plains Avenue, Johnny said, "Hell of a night."

"Yeah."

He drove past the Catholic church, past the ball field belonging to the high school, and then slowed down as we cruised up to the school itself.

"There he is," Johnny said.

He motioned with his head, and I saw a thin man standing on the sidewalk, flagging us down. He stood hunched against the rain, his fedora pulled down over his ears. Johnny pulled up alongside him, and I opened the door on my side. A sheet of rain washed into the car, and the guy stuck in his head.

"Right around the corner," he said.

"Get in," I told him. I moved over to make room, and he squeezed onto the seat, bringing the clinging wetness of the rain with him. Johnny turned the corner, and the old man pointed through the windshield. "There," he said. "Right there."

We pulled the car over to the curb, and Johnny got out from behind the wheel before the man next to me had moved. The man shrugged, sighed and stepped out into the rain. I followed close behind him.

The girl was sprawled against the iron-barred fence that surrounded the school. She'd been wearing a raincoat, but it had been forcibly ripped down the front, pulling all the buttons loose. Her blouse had been torn down the center, her bra cruelly ripped from her breasts. Johnny played his flash over her, and we saw the ugly welts covering her wet skin. Her skirt and underclothing had been shredded, too, and she lay grotesque in death, her legs twisted at a curious wide-spread angle.

"Better get a blanket, Mike," Johnny said.

I nodded and walked to the car. I took a blanket from the back, and when I walked over to the girl again, Johnny was getting the man's name and address.

"The ambulance should be along soon," I said.

"Yeah." Johnny closed his pad, took the blanket and draped it over the girl. The rain thudded at it, turning it into a sodden, black mass on the pavement.

"How'd you find her?" I asked the man.

"I been workin' the four to twelve at my plant," he said, "out on Long Island. I usually get home about this time when I got that shift. I live right off Bronxwood, get off the train at Gun Hill."

"You were walking home when you found the girl?"

"Yes, sir."

"What'd you do then?"

"I walked clear back to White Plains Avenue, found an open candy store and called you fellows. Then I came back to wait for you."

"What'd you tell the man who answered the phone?"

"All about the girl. That I'd found her. That's all."

"Did you say she was dead?"

"Well, yes. Yes, I did." He stared down at the girl. "My guess is she was raped." He looked at me for confirmation, but I said nothing.

"I think you can go home now, sir," Johnny said. "Thanks a lot for reporting this. We'll call you if we need you."

"Glad to help," the old man said. He nodded at us briefly, and then glanced down at the girl under the blanket again. He shook his head, and started off down Bronxwood Avenue. We watched him go, the rain slicing at the pavement around us. Johnny looked off down the street, watching for the ambulance.

"Might be rape at that," he said.

I pulled my collar up against the rain.

We got the autopsy report at six that morning. We'd already found a wallet in the dead girl's coat pocket, asking anyone to call a Mrs. Iris Ferroni in case of accident. We'd called Mrs. Ferroni, assuming her to be the girl's mother, and she'd identified the body as that of her daughter, Jean Ferroni. She'd almost collapsed after that, and we were holding off questioning her until she pulled herself together.

Johnny brought the report in and put it next to my coffee cup on the table.

I scanned it quickly, my eyes skimming to the "Cause of death" space. In neat typescript, I read:

Sharp instrument entering heart from below left breast.

I flipped the page and looked at the attached detailed report. The girl had been raped, all right, consecutively, brutally.

I turned back to the first page and looked at it once more. My eyes lingered on one item.

Burial Permit No: 63-7501-H.

"Now she's just a number," I said. "Sixteen year old kid with a grave-number."

"She was seventeen," Johnny said.

"That makes a big difference."

"I think we can talk to her mother now," Johnny said.

I rubbed my forehead and said, "Sure. Why don't you bring her in?"

Johnny nodded and went out, to return in a few minutes with a small, dark woman in a plain black coat. The woman's eyes were red, and her lip trembled. She still looked dazed from the shock of having seen her daughter with the life torn from her.

"This is Detective Hannigan," Johnny said, "and I'm his partner, Detective Knowles. We'd like to ask you a few questions, if you don't mind."

Mrs. Ferroni nodded, but said nothing.

"What time did your daughter leave the house last night, Mrs. Ferroni?" I asked.

The woman sighed. "Eight o'clock, I think," she said. There was the faintest trace of an accent in her voice.

"Did she leave with anyone?"

"Yes."

"Who?"

"A boy. He takes her out sometimes. Ricky. Ricky Tocca."

"Do you know the boy well?"

"He's from the neighborhood. He's a good boy."

"Did they say where they were going?"

"To a movie. I think they go up to Mount Vernon a lot. That's where they were going."

"Does this Tocca have a car?"

"Yes."

"Would you know the year and make, Mrs. Ferroni?"

"A Plymouth," she said. "Or a Chevy, I think. I don't know. It's a new car." She paused and bit her lip. "He wouldn't hurt my daughter. He's a nice boy."

"We're not saying he would," Johnny said gently. "We're just trying to get some sort of a lead, Mrs. Ferroni."

"I understand."

"They left the house at eight, you say?"

"About that time."

"What time does your daughter usually come home?"

"One, two. On weekends. During the week . . . well, I liked her to come home early . . ."

"But she didn't, is that it?"

"You know how it is with a young girl. They think they know everything. She stayed out late every night. I told her to be careful . . . I *told* her . . . I *told* her . . ."

She bit her lip, and I expected tears again, but there were none. Johnny cleared his throat, and asked, "Weren't you worried when she didn't show up this morning? I mean, we didn't call you until about four a.m."

Mrs. Ferroni shook her head. "She comes in very late sometimes. I worry . . . but she always comes home. This time . . ."

There was a strained, painful silence. "I think you can go now, Mrs. Ferroni," I said. "We'll have one of our men drive you home. Thank you very much."

"You'll . . . you'll find who did it, won't you?" she asked.

"We'll sure as hell try," I told her.

We picked up Richard Tocca, age twenty, as he was leaving for work the next morning. He stepped out of a two-story frame on Burke Avenue, looked up at the overcast sky, and then began walking quickly to a blue Ford parked at the curb. Johnny collared him as he was opening the door on the driver's side.

"Richard Tocca?" he asked.

The kid looked up suspiciously. "Yeah." He looked at Johnny's fist tightened in his coat sleeve and said, "What is this?"

I pulled up and flashed my buzzer. "Police officers, Tocca. Mind answering a few questions?"

"What's the matter?" he asked. "What did *I* do?"

"Routine," Johnny said. "Come on over to our car, won't you?"

"All right," Tocca said. He glanced at his watch. "I hope this doesn't take long. I got to be at work at nine."

"It may not take long," I said.

We walked over to the car and I held the door for him. He climbed in, and Johnny and I sat on either side of him. He was a thin-faced kid with straight blond hair and pale blue eyes. Clear complexioned, clean shaven. Slightly protruding teeth. Dressed neatly and conservatively for a kid his age.

"What's this all about?" he asked.

"You date Jean Ferroni last night?" Johnny asked.

"Yes. Jesus, don't tell me she's in some kind of trouble."

"What time'd you pick her up?"

"About eight-fifteen, I guess. Listen, is she . . ."

"Where'd you go?"

"Well, that's just it. We were *supposed* to have a date, but she told me it was off, just like that. She made me drive her to Gun Hill and then she got out of the car. If she's in any trouble, I didn't have anything to do with it."

"She's in big trouble," Johnny said. "The biggest trouble."

"Yeah, well, I didn't have . . ."

"She's dead," I said.

The kid stopped talking, and his jaw hung slack for a minute. He blinked his eyes rapidly two or three times and then said, "Jesus. Jesus."

"You date her often, Ricky?"

"Huh?" He still seemed shocked. "Yeah, pretty often."

"How often?"

"Two, three times a week. No, less."

"When'd you see her last?"

"Last night."

"Before that."

"Last . . . Wednesday, I guess it was. Yeah."

"Why'd you date her?"

"I don't know. Why do you date girls?"

"Why'd you date *this* girl? Why'd you date Jean Ferroni?"

"I don't know. She's . . . she was a nice kid. That's all."

"You serious about her?" Johnny asked.

"Well . . ."

"You been sleeping with her?"

"No. *No.* I mean . . . well no, I wasn't."

"Yes or no?"

"No."

"What time did you pick her up last night?"

"Eight-fifteen. I told you . . ."

"Where'd you drop her off?"

"Gun Hill and White Plains."

"What time was this?"

"About eighty-thirty."

"Why'd you date her so much?"

"I heard she was . . . hell, I don't like to say this. I mean, the girl's dead . . ."

"You heard what?"

"I heard she was . . . hot stuff."

"Where'd you hear that?"

"Around. You know how the word spreads."

"Who'd you hear it from?"

"Just around, that's all."

"And you believed it?"

"Well, yeah. You see, I . . ." He stopped short, catching himself and his tongue.

"You what?"

"Nothing."

"Let's hear it," Johnny said. "Now."

"All right, all right." He fell into a surly silence, and Johnny and I waited. Finally, he said, "I saw pictures."

"What kind of pictures?"

"You know. Pictures. Her. And a guy. You know."

"You mean pornographic pictures?"

"Yeah."

"Then say what you mean. Where'd you see these pictures?"

"A guy had them."

"Have *you* got any?"

"No. Well . . . I got one," the kid admitted. "Just one."

"Let's see it."

He fished into his wallet and said, "I feel awful funny about this. You know, Jean is dead and all."

"Let's see the picture."

He handed a worn photograph to Johnny, and Johnny studied it briefly and passed it to me. It was Jean Ferroni, all right, and I couldn't very much blame the Tocca kid for his assumption about her.

"Know the guy in this picture?" I asked.

"No."

"Never seen him around?"

"No."

"All right, kid," Johnny said. "You can go to work now."

Richard Tocca looked at the picture in my hand longingly, reluctant to part with it. He glanced up at me hopefully, saw my eyes, and changed his mind about the question he was ready to ask. I got out of the car to let him out, and he walked to his Ford without looking back at us. The questioning had taken exactly seven minutes.

Johnny started the car, and threw it into gear.

"Want me to drive?" I asked.

"No, that's okay."

"This puts a different light on it, huh?"

Johnny nodded.

We staked out every candy store and ice cream parlor in the Gun Hill Road to 219th Street area, figuring we might pick up someone passing the pornos there. We also set up four policewomen in apartments, thinking there was an off chance someone might contact them for lewd posing. The policewomen circulated at the local dances, visited the local bars, bowling alleys, movies. We didn't get a rumble. The Skipper kept us on the case, but it seemed to have bogged down temporarily.

We'd already gone over the dead girl's belongings at her home. She'd had an address book, but we'd checked on everyone in it, and they were all apparently only casual acquaintances. We'd checked the wallet the girl was carrying on the night of her murder. Aside from the In-Case-Of card, a social security card, and some innocent pictures taken outside the high school with her girl friends, there was nothing.

Most of her high school friends said, under questioning, that

Jean Ferroni didn't hang around with them much anymore. They said she'd gone snooty and was circulating with an older crowd. None of them knew who the people in the older crowd were.

Her teachers at school insisted she was a nice girl, a little subdued and quiet in class, but intelligent enough. Several of them complained that she'd been delinquent in homework assignments. None of them knew anything about her outside life.

We got our first real break when Mrs. Ferroni showed up with the key. She placed it on the desk in front of Johnny and said, "I was cleaning out her things. I found this. It doesn't fit any of the doors in the house. I don't know what it's for."

"Maybe her gym locker at school," I said.

"No. She had a combination lock. I remember she had to buy one when she first started high school."

Johnny took the key, looked at it, and passed it to me. "Post office box?" he asked.

"Maybe." I turned the key over in my hands. The numerals 894 were stamped into its head.

"Thanks, Mrs. Ferroni," Johnny said. "We'll look into it right away."

We started at the Williamsbridge Post Office right on Gun Hill Road. The mailmen were very cooperative, but the fact remained it wasn't a key to any of their boxes. In fact, it didn't look like a post office key at all. We tried the Wakefield Branch, up the line a bit, and got the same answer.

We started on the banks then.

Luckily, we hit it on the first try. The bank was on 220th Street, and the manager was cordial and helpful. He took one look at the key and said, "Yes, that's one of ours."

"Who rents the box?" we asked.

He looked at the key again. "Safety deposit 894. Just a moment, and I'll have that checked."

We stood on either side of his polished desk while he picked up a phone, asked for a Miss Delaney, and then questioned her about the key. "Yes," he said. "I see. Yes, thank you." He cradled the phone, put the key on the desk and said, "Jo Ann Ferris. Does that help you, gentlemen?"

"Jo Ann Ferris," Johnny said. "Jean Ferroni. That's close enough." He looked directly at the manager. "We'll be back in a little while with a court order to open that box. We'll ask for you."

"Certainly," the manager said, nodding gravely.

In a little over two hours, we were back, and we followed the manager past the barred gate at the rear of the bank, stepped into the vault, and walked back to the rows of safety deposit boxes. "894," he said. "Yes, here it is."

He opened the box, pulled out a slab and rested the box on it. Johnny lifted the lid.

"Anything?" I asked.

He pulled out what looked like several rolled sheets of stiff white paper. They were secured with rubber bands, and Johnny slid the bands off quickly. When he unrolled them, they turned out to be eight by ten glossy prints. I took one of the prints and looked at Jean Ferroni's contorted body. Beside me, the manager's mouth fell open.

"Well," I said, "this gives us something."

"We'll just take the contents of this box," Johnny said to the manager. "Make out a receipt for it, will you, Mike?"

I made out the receipt and we took the bundle of pornographic photos back to the lab with us. Whatever else Jean Ferroni had done, she had certainly posed in a variety of compromising positions. She'd owned a ripe, young body, and the pictures left nothing whatever to the imagination. But we weren't looking for kicks. We were looking for clues.

Dave Alger, one of the lab men, didn't hold out much hope.

"Nothing," he said. "What did you expect? Ordinary print paper. You can get the same stuff in any home developing kit."

"What about fingerprints?"

"The girl's mostly. A few others, but all smeared. You want me to track down the rubber bands?"

"Comedian," Johnny said.

"You guys expect miracles, that's all. You forget this is science and not witchcraft."

I was looking at the pictures spread out on the lab counter. They were all apparently taken in the same room, on the same bed. The bed had brass posts and railings at the head and foot. Behind the bed was an open window, with a murky city display of buildings outside. The pictures had evidently been taken at night, and probably recently because the window was wide open. Alongside the window on the wall was a picture of an Indian sitting on a black horse. A wide strip of wallpaper had been torn almost from ceiling to floor, leaving a white path on the wall. The room did not have the feel of a private apartment. It looked like any third-rate hotel room. I kept looking at the pictures and at the open window with the buildings beyond.

"You think all we do is wave a rattle and shake some feathers and wham! we got your goddam murderer. Well, it ain't that simple. We put in a lot of time on . . ."

"Blow this one up, will you?" I said.

"Why? You looking for tattoo marks?"

"No. I want to look through that window."

Dave suddenly brightened. "How big you want it, Mike?"

"Big enough to read those neon signs across the street."

"Can do," he said.

He scooped up all the pictures and ran off, his heels clicking against the asphalt tile floor.

"Think we got something?" Johnny asked.

"Maybe. We sure as hell can't lose anything."

"Besides, you'll have something to hang over your couch," Johnny cracked.

"Another comedian," I said, but I was beginning to feel better already. I smoked three cigarettes down to butts, and then Dave came back.

"One Rheingold beer billboard," he said.

"Yeah?"

"And one Hotel Mason. That help?"

The Hotel Mason was a dingy, grey-faced building on West Forty-Seventh. We weren't interested in it. We were interested in the building directly across the way, an equally dingy, gray-faced edifice that was named the Allistair Arms.

We walked directly to the desk and flashed our buzzers, and the desk clerk looked hastily to the elevator bank.

"Relax," Johnny said.

He pulled one of the pictures from under his jacket. The lab had whitened out the figures of Jean Ferroni and her male companion, leaving only the bed, the picture on the wall, and the open window. Johnny showed the picture to the desk clerk.

"What room is this?" he said.

"I . . . I don't know."

"Look hard."

"I tell you I don't know. Maybe one of the bellhops." He

pounded a bell on the desk, and an old man in a bellhop's rig hobbled over. Johnny showed him the picture and repeated his question.

"Damned if I know," the old man said. "All these rooms look alike." He stared at the picture again, shaking his head. Then his eyes narrowed and he bent closer and looked harder. "Oh," he said, "that's 305. That picture of the Injun and the ripped wallpaper there. Yep, that's 305." He paused. "Why?"

I turned. "Who's in 305?"

The desk clerk made a show of looking at the register. "Mr. Adams. Harley Adams."

"Let's go, Johnny," I said.

We started up the steps, and I saw Johnny's hand flick to his shoulder holster. When the hand came out from under his coat, it was holding a .38. I took out my own gun and we padded up noiselessly.

We stopped outside room 305, flattening ourselves against the walls on either side of the door.

Johnny reached out and rapped the butt of his gun against the door.

"Who is it?" a voice asked.

"Open up!"

"Who is it?"

"Police officers. Open up!"

"Wha . . ."

There was a short silence inside, and then we heard the frantic slap of leather on the floor.

"Hit it, Johnny," I shouted.

Johnny backed off against the opposite wall, put the sole of his shoe against it, and shoved off toward the door. His shoulder hit the wood, and the door splintered inward.

Adams was in his undershirt and trousers, and he had one leg over the windowsill, heading for the fire escape, when we came in. I swung my .38 in his direction and yelled, "You better hold it, Adams."

He looked at the gun, and then slowly lowered his leg to the floor.

"Sure," he said. "I wasn't going anyplace."

We found piles of pictures in the room, all bundled neatly. Some of them were of Jean Ferroni. But there were other girls and other men. We found an expensive camera in the closet, and a darkroom setup in the bathroom. We also found a switch knife with a six-inch blade in the top drawer of his dresser.

"I don't know anything about it," Adams insisted.

He kept insisting that for a long time, even after we showed him the pictures we'd taken from Jean Ferroni's safety deposit box. He kept insisting until we told him his knife would go down to the lab and they'd sure as hell find *some* trace of the dead girl on it, no matter how careful he'd been. We were stretching the truth a little, because a knife can be washed as clean as anything else. But Adams took the hook and told us everything.

He'd given the kid a come-on, getting her to pose alone at first, in the nude. From there, it had been simple to get her to pose for the big stuff, the stuff that paid off.

"She was getting classy," Adams said. "A cheap tramp like that getting classy. Wanted a percentage of the net. I gave her a percentage, all right. I arranged a nice little party right in my hotel room. Six guys. They fixed her good, one after the other. Then I drove her up to her own neighborhood and left her the way you found her—so it would look like a rape kill."

He paused and shifted in his chair, making himself comfortable.

"Imagine that broad," he continued. "Wanting to *share* with me. I showed her."

"You showed her, all right," Johnny said tightly.

That was when I swung out with my closed fist, catching Adams on the side of the jaw. He fell backward, knocking the chair over, sprawling onto the floor.

He scrambled to his feet, crouched low and said, "Hey, what the hell? Are you crazy?"

I didn't answer him. I left the Interrogation Room, walking past the patrolman at the door. Johnny caught up with me in the corridor, clamped his hand onto my shoulder.

"Why'd you hit him, Mike?" he asked.

"I wanted to," I said. "I just wanted to."

Johnny's eyes met mine for a moment, held them. His hand tightened on my shoulder, and his head nodded almost imperceptibly.

We walked down the corridor together, our heels clicking noisily on the hard floor.

A Very Merry Christmas

Sitting at the bar, Pete Charpens looked at his own reflection in the mirror, grinned, and said, "Merry Christmas."

It was not Christmas yet, true enough, but he said it anyway, and the words sounded good, and he grinned foolishly and lifted his drink and sipped a little of it and said again, "Merry Christmas," feeling very good, feeling very warm, feeling in excellent high spirits. Tonight, the city was his. Tonight, for the first time since he'd arrived from Whiting Center eight months ago, he felt like a part of the city. Tonight, the city enveloped him like a warm bath, and he lounged back and allowed the undulating waters to cover him. It was Christmas Eve, and all was right with the world, and Pete Charpens loved every mother's son who roamed the face of the earth because he felt as if he'd finally come home, finally found the place, finally found himself.

It was a good feeling.

This afternoon, as soon as the office party was over, he'd gone into the streets. The shop windows had gleamed like pot-bellied stoves, cherry hot against the sharp bite of the air. There was a promise of snow in the sky, and Pete had walked the tinseled streets of New York with his tweed coat collar against the back of his neck, and he had felt warm and happy. There were shoppers in the streets, and Santa Clauses with bells, and giant wreaths and giant trees, and music coming from speakers, the timeless carols of the holiday season. But more than that. For the first time in eight months, he had felt the pulse beat of the city, the people, the noise, the clutter, the rush, and above all the warmth. The warmth had engulfed him, surprising him. He had watched it with the foolish smile of a spectator and then, with sudden realization, he had known he was part of it. In the short space of eight months, he had become a part of the city—and the city had become a part of him. He had found a home.

"Bartender," he said.

The bartender ambled over. He was a big red-headed man with freckles all over his face. He moved with economy and grace. He seemed like a very nice guy who probably had a very nice wife and family decorating a Christmas tree somewhere in Queens.

"Yes, sir?" he asked.

"Pete. Call me Pete."

"Okay, Pete."

"I'm not drunk," Pete said, "believe me. I know all drunks say that, but I mean it. I'm just so damn happy I could bust. Did you ever feel that way?"

"Sure," the bartender said, smiling.

"Let me buy you a drink."

"I don't drink."

"Bartenders never drink, I know, but let me buy you one. Please. Look, I want to thank people, you know? I want to thank everybody in this city. I want to thank them for being here, for making it a city. Do I sound nuts?"

"Yes," the bartender said.

"Okay. Okay then, I'm nuts. But I'm a hick, do you know?

I came here from Whiting Center eight months ago. Straw sticking out of my ears. The confusion here almost killed me. But I got a job, a good job, and I met a lot of wonderful people, and I learned how to dress, and I . . . I found a home. That's corny. I know it. That's the hick in me talking. But I love this damn city, I *love* it. I want to go around kissing girls in the streets. I want to shake hands with every guy I meet. I want to tell them I feel like a person, a human being, I'm alive, alive! For Christ's sake, I'm alive!"

"That's a good way to be," the bartender agreed.

"I know it. Oh, my friend, do I know it! I was dead in Whiting Center, and now I'm here and alive and . . . look, let me buy you a drink, huh?"

"I don't drink," the bartender insisted.

"Okay. Okay, I won't argue. I wouldn't argue with anyone tonight. Gee, it's gonna be a great Christmas, do you know? Gee, I'm so damn happy I could bust." He laughed aloud, and the bartender laughed with him. The laugh trailed off into a chuckle, and then a smile. Pete looked into the mirror, lifted his glass again, and again said, "Merry Christmas. Merry Christmas."

He was still smiling when the man came into the bar and sat down next to him. The man was very tall, his body bulging with power beneath the suit he wore. Coatless, hatless, he came into the bar and sat alongside Pete, signalling for the bartender with a slight flick of the hand. The bartender walked over.

"Rye neat," the man said.

The bartender nodded and walked away. The man reached for his wallet.

"Let me pay for it," Pete said.

The man turned. He had a wide face with a thick nose and small brown eyes. The eyes came as a surprise in his otherwise large body. He studied Pete for a moment and then said, "You a queer or something?"

Pete laughed. "Hell, no," he said. "I'm just happy. It's Christmas Eve, and I feel like buying you a drink."

The man pulled out his wallet, put a five dollar bill on the bar top and said, "I'll buy my own drink." He paused. "What's the matter? Don't I look as if I can afford a drink?"

"Sure you do," Pete said. "I just wanted to . . . look, I'm happy. I want to share it, that's all."

The man grunted and said nothing. The bartender brought his drink. He tossed off the shot and asked for another.

"My name's Pete Charpens," Pete said, extending his hand.

"So what?" the man said.

"Well . . . what's your name?"

"Frank."

"Glad to know you, Frank." He thrust his hand closer to the man.

"Get lost, Happy," Frank said.

Pete grinned, undismayed. "You ought to relax," he said, "I mean it. You know, you've got to stop . . ."

"Don't tell me what I've got to stop. Who the hell are you, anyway?"

"Pete Charpens. I told you."

"Take a walk, Pete Charpens. I got worries of my own."

"Want to tell me about them?"

"No, I don't want to tell you about them."

"Why not? Make you feel better."

"Go to hell, and stop bothering me," Frank said.

The bartender brought the second drink. He sipped at it, and then put the shot glass on the bar top.

"Do I look like a hick?" Pete asked.

"You look like a goddamn queer," Frank said.

"No, I mean it."

"You asked me, and I told you."

"What's troubling you, Frank?"

"You a priest or something?"

"No, but I thought . . ."

"Look, I come in here to have a drink. I didn't come to see the chaplain."

"You an ex-Army man?"

"Yeah."

"I was in the Navy," Pete said. "Glad to be out of that, all right. Glad to be right here where I am, in the most wonderful city in the whole damn world."

"Go down to Union Square and get a soap box," Frank said.

"Can't I help you, Frank?" Pete asked. "Can't I buy you a drink, lend you an ear, do something? You're so damn sad, I feel like . . ."

"I'm not sad."

"You sure look sad. What happened? Did you lose your job?"

"No, I didn't lose my job."

"What do you do, Frank?"

"Right now, I'm a truck driver. I used to be a fighter."

"Really? You mean a boxer? No kidding?"

"Why would I kid you?"

"What's your last name?"

"Blake."

"Frank Blake? I don't think I've heard it before. Of course, I didn't follow the fights much."

"Tiger Blake, they called me. That was my ring name."

"Tiger Blake. Well, we didn't have fights in Whiting Center. Had to go over to Waterloo if we wanted to see a bout. I guess that's why I never heard of you."

"Sure," Frank said.

"Why'd you quit fighting?"

"They made me."

"Why?"

"I killed a guy."

Pete's eyes widened. "In the ring?"

"Of course in the ring. What the hell kind of a moron are you, anyway? You think I'd be walking around if it wasn't in the ring? Jesus!"

"Is that what's troubling you?"

"There ain't nothing troubling me. I'm fine."

"Are you going home for Christmas?"

"I got no home."

"You must have a home," Pete said gently. "*Everybody's* got a home."

"Yeah? Where's your home? Whiting Center or wherever the hell you said?"

"Nope. This is my home now. New York City. New York, New York. The greatest goddamn city in the whole world."

"Sure," Frank said sourly.

"My folks are dead," Pete said. "I'm an only child. Nothing for me in Whiting Center anymore. But in New York, well, I get the feeling that I'm here to stay. That I'll meet a nice girl here, and marry her, and raise a family here and . . . and this'll be home."

"Great," Frank said.

"How'd you happen to kill this fellow?" Pete asked suddenly.

"I hit him."

"And killed him?"

"I hit him on the Adam's apple. Accidentally."

"Were you sore at him?"

"We were in the ring. I already told you that."

"Sure, but were you sore?"

"A fighter don't have to be sore. He's paid to fight."

"Did you like fighting?"

"I loved it," Frank said flatly.

"How about the night you killed that fellow?"

Frank was silent for a long time. Then he said, "Get lost, huh?"

"I could never fight for money," Pete said. "I have a quick temper, and I get mad as hell, but I could never do it for money. Besides, I'm too happy right now to . . ."

"Get lost," Frank said again, and he turned his back. Pete sat silently for a moment.

"Frank?" he said at last.

"You back again?"

"I'm sorry. I shouldn't have talked to you about something that's painful to you. Look, it's Christmas Eve. Let's . . ."

"Forget it."

"Can I buy you a drink?"

"No. I told you no a hundred times. I buy my own damn drinks!"

"This is Christmas E . . ."

"I don't care what it is. You happy jokers give me the creeps. Get off my back, will you?"

"I'm sorry. I just . . ."

"Happy, happy, happy. Grinning like a damn fool. What the hell is there to be so happy about? You got an oil well someplace? A gold mine? What is it with you?"

"I'm just . . ."

"You're just a jerk! I probably pegged you right the minute I laid eyes on you. You're probably a damn queer."

"No, no," Pete said mildly. "You're mistaken, Frank. Honestly, I just feel . . ."

"Your old man was probably a queer, too. Your old lady probably took on every sailor in town."

The smile left Pete's face, and then tentatively reappeared. "You don't mean that, Frank," he said.

"I mean everything I ever say," Frank said. There was a strange gleam in his eyes. He studied Pete carefully.

"About my mother, I meant," Pete said.

"I know what you're talking about. And I'll say it again. She probably took on every sailor in town."

"Don't say that, Frank," Pete said, the smile gone now, a perplexed frown teasing his forehead, appearing, vanishing, reappearing.

"You're a queer, and your old lady was a . . ."

"Stop it, Frank."

"Stop what? If your old lady was . . ."

Pete leaped off the bar stool. "Cut it out!" he yelled.

From the end of the bar, the bartender turned. Frank caught the movement with the corner of his eye. In a cold whisper, he said, "Your mother was a slut," and Pete swung at him.

Frank ducked, and the blow grazed the top of his head. The bartender was coming towards them now. He could not see the strange light in Frank's eyes, nor did he hear Frank whisper again, "A slut, a slut."

Pete pushed himself off the bar wildly. He saw the beer bottle then, picked it up, and lunged at Frank.

The patrolman knelt near his body.

"He's dead, all right," he said. He stood up and dusted off his trousers. "What happened?"

Frank looked bewildered and dazed. "He went berserk," he

said. "We were sitting and talking. Quiet. All of a sudden, he swings at me." He turned to the bartender. "Am I right?"

"He was drinking," the bartender said. "Maybe he was drunk."

"I didn't even swing back," Frank said, "not until he picked up the beer bottle. Hell, this is Christmas Eve. I didn't want no trouble."

"What happened when he picked up the bottle?"

"He swung it at me. So I . . . I put up my hands to defend myself. I only gave him a push, so help me."

"Where'd you hit him?"

Frank paused. "In . . . in the throat, I think." He paused again. "It was self-defense, believe me. This guy just went berserk. He musta been a maniac."

"He *was* talking kind of queer," the bartender agreed.

The patrolman nodded sympathetically. "There's more nuts outside than there is in," he said. He turned to Frank. "Don't take this so bad, Mac. You'll get off. It looks open and shut to me. Just tell them the story downtown, that's all."

"Berserk," Frank said. "He just went berserk."

"Well . . ." The patrolman shrugged. "My partner'll take care of the meat wagon when it gets here. You and me better get downtown. I'm sorry I got to ruin your Christmas, but . . ."

"It's *him* that ruined it," Frank said, shaking his head and looking down at the body on the floor.

Together, they started out of the bar. At the door, the patrolman waved to the bartender and said, "Merry Christmas, Mac."

Small Homicide

Her face was small and chubby, the eyes blue and innocently rounded, but seeing nothing. Her body rested on the seat of the wooden bench, one arm twisted awkwardly beneath her.

The candles near the altar flickered and cast their dancing shadows on her face. There was a faded, pink blanket wrapped around her, and against the whiteness of her throat were the purple bruises that told us she'd been strangled.

Her mouth was open, exposing two small teeth and the beginnings of a third.

She was no more than eight months old.

The church was quiet and immense, with early-morning sunlight lighting the stained-glass windows. Dust motes filtered down the long, slanting columns of sunlight, and Father Barron stood tall and darkly somber at the end of the pew, the sun touching his hair like an angel's kiss.

"This is the way you found her, Father?" I asked.

"Yes. Just that way." The priest's eyes were a deep brown against the chalky whiteness of his face. "I didn't touch her."

Pat Travers scratched his jaw and stood up, reaching for the pad in his back pocket. His mouth was set in a tight, angry line. Pat had three children of his own. "What time was this, Father?"

"At about five-thirty. We have a six o'clock mass, and I came out to see that the altar was prepared. Our altar boys go to school, you understand, and they usually arrive at the last moment. I generally attend to the altar myself."

"No sexton?" Pat asked.

"Yes, we have a sexton, but he doesn't arrive until about eight every morning. He comes earlier on Sundays."

I nodded while Pat jotted the information in his pad. "How did you happen to see her, Father?"

"I was walking to the back of the church to open the doors. I saw something in the pew, and I . . . well, at first I thought it was just a package someone had forgotten. When I came closer, I saw it was . . . was a baby." He sighed deeply and shook his head.

"The doors were locked, Father?"

"No. No, they're never locked. This is God's house, you know. They were simply closed. I was walking back to open them. I usually open them before the first mass in the morning."

"They were all unlocked all night?"

"Yes, of course."

"I see." I looked down at the baby again. "You . . . you wouldn't know who she is, would you, Father?"

Father Barron shook his head again. "I'm afraid not. She may have been baptized here, but infants all look alike, you know. It would be different if I saw her every Sunday. But . . ." He spread his hands wide in a helpless gesture.

Pat nodded, and kept looking at the dead child. "We'll have to send some of the boys to take pictures and prints, Father. I hope you don't mind. And we'll have to chalk up the pew. It shouldn't take too long, and we'll have the body out as soon as possible."

Father Barron looked down at the dead baby. He crossed himself then and said, "God have mercy on her soul."

I was sipping at my hot coffee when the buzzer on my desk sounded. I pushed down the toggle and said, "Levine here."

"Dave, want to come into my office a minute? This is the lieutenant."

"Sure thing," I told him. I put down the cup and said, "Be right back," to Pat, and headed for the Skipper's office.

He was sitting behind his desk with our report in his hands. He glanced up when I came in and said, "Sit down, Dave. Hell of a thing, isn't it?"

"Yes," I said.

"I'm holding it back from the papers, Dave. If this breaks, we'll have every mother in the city telephoning us. You know what that means?"

"You want it fast."

"I want it damned fast. I'm pulling six men from other jobs to help you and Pat. I don't want to go to another precinct for help because the bigger this gets, the better its chances of breaking print are. I want it quiet and small, and I want it fast." He stopped and shook his head, and then muttered, "Goddamn thing."

"We're waiting for the autopsy report now," I said. "As soon as we get it, we may be able to—"

"What did it look like to you?"

"Strangulation. It's there in our report."

The lieutenant glanced at the typewritten sheet in his hands, mumbled, "Uhm," and then said, "While you're waiting, you'd better start checking the Missing Persons calls."

"Pat's doing that now, sir."

"Good, good. You know what to do, Dave. Just get me an answer to it fast."

"We'll do our best, sir."

He leaned back in his leather chair, "A little girl, huh?" He shook his head. "Damn shame. Damn shame." He kept shaking his head and looking at the report, and then he dropped the report on his desk and said, "Here're the boys you're got to work with." He handed me a typewritten list of names. "All good, Dave. Get me results."

"I'll try, sir."

Pat had a list of calls on his desk when I went outside again. I picked it up and glanced through it rapidly. A few older kids were lost, and there had been the usual frantic pleas from frantic mothers who should have watched their kids more carefully in the first place.

"What's this?" I asked. I put my forefinger alongside a call clocked in at eight-fifteen. A Mrs. Wilkes had phoned to say she'd left her baby outside in the carriage, and the carriage was gone.

"They found the kid," Pat said. "Her older daughter had simply taken the kid for a walk. There's nothing there, Dave."

"The Skipper wants action, Pat. The photos come in yet?"

"Over there." He indicated a pile of glossy photographs on his desk. I picked up the stack and thumbed through it. They'd shot the baby from every conceivable angle, and there were two good close-ups of her face. I fanned the pictures out on my desk top and phoned the lab. I recognized Caputo's voice at once.

"Any luck, Cappy?"

"That you, Dave?"

"Yep."

"You mean on the baby?"

"Yeah."

"The boys brought in a whole slew of stuff. A pew collects a lot of prints, Dave."

"Anything we can use?"

"I'm running them through now. If we get anything, I'll let you know."

"Fine. I want the baby's footprints taken and a stat sent to every hospital in the state."

"Okay. It's going to be tough if the baby was born outside, though."

"Maybe we'll be lucky. Put the stat on the machine, will you? And tell them we want immediate replies."

"I'll have it taken care of, Dave."

"Good. Cappy, we're going to need all the help we can get on this one. So . . ."

"I'll do all I can."

"Thanks. Let me know if you get anything."

"I will. So long, Dave. I've got work."

He clicked off, and I leaned back and lighted a cigarette. Pat picked up one of the baby's photos and glumly studied it.

"When they get him, they should cut off his . . ."

"He'll get the chair," I said. "That's for sure."

"I'll pull the switch. Personally. Just ask me. Just ask me and I'll do it."

The baby was stretched out on the long white table when I went down to see Doc Edwards. A sheet covered the corpse, and Doc was busy typing up a report. I looked over his shoulder:

POLICE DEPARTMENT
City of New York

Date: _____June 12, 1953_____

From: Commanding Officer, _____Charles R. Brandon, 77th Pct._____

To: Chief Medical Examiner

SUBJECT: DEATH OF _____Baby girl (unidentified)_____

     Please furnish information on items checked below in connection with the death of the above named. Body was found on ___June 12,___ ___1953___ at ___Church of the Holy Mother,___ ___1220 Benson Avenue, Bronx, New York___

Autopsy performed or examination made? ___Yes___

By Dr. ___James L. Edwards, Fordham Hospital Mortuary___

Date: ___June 12, 1953___ Where? ___Bronx County___

Cause of death: ___Broken neck___

Doc Edwards looked up from the typewriter.

"Not nice, Dave."

"No, not nice at all." I saw that he was ready to type in the *Result of chemical analysis* space. "Anything else on her?"

"Not much. Dried tears on her face. Urine on her abdomen, buttocks, and genitals. Traces of Desitin and petroleum jelly there, too. That's about it."

"Time of death?"

"I'd put it at about three a.m. last night."

"Uh-huh."

"You want a guess?"

"Sure."

"Somebody doesn't like his sleep to be disturbed by a crying kid. That's my guess."

"Nobody likes his sleep disturbed," I said. "What's the Desitin and petroleum jelly for? That normal?"

"Yeah, sure. Lots of mothers use it. Mostly for minor irritations. Urine burn, diaper rash, that sort of thing."

"I see."

"This shouldn't be too tough, Dave. You know who the kid is yet?"

"We're working on that now."

"Well, good luck."

"Thanks."

I turned to go, and Doc Edwards began pecking at the typewriter again, completing the autopsy report on a dead girl.

There was good news waiting for me back at the office. Pat rushed over with a smile on his face and a thick sheet of paper in his hands.

"Here's the ticket," he said.

I took the paper and looked at it. It was the photostat of a birth certificate.

U. S. NAVAL HOSPITAL St. Albans, N. Y. **Birth Certificate**

This certifies that **Louise Ann Dreiser** was born to **Alice Dreiser** in this hospital at **4:15 P.M.** on the **tenth** day of **November, 1952**

Weight **7** lbs. **6** ozs.

In witness whereof, the said hospital has caused this certificate to be issued, properly signed and the seal of the hospital hereunto affixed.

Gregory Freeman, Lt(jg) MC USN

Gregory Freeman, LTJG MC USN
Attending Physician

Frederick L. Mann

Frederick L. Mann, CAPTAIN MC
Commanding Officer USN

"Here's how they got it," Pat said, handing me another stat. I looked at it quickly. It was obviously the reverse side of the birth certificate.

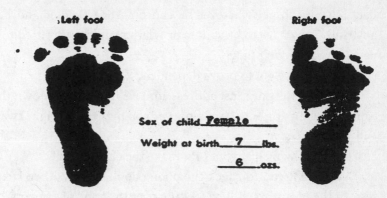

Left foot   **Right foot**

Sex of child _Female_

Weight at birth___ **7** ___lbs.

___ **6** ___ozs.

Certificate of birth should be carefully preserved as record of value for future use:

1. To identify relationship

2. To establish age to enter school

There were several more good reasons why a birth certificate should be kept in the sugar bowl, and then below that:

Official registration at **148-15 Archer Avenue,**
Jamaica, L.I., N.Y.

Mother's left thumb   **Mother's right thumb**

"Alice Dreiser," I said.

"That's the mother. Prints and all. I've already sent a copy down to Cappy to check against the ones they lifted from the pew."

"Fine. Pick one of the boys from the list the Skipper gave us, Pat. Tell him to get whatever he can on Alice Drieser and her husband. They have to be sailors or relations to get admitted to a naval hospital, don't they?"

"Yeah. You've got to prove dependency."

"Fine. Get the guy's last address, and we'll try to run down the woman, or him, or both. Get whoever you pick to call right away, will you?"

"Right. Why pick anyone? I'll make the call myself."

"No, I want you to check the phone book for any Alice Dreisers. In the meantime, I'll be looking over the baby's garments."

"You'll be down at the lab?"

"Yeah. Phone me, Pat."

"Right."

Caputo had the garments separated and tagged when I got there.

"You're not going to get much out of these," he told me.

"No luck, huh?"

He held out the pink blanket. "Black River Mills. A big trade name. You can probably buy it in any retail shop in the city." He picked up the small pink sweater with the pearl buttons. "Toddlers, Inc., ditto. The socks have no markings at all. The undershirt came from Gilman's here in the city. It's the largest department store in the world, so you can imagine how many of these they sell every day. The cotton pajamas were bought there, too."

"No shoes?"

"No shoes."

"What about the diaper?"

"What about it? It's a plain diaper. No label. You got any kids, Dave?"

"One."

"You ever see a diaper with a label?"

"I don't recall."

"If you did, it wasn't in it long. Diapers take a hell of a beating."

"Maybe this one came from a diaper service."

"Maybe. You can check that."

"Safety pins?"

"Two. No identifying marks. Look like five-and-dime stuff."

"Any prints?"

"Yeah. There are smudged prints on the pins, but there's a good partial thumbprint on one of the pajama snaps."

"Whose?"

"It matches the right thumbprint on the stat you sent down. Mrs. Dreiser's."

"Uh-huh. Did you check her prints against the ones from the pew?"

"Nothing, Dave. None of her, anyway."

"Okay, Cappy. Thanks a lot."

Cappy shrugged. "I get paid," he said. He grinned and waved as I walked out and headed upstairs again. I met Pat in the hallway, coming down to the lab after me.

"What's up?" I asked.

"I called the Naval Hospital. They gave me the last address they had for the guy. His name is Carl Dreiser, lived at 831 East 217th Street, Bronx, when the baby was born."

"How come?"

"He was a yeoman, working downtown on Church Street.

Lived with his wife uptown, got an allotment. You know the story."

"Yeah. So?"

"I sent Artie to check at that address. He should be calling in soon now."

"What about the sailor?"

"I called the Church Street office, spoke to the commanding officer, Captain"—he consulted a slip of paper—"Captain Thibot. This Dreiser was working there back in November. He got orders in January, reported aboard the U.S.S. Hanfield, DD 981, at the Brooklyn Navy Yard on January fifth of this year."

"Where is he now?"

"That's the problem, Dave."

"What kind of problem?"

"The Hanfield was sunk off Pyongyang in March."

"Oh."

"Dreiser is listed as missing in action."

I didn't say anything. I nodded, and waited.

"A telegram was sent to Mrs. Dreiser at the Bronx address. The Navy says the telegram was delivered and signed for by Alice Dreiser."

"Let's wait for Artie to call in," I said.

We ordered more coffee and waited. Pat had checked the phone book, and there'd been no listing for either Carl or Alice Dreiser. He'd had a list typed of every Dreiser in the city, and it ran longer than my arm.

"Why didn't you ask the Navy what his parents' names are?" I said.

"I did. Both parents are dead."

"Who does he list as next of kin?"

"His wife. Alice Dreiser."

"Great."

In a half hour, Artie called in. There was no Alice Dreiser living at the Bronx address. The landlady said she'd lived there until April and had left without giving a forwarding address. Yes, she'd had a baby daughter. I told Artie to keep the place staked out, and then buzzed George Tabin and told him to check the Post Office Department for any forwarding address.

When he buzzed back in twenty minutes, he said, "Nothing, Dave. Nothing at all."

We split the available force of men, and I managed to wangle four more men from the lieutenant. Half of us began checking on the Dreisers listed in the phone directory, and the rest of us began checking the diaper services.

The first diaper place I called on had a manager who needed only a beard to look like Santa Claus. He greeted me affably and offered all his assistance. Unfortunately, they'd never had a customer named Alice Dreiser.

At my fourth stop, I got what looked like a lead.

I spoke directly to the vice-president, and he listened intently.

"Perhaps," he said, "perhaps." He was a big man, with a wide waist, a gold watch chain spraddling it. He leaned over and pushed down on his intercom buzzer.

"Yes, sir?"

"Bring in a list of our customers. Starting with November of 1952."

"Sir?"

"Starting with November of 1952."

"Yes, sir."

We chatted about the diaper business in general until the list came, and then he handed it to me and I began checking off the names. There were a hell of a lot of names on it. For the month of December, I found a listing for Alice Dreiser. The address given was the one we'd checked in the Bronx.

"Here she is," I said. "Can you get her records?"

The vice-president looked at the name. "Certainly, just a moment." He buzzed his secretary again, told her what he wanted, and she brought the yellow file cards in a few minutes later. The cards told me that Alice Dreiser had continued the diaper service through February. She'd been late on her February payment, and had cancelled service in March. She'd had the diapers delivered for the first week in March but had not paid for them. She did not notify the company that she was moving. She had not returned the diapers they'd sent her that first week in March. The company did not know where she was.

"If you find her," the vice-president told me, "I'd like to know. She owes us money."

"I'll keep that in mind," I said.

The reports on the Dreisers were waiting for me back at the precinct. George had found a couple who claimed to be Carl's aunt and uncle. They knew he was married. They gave Alice's maiden name as Grant. They said she lived somewhere on Walton Avenue in the Bronx, or at least *had* lived there when Carl first met her, they hadn't seen either her or Carl for months. Yes, they knew the Dreisers had had a daughter. They'd received an announcement card. They had never seen the baby.

Pat and I looked up the Grants on Walton Avenue, found a listing for Peter Grant, and went there together.

A bald man in his undershirt, his suspenders hanging over his trousers, opened the door.

"What is it?" he asked.

"Police officers," I said. "We'd like to ask a few questions."

"What about? Let me see your badges."

Pat and I flashed our buzzers and the bald man studied them.

"What kind of questions do you want to ask?"

"Are you Peter Grant?"

"Yeah, that's right. What's this all about?"

"May we come in?"

"Sure, come on in." We followed him into the apartment, and he motioned us to chairs in the small living room. "Now, what is it?" he asked.

"Your daughter is Alice Dreiser?"

"Yes," he said.

"Do you know where she lives?"

"No."

"Come on, mister," Pat said. "You know where your daughter lives."

"I don't," Grant snapped, "and I don't give a damn, either."

"Why? What's wrong, mister?"

"Nothing. Nothing's wrong. It's none of your business, anyway."

"Her daughter had her neck broken," I said. "It is our business."

"I don't give a . . ." he started to say. He stopped then and looked straight ahead of him, his brows pulled together into a tight frown. "I'm sorry. I still don't know where she lives."

"Did you know she was married?"

"To that sailor. Yes, I knew."

"And you knew she had a daughter?"

"Don't make me laugh," Grant said.

"What's funny, mister?" Pat said.

"Did I know she had a daughter? Why the hell do you think she married the sailor? Don't make me laugh!"

"When was your daughter married, Mr. Grant?"

"Last September." He saw the look on my face, and added, "Go ahead, you count it. The kid was born in November."

"Have you seen her since the marriage?"

"No."

"Have you ever seen the baby?"

"No."

"Do you have a picture of your daughter?"

"I think so. Is she in trouble? Do you think she did it?"

"We don't know who did it yet."

"Maybe she did," Grant said softly. "She just maybe did. I'll get you the picture."

He came back in a few minutes with a picture of a plain girl wearing a cap and gown. She had light eyes and straight hair, and her face was intently serious.

"She favors her mother," Grant said, "God rest her soul."

"Your wife is dead?"

"Yes. That picture was taken when Alice graduated high school. She graduated in June and married the sailor in September. She's . . . she's only just nineteen now, you know."

"May we have this?"

He hesitated and said, "It's the only one I've got. She . . . she didn't take many pictures. She wasn't a very . . . pretty kid."

"We'll return it."

"All right," he said. His eyes began to blink. "She . . . If she's in trouble, you'll . . . you'll let me know, won't you?"

"We'll let you know."

"Kids . . . kids make mistakes sometimes." He stood up abruptly. "Let me know."

We had copies of the photo made, and then we staked out every church in the neighborhood in which the baby was found. Pat and I covered the Church of the Holy Mother, because we figured the suspect was most likely to come back there.

We didn't talk much. There is something about a church of any denomination that makes a man think rather than talk. Pat and I knocked off at about seven every night, and the night boys took over then. We were back on the job at seven in the morning, every morning.

It was a week before she came in.

She was a thin girl, with the body of a child and a pinched, tired face. She stopped at the font in the rear of the church, dipped her hand in the holy water, and crossed herself. Then she walked to the altar, stopped before an idol of the Virgin Mary, lighted a candle, and knelt before it.

"That's her," I said.

"Let's go," Pat answered.

"Not here. Outside."

Pat's eyes locked with mine for an instant. "Sure," he said.

She knelt before the idol for a long time, and then got to her feet slowly, drying her eyes. She walked up the aisle, stopped at the font, crossed herself, and then walked outside.

We followed her out, catching up with her at the corner. I pulled up on one side of her and Pat on the other.

"Mrs. Dreiser?" I asked.

She stopped walking. "Yes?"

I showed my buzzer. "Police officers," I said. "We'd like to ask some questions."

She stared at my face for a long time. She drew a trembling breath then, and said, "I killed her. I . . . Carl was dead, you see. I . . . I guess that was it. It wasn't right—his getting killed, I mean. And she was crying." She nodded blankly. "Yes, that was it. She just cried all the time, not knowing that I was crying inside. You don't know how I cried inside. Carl . . . he was all I had. I . . . I couldn't stand it anymore. I told her to shut up and when she didn't I . . . I . . ."

"Come on now, ma'am," I said.

"I brought her to the church." She nodded, remembering it all now. "She was innocent, you know. So I brought her to the church. Did you find her there?"

"Yes, ma'am," I said. "That's where we found her."

She seemed pleased. A small smile covered her mouth and she said, "I'm glad you found her."

She told the story again to the lieutenant. Pat and I checked out and on the way to the subway, I asked him, "Do you still want to pull the switch, Pat?"

He didn't answer.

Hot

I wore moccasins, which were against Navy regulations, and the heat of the deck plates scorched up through the thin soles of the shoes, blistering my feet. I sat aft on the fantail, looking out over the heat of Guantanamo Bay, watching the guys from one of the other ships diving over the side and into the water. The water looked cool and clear, and the guys from the other can seemed to be enjoying it. They didn't seem to be afraid of any barracuda. They seemed to be ordinary guys taking an ordinary swim in the drink.

The Cuban sun beat down on my head, scorched through the white hat there, left a soggy ring of sweat where the hat band met my forehead. The Old Man made sure we wore hats, and he posted a notice on the quarterdeck saying no man would be allowed to roam the ship without a shirt on. He was worried about us getting sunburned. He was worried about all that sun up there beating down and turning us lobster red.

But he wouldn't let us swim.

He said there were barracuda in the water. He knew. He was a bigshot Commander who'd politicked his way through Annapolis, and he knew. Sure. He couldn't tell a barracuda from a goldfish, but he'd pursed his fat lips and scratched his bald head and said, "No swimming. Barracuda." And that was that.

Except every other ship in the squadron was allowing its crew to swim. Every other ship admitted there were no barracuda in the waters, or maybe there were, but who the hell cared? They were all out there swimming, jumping over the sides and sticking close to the nets the ships had thrown over, and nobody'd got bitten yet.

I wiped the sweat from my forehead, and I sucked in a deep breath, trying to get some air, trying to sponge something fresh out of the hot stillness all around me. I sucked in garbage fumes and that was all. The garbage cans were stacked on the fantail like rotting corpses. We weren't supposed to dump garbage in port, and the garbage scow was late, but did the Old Man do anything about that? No, he just issued stupid goddamn orders about no swimming, orders he . . .

"Resting, Peters?"

I jumped to my feet because I recognized the voice. I snapped to and looked into the skipper's face and said, "Yes, sir, for just a moment, sir."

"Haven't you got a work station?" he asked. I looked at his fat lips, pursed now, cracking and dried from the heat. I looked at his pale blue eyes and the deep brown color of his skin, burned from the sun and the wind on the open bridge. My captain, my skipper. The Commander. The louse.

"Yes, sir," I said. "I have a work station."

"Where, Peters?"

"The radar shack, sir."

"Then what are you doing on the fantail?"

"It was hot up there, sir. I came down for a drink at the scuttlebutt, and I thought I'd catch some air while I was at it."

"Uh-huh." He nodded his head, the braided peak of his cap

catching the hot rays of the sun. The silver maple leaf on the collar of his shirt winked up like a hot eye. He looked down at the deck, and then he looked at my feet, and then he said, "Are those regulation shoes, Peters?"

"No, sir," I said.

"Why not?"

"My feet were sweating in . . ."

"Are you aware of my order about wearing loafers and moccasins aboard ship?"

"Yes, sir."

"Then why are you wearing moccasins?"

"I told you, sir. My feet . . ."

"Why are you wearing white socks, Peters?"

"Sir?"

"You heard me, goddamnit. Regulation is black socks. The uniform of the day is posted every day in the midships passageway, Peters. The uniform for today is dungarees, white hats, black socks and black shoes. Are you aware of that?"

"Yes, sir."

"Do you know that we are here on shakedown cruise, Peters?"

"Yes, sir."

"Do you know that the squadron commander may pop in on this ship at any moment? Do you know that? What do you think he'd say to me if he found men in white socks and moccasins? What the hell do you think this is, Peters? A goddamn country club?"

"No, sir."

"When's the last time you had a haircut, Peters?"

"Last week, sir."

"Don't lie to me, Peters."

"Last week, sir," I repeated.

"Then get down to the barber shop after sweepdown, do you understand? And you'd better shave, too, Peters. I don't like any man in my crew looking like a bum."

"I'm sorry, sir. I . . ."

"Get back to your station. And if I find you goofing off again, Peters, it's going to be your hide, remember that. Now get going."

"Yes, sir," I said.

"Change those socks and shoes first."

"Yes, sir."

"And on the double, Peters."

"Yes, sir."

I left him and went down to the aft sleeping compartment. It was hotter down there, and you could feel the sweat clinging to the sides of the ship, dripping from the bulkheads. There was a stink down there, too, a stink worse than garbage, the stink of men living in cramped quarters. I went to my locker and lifted the top, and Ramsey, a Radioman Second, looked down from his sack. He was in his skivvies, and his bare chest and legs were coated with perspiration.

"Man," he said, "and I thought it was hot in Georgia."

"The Old Man is prowling," I told him. "You better move your ass."

"Let him prowl," Ramsey said. "That one don't scare me none."

"No, huh?" I said. I took out a pair of black socks and the regulation black shoes, and then I kicked off the moccasins and pulled off the white socks. "Maybe you like losing liberty, huh, Ramsey? If the Old Man catches you sprawled out like that, you'll get a Captain's Mast, at least."

"You know what he can do with his Mast, don't you?" Ramsey asked, smiling and stretching out.

"How come you're so brave, Ramsey?" I asked, putting on the black socks.

"How come? I'll let you in on a secret, Dave. You really want to know?"

"Yeah, how come?"

"I'm sick, man. I got me cat fever. The Chief Pharmacist's Mate himself, he said I got to lay flat on my keester. That's what he said. So let the Old Man come down here and say something, just let him. I'll tell him just where the crowbar goes."

"You wouldn't tell him nothing," I said, smiling. "You and the skipper are buddies."

"Sure," Ramsey said.

"I think you really like the Old Man."

"Only one way I'd like him," Ramsey said.

"How's that?"

Ramsey rolled over. "Dead," he said.

I went up to the radar shack after changing, and I got to work, piddling around with a bucket and a rag, wiping off the radar scopes, fooling with the plotting boards, making like I was working. The radar shack was about as big as a flea's nose, and I'd already cleaned it thoroughly after chow. That made no difference to the Navy. In the Navy, you cleaned it again, or you pretended to clean it again. Anything to keep you busy. Anything to keep you from enjoying a swim when the thermometer was ready to pop.

Gary came in while I was behind the vertical plotting board, and he said, "What're you doing, Peters?"

"What the hell does it look like I'm doing?" I asked him.

"It looks like you're working," he said, "but I know that can't be so."

"Yeah, stow it," I told him.

"You shouldn't be nasty to non-commissioned officers, Peters," he said. He smiled a crooked smile, and his buck teeth showed in his narrow face. "I could report you to the Old Man, you know."

"You would, too," I said.

"He don't like you to begin with." Gary smiled again, enjoying the three stripes he wore on his dress blues, enjoying the three stripes he'd inked onto his denim shirt. "What'd you do to the old boy, Dave?"

"Nothing," I said.

"Well, he sure don't like you."

"The feelings are mutual," I said.

"You like mid watches, Dave?"

"Whattya mean?" I asked.

"We got to stand voice radio watch in port, you know that. Not enough radiomen. I showed the Old Man the watch list. Had you slated for a four to eight this afternoon."

"So?"

"The Old Man told me to put you on the mid watch."

"The mid watch? What the hell for? Why . . ."

"Nobody likes to drag up here at midnight, Dave," Gary said. "But don't be bitter."

"What the hell did he do that for?" I asked.

Gary shook his head. "He just don't like you, chum. Hell, he don't like any enlisted man on this ship—but you he likes least of all."

"The hell with him," I said. "I've stood mid watches before. Ain't no mid watch going to break me."

"That's the spirit," Gary said drily. He paused a moment, and then said, "But you know something, Dave?"

"What?"

"If I had a character like the Old Man riding my tail, you know what I'd do?"

"No. What would you do?"

"I'd kill him," he said softly. He looked at me steadily, and then turned. "Don't want to interrupt your work, chum," he said, and then he was gone.

I thought about that mid watch all morning and, when the chow whistle sounded, I dropped the bucket and rags and headed down for the main deck. I got in line and started talking with one of the guys, Crawley, a gunner's mate. I had my back to the railing so I naturally couldn't see what was going on behind me. Nobody yelled, "Attention!" either, so I didn't know what was happening until I heard the Old Man's voice say, "How about it, Peters?"

I turned slowly, and he was standing there with his hands on his hips and a smile on his face, but the smile didn't reach those cold blue eyes of his.

"Sir?" I said.

"You know what this leaf on my collar means, Peters?"

"Yes, sir," I said. I was standing at attention now, and the sweat was streaming down my face, and my feet were sweating inside the black socks and black shoes.

"Do you know that an enlisted man is supposed to come to attention when an officer appears? Do you know that I am the captain of this ship, Peters?"

"Yes, sir. I know that."

"I don't think I like the tone of your voice, Peters."

"I'm sorry, sir."

"Hereafter, Peters, you keep your eyes peeled, understand? And whenever you see me coming, I want you to shout, 'Attention!' in case there are any other members of the crew who don't understand the meaning of respect. Do you understand that, Peters?"

"Yes, sir."

"Good. And so you won't forget it, Peters, perhaps we'll forego liberty for a week when we get back to the States."

"Sir, I . . ."

"That'll do, Peters. I'll discuss this with the Communications Officer, and you'll be restricted to the ship for a week after we return to Norfolk."

"I didn't even see you, sir," I said doggedly. "My back was . . ."

"It's your business to see me, Peters. And from now on, you'd damn well better see me."

"You're the boss," I said angrily.

"Yes, Peters," the captain said coldly. "I am."

He looked at me steadily for another moment, and then addressed the other guys standing in line. "At ease," he said, and walked through the passageway near the mess hall.

I watched his back disappear, and then I slouched against the bulkhead, and Crawley, the gunner's mate, said, "That rotten louse."

I didn't answer him. I was thinking of the mid watch, and now the loss of a week's liberty, after three weeks of shakedown cruise when we'd all been restricted to base. The swabbies on the base all got liberty in Havana, but not the poor slobs who came down to play war games, not us. We roamed the base and bought souvenirs for the folks at home, but you can buy only so many souvenirs in three weeks, and after that you don't even bother going ashore. Sure, Norfolk was a rat town, but it was a town at least, and there were women there—if you weren't too particular—and Stateside liberty wasn't to be sneezed at, not after three weeks in Guantanamo.

And tomorrow we'd be going out with the cruiser again, and that meant a full day of Battle Stations, the phony General Quarters stuff that was supposed to knit us together into a fighting crew. I didn't mind that business because it wasn't too bad, but after a mid watch—even if you went to sleep right after evening chow, which you never did—it was a back breaker. You got off at four in the morning, provided your relief wasn't goofing, and you hit the sack until reveille. If you averaged two hours sleep, you were doing good. And then Battle Stations all day.

"He rides everybody," Crawley said. "Everybody. He's crazy, that's all."

"Yeah," I said.

"I come off a DE," Crawley said. "We hit more Pacific islands than I can count. This was in the last war, Peters."

"Yeah," I said dully.

"We had a guy like this one, too. So we were coming in on Tarawa the night of the invasion and three quartermasters got ahold of him, right on the bridge, right in front of the exec and a pile of other officers. They told that boy that he better shape up damn soon or he was gonna be swimmin' with the sharks. He looked to the exec and the other brass for help, but they didn't budge an inch. Boy, he read the deep-six in everybody's eyes."

"What'd he do?" I asked.

"He gave the con to the exec, right then and there, and we were never bothered by him again. He transferred off the ship inside a month."

"He must've come onto this tub," I said.

"No, he couldn't hold a candle to our Old Man. Our Old Man

is the worst I ever met in the Navy, and that includes boot camp. He's a guy who really deserves it."

"Deserves what?" I asked.

"A hole between the eyes maybe. Or some arsenic in his goddamned commanding officer's soup. Or a dunk in the drink with his damn barracuda."

"You can land in Portsmouth for that," I said.

"Not if they don't catch you, Peters," Crawley said.

"Fat chance of getting away with it," I said.

"You think they'd know who did it?" he asked. "Suppose the Old Man gets a hole in his head from a .45 swiped from the gun locker? Suppose . . ."

"You better knock that kind of talk off," I warned. "That's mutiny, pal."

"Mutiny, my ass. Suppose the .45 was dumped over the side? How would they prove who did it? You know how many guys are on this ship, Peters?"

"Yeah," I said slowly.

"You wait and see," he said. "Someday, somebody'll have the guts to do it. Goodbye, Old Man. And good riddance."

"Yeah, but suppose . . ."

"The line's moving, Peters," Crawley said.

The base sent out a drone that afternoon, and we went out and shot at it. We didn't get back to the bay until about 1930, and then we had a late chow, and the Old Man announced that no movies would be shown on the boat deck that night because we'd missed the launch that brought the reels around. Findlay, the Chief Bo'sun asked him if we couldn't see the same movie we'd seen the night before, but he said, "I don't like seeing movies twice," and that was the end of it.

I suppose I should have gone straight to bed because the mid watch was coming up, but instead I hung around abovedecks, trying to get some air. Guys had dumped their mattresses all over the ship, sleeping up there under the stars in their skivvies. There was no breeze, and it was hot as hell, and I'd already taken more salt pills than I should have. The sweat kept coming, the kind of sweat that stuck all your clothes to you and made you want to crawl out of your skin. A poker game was in session near the torpedo tubes amidships on the boat deck, and I watched it for a while, and then climbed the ladder down to the main deck.

Mr. Gannson was OD, and he slouched against the metal counter and threw the bull with Ferguson, the gunner's mate who was on with him as messenger. They both wore .45's strapped to their hips, and I passed them silently, nodding as I went by. I leaned over the rail just aft of the quarterdeck, looking down at the fluorescent sprinkles of water that lapped the sides of the ship. The water looked cool, and it made me feel more uncomfortable. I fired a cigarette and looked out to the lights of the base, and then I heard Mr. Gannson say, "You got a clip in that gun, Ferguson?"

I turned as Ferguson looked up with a puzzled look on his face. "Why, no, sir. You remember the ditty bag thing. We . . ."

"This is shakedown, Ferguson. The captain catch you with an empty sidearm, and you're up the creek."

"But the ditty bag . . ."

"Never mind that. Get to the gun locker and load up."

"Yes, sir," Ferguson said.

The ditty bag he'd referred to had been hanging from one of the stanchions in the forward sleeping compartment. Davis, on fire watch, had gone down to relieve Pierto. The fire watch is just a guy who roams the ship, looking for fires and crap games and making sure all the lights are out in the sleeping compartments after taps. I don't know why he rates a .45 on his hip, but he does. When you relieve the watch, you're supposed to check the weapon he gives you, make sure it's loaded, and all that bull. So Pierto handed Davis the gun, and Davis probably wasn't too used to .45's because he'd just made Radarman Third, and only noncommissioned officers stood fire watch on our ship. He yanked back the slide mechanism, looked into the breach the way he was supposed to, and then squeezed the trigger, and a goddamn big bullet came roaring out of the end of his gun. The bullet went right through the ditty bag, and then started ricocheting all over the compartment, bouncing from one bulkhead to another. It almost killed Klein when it finally lodged in his mattress. It had sounded like a goddamned skirmish down there, and it had attracted the OD.

Well, this was about two months ago, when we were still in Norfolk, and the skipper ordered that any sidearms carried aboard his ship would have no magazines in them from then on. That went for the guys standing gangway watch when we were tied up, too. They'd carry nothing in their rifles and nothing in the cartridge belts around their waists. Nobody gave a damn because there was nothing to shoot in the States anyway.

I watched Ferguson walk away from the quarterdeck and then head for the gun locker right opposite Sick Bay, the key to the heavy lock in his hands. I walked past the quarterdeck, too, and hung around in the midships passageway reading the dope sheet. I saw Ferguson twist the key in the hanging lock, and then undog the hatch. He pulled the hatch open, and stepped into the gun locker, and I left the midships passageway just as he flicked the light on inside.

"Hi," I said, walking in.

He looked up, startled, and then said, "Oh, hi, Peters."

The rifles were stacked in a rack alongside one bulkhead, and a dozen or so .45's hung from their holster belts on a bar welded to another bulkhead. Ferguson rooted around and finally came up with a metal box which he opened quickly. He turned his back to me and pulled out a magazine, and the ship rolled a little and the .45's on the bar swung a little. He moved closer to the light so he could see what the hell he was doing, his back still turned to me.

I threw back the flap on one of the holsters and yanked out a .45, the walnut stock heavy in my hand. I stuck the gun inside my shirt and into the band of my trousers, cold against my sweating stomach. I heard Ferguson ram the clip home into his own .45, and then he said, "Come on, Peters. I got to lock up."

I followed him out, and even helped him dog the hatch. He snapped the lock, and I said, "Think I'll turn in."

Ferguson nodded sourly. "You can sleep in this heat, you're a better man than I am, Gunga Din."

I smiled and walked back aft toward the fantail. I wanted to sit down someplace and feel the gun in my hands. But it was so damned hot that every guy and his brother was abovedecks, either hanging around smoking or getting his mattress ready for the night. I went into the head, and the place was packed, as usual.

The gun was hot against my skin now, and I wanted to take it out and look at it, but I couldn't do that because I didn't want anyone to remember they'd seen me with a .45.

I kept hanging around waiting for the crowd to thin, but the crowd didn't thin. You couldn't sleep in all that heat, and nobody felt like trying. Before I knew it, it was 2345, and Ferguson was coming around to wake me for the mid watch. Only I wasn't sleeping, and he found me gassing near the aft five-inch mount.

"You're being paged, Peters," he said.

"Okay," I told him. I went forward, and then up the ladder to the passageway outside the radar shack. Centrella was sitting in front of the Sugar George, a writing pad open on his lap.

"Hi, boy," I said. "You're liberated."

"Allah be praised," he said, smiling. He got to his feet and pointed to a speaker bolted into the overhead. "That's the only speaker you got, boy," he said. "Nothing on it all night. Just static."

"You're sure it's plugged in?"

"I'm sure. You take down anything for Cavalcade. That's 'All ships.' You also take down anything for Wonderland. That's us."

"No kidding," I said.

"In case you didn't know, Peters."

"Well, thanks," I said, smiling.

"You'll probably get a weather report for Guantanamo Bay and vicinity pretty soon." Centrella shrugged. "There's some joe in the pot, and I think those radio guys got a pie from the cook. They wouldn't give me none, and it's probably all gone by now. But maybe you got influence."

"Yeah," I said.

"Okay, you relieving me?"

"The watch is relieved," I said. "Go hit the sack."

Centrella nodded and headed for the door. "Oh, yeah," he said, turning, "the Old Man's in his cabin. He wants anything important brought right to him."

"What does he consider important?" I asked.

"How the hell do I know?"

"That's a big help. Go to sleep, Centrella."

" 'Night," he said, and then he stepped out into the passageway.

I was ready to close the door after him. I had the knob in my hand, when Parson stuck his wide palm against the metal.

"Hey, boy," he said, "you ain't going to close the door in this heat?"

"Hi, Parson," I said dully. I'd wanted to close the door so I could get a better look at the gun.

"You got any hot joe, man?" he asked.

"I think there's some," I told him.

"Well, I got some pie. You like apple pie?"

He didn't wait for an answer. He shoved his way in, and put the pie down on one of the plotting boards. Then he went to the electric grill, shook the joe pot, and said, "Hell, enough here for a regiment."

He took two white cups from the cabinet under the grille, and poured the joe. Then he reached under for the container of evap, and the sugar bowl. The radio shack was right down the passage-way, you see, and most of the radio guys knew just where we kept everything. We went in there for coffee, too, whenever none was brewing in the radar shack, so that made things sort of even. Only, I could have done without Parson's company tonight.

"Come on, man," he said, "dig in."

I walked over to the plotting board and lifted a slice of pie, and Parson said, "How many sugars?"

"Two."

He spooned the sugar into my coffee, stirred it for me, and handed me the steaming mug.

"This is great stuff on a hot night," I told him.

"You should've asked for battleship duty," Parson said. "They got ice cream parlors aboard them babies."

"Yeah," I said. The steam from the coffee rose up and touched my face, and I began to sweat more profusely. I put down the cup and reached for a handkerchief, and I was wiping my face when the Old Man popped in.

"Atten*tion!*" I shouted, and Parson leaped to his feet, almost knocking over his cup. The Old Man was in silk pajamas, and he stormed into the shack like something on a big black horse.

"At ease," he shouted, and then he yelled, "What the hell is going on here, Peters?"

"We were just having a little coffee, sir. We . . ."

"What is this, the Automat? Where'd you get that pie?"

I looked to Parson, and Parson said, "One of the cooks, sir. He . . ."

"That's against my orders, Parson," the skipper bellowed. "I don't like thieves aboard my . . ."

"Hell, sir, I didn't steal . . ."

"And I don't like profanity, either. Who's on watch here?"

"I am, sir," I said.

"Where are you supposed to be, Parson?"

"Next door, sir. In the radio . . ."

"Am I to understand that you're supposed to be standing a radio watch at this time, Parson?"

"Yes, sir, but . . ."

"Then what the hell are you doing in here?" the Old Man roared.

"I thought I'd . . ."

"Get down to the OD, Parson. Tell him I've put you on report. This'll mean a Captain's Mast for you, sailor."

"Sir," I said, "he was only . . ."

"You shut up, Peters! I see you still haven't got that haircut."

"We were out with the drone, sir. I couldn't . . ."

"Get it first thing tomorrow," he said, ignoring the fact that we'd be out with the cruiser tomorrow. "And now you can dump that coffee pot over the side, and I want that sugar and milk returned to the mess hall."

"I'm on watch, sir," I said coldly.

"Do it when you're relieved, Peters." He stood glaring at me, and then asked, "Were there any important messages, or were you too busy dining?"

"None, sir," I said.

"All right. I'm going out to the boat deck now to get those men below. I don't like my ship looking like a garbage scow. Men aren't supposed to sleep abovedecks."

"Yes, sir," I said.

"I'll be there if anything comes for me. When I come back, you'll hear me going up the ladder outside. I'll be in my cabin then. Is that clear?"

"Yes, sir," I said tightly.

"All right." He walked out, and Parson watched him go and then said, "Someday that man's gonna get it, Dave. Someday."

I didn't say anything. I watched Parson go down to the OD, and I thought: *Not someday. Now.*

I heard the Old Man yelling out on the boat deck, and then I heard the grumbling as the guys out there stirred and began packing their mattresses and gear. I was sweating very heavily, and I didn't think it was from the heat this time. I could feel the hard outline of the .45 against my belly, and I wanted to rip the gun out and just run out onto the boat deck and pump the bastard full of holes, but that wasn't the smart way.

The smart way was to be in a spot where I could dump the gun over the side. I stepped out of the radar shack and looked down the passageway to where the skipper was waving his arms and ranting on the boat deck. There was a gun mount tacked to the side of the ship just outside the passageway and the radar shack. The hatch was closed, and I undid the dogs on it, and shoved it out, and then stepped outside, stationing myself near the magazine box alongside the 20mm mount. I could see the ladder leading up to the bridge and the captain's cabin from where I was standing. My idea was to plug the captain, dump the gun, and then rush inside, as if I was just coming out of the radar shack after hearing the shot.

I could hear the captain ending his tirade, and I thought to myself that it was the last time he'd chew anybody out. I thought everybody was going to be real tickled about this. Hell, I'd probably get a medal from the crew. It was all over out there on the boat deck now, and I peeked into the passageway and saw the Old Man step through the hatch and glance briefly into the radio shack.

I pulled the .45 out of my shirt.

The gun was very heavy and very hot. My hand slipped on the walnut grip, and I shifted hands and wiped the sweat off on the back of my dungarees. I took a firmer grip on the gun, with the sweat running down my face and over my neck and trickling down my back, sticky and warm. I thumbed off the safety, and the Old Man passed the radar shack and didn't even look in, and I sucked in a deep breath and waited.

And then he was starting up the ladder, and I thought, *Now, you louse, now!* and I sighted the gun at the back of his neck.

I squeezed the trigger.

There was a dull click and nothing else, and I was shocked for a second, but I squeezed off again, and there was another dull click, and the Old Man was already halfway up the steps, and he still hadn't turned. I squeezed the trigger twice more, but I got empty clicks both times, and then the Old Man was out of sight, heading toward his cabin.

I looked down at the gun in my hand, realizing it was empty, realizing there was no clip in it. I remembered the captain's orders about no magazines allowed in sidearms or pieces, and I remembered that Ferguson had gone to the gun locker to get a clip for his own empty .45.

I was still sweating, and the hand holding the gun was trembling now, as if I was just realizing what I'd almost done, just realizing that I'd almost killed a man.

I felt kind of foolish. Maybe an empty gun makes you feel that way. Or maybe the anger had burned itself out when I'd heard those stupid empty clicks. Maybe that, and maybe I was a little glad the gun had been empty, because chewing out a man is one thing, but killing a man is another. He chewed everybody out, when you got down to it, and nobody had gunned him down yet. Just me, who would have already committed murder if it hadn't been for an order the captain had issued a long time ago. Me, from Red Bank, New Jersey—a murderer.

I dumped the gun over the side, and I heard the small splash when it hit the water, and then I heard the speaker in the radar shack calling, "Cavalcade, Cavalcade . . ."

I ran in and began copying down the weather forecast for Guantanamo Bay, and the weather forecast said there would be rain tonight, and all at once I felt a lot cooler.

Kid Kill

It was just a routine call. I remember I was sitting around with
Ed, talking about a movie we'd both seen, when Marelli walked
in, a sheet of paper in his hand.

"You want to take this, Art?"

I looked up, pulled a face, and said, "Who stabbed who now?"

"This is an easy one," Marelli said, smiling. He smoothed
his mustache in an unconscious gesture and added, "Accidental
shooting."

"Then why bother Homicide?"

"Accidental shooting resulting in death," Marelli said.

I got up, hitched up my trousers, and sighed. "They always pick
the coldest goddamn days of the year to play with war souvenirs."
I looked at the frost edging the windows and then turned back to
Marelli. "It *was* a war sourvenir, wasn't it?"

"A Luger," Marelli said. "9mm with a 3⅝ inch barrel. The man
on the beat checked it."

"Was it registered?"

"You tell me."

"Stupid characters," I said. "You'd think the law wasn't for their own protection." I sighed again and looked over to where Ed was trying to make himself small. "Come on, Ed, time to work."

Ed shuffled to his feet. He was a big man with bright red hair, and a nose broken by an escaped con back in '45. It happened that the con was a little runt, about five feet high in his Adler elevators, and Ed had taken a lot of ribbing about that broken nose—even though we all knew the con had used a lead pipe.

"Trouble with you, Marelli," he said in his deep voice, "you take your job too seriously."

Marelli looked shocked. "Is it my fault some kid accidentally plugs his brother?"

"What?" I asked. I had taken my overcoat from the peg and was shrugging into it now. "What was that, Marelli?"

"It was a kid," Marelli said. "Ten years old. He was showing his younger brother the Luger when it went off. Hell, you know these things."

I pulled my muffler tight around my neck and then buttoned my coat. "This is just a waste of time," I said. "Why do the police always have to horn in on personal tragedies?"

Marelli paused near the table, dropping the paper with the information on it. "Every killing is a personal tragedy for someone," he said. I stared at him as he walked to the door, waved, and went out.

"Pearls from a flatfoot," Ed said. "Come on, let's get this over with."

It was bitterly cold, the kind of cold that attacks your ears and your hands, and makes you want to huddle around a potbelly stove. Ed pulled the Mercury up behind the white-topped squad car, and we climbed out, losing the warmth of the car heater. The beat man was standing near the white picket fence that ran around the small house. His uniform collar was pulled high onto the back of his neck, and his eyes and nose were running. He looked as cold as I felt.

Ed and I walked over to him, and he saluted, then began slapping his gloved hands together.

"I been waitin' for you, sir," he said. "My name's Connerly. I put in the call."

"Detective Willis," I said. "This is my partner, Ed Daley."

"Hiya," Ed said.

"Hell of a thing, ain't it, sir?"

"Sounds routine to me," Ed put in. "Kid showing off his big brother's trophy, bang! His little brother is dead. Happens every damned day of the week."

"Sure, sir, but I mean . . ."

"Family inside?" I asked.

"Just the mother, sir. That's what makes it more of a tragedy, you see."

"What's that?" I asked.

"Well, sir, she's a widow. Three sons. The oldest was killed in the war. He's the one sent the Luger home. Now this. Well, sir, you know what I mean."

"Sure," I said. "Let's get inside."

Connerly led us to the front door, and rapped on it with a gloved hand. Ed stole a glance at me, and I knew he didn't relish this particular picnic any more than I did.

The door opened quickly, and a small woman with dark brown eyes opened the door. She might have been pretty once, but that was a long time ago, and all the beauty had fled from her, leaving her tired and defeated.

"Mrs. Owens, this is Detective Willis and his partner," Connerly said.

Mrs. Owens nodded faintly.

"May we come in, ma'am?" I asked.

She seemed to remember her manners all at once. "Yes, please do." Her voice was stronger than her body looked, and I wondered if she were really as old as she seemed. A widow, one son killed in the war. Death can sometimes do that to a person. Leave them more withered than the corpse.

"We're sorry to bother you, ma'am," I said, feeling foolish as hell, the way I always did in a situation like this. "The law requires us to make a routine check, however, and . . ."

"That's quite all right, Mr. Willis." She moved quickly to the couch and straightened the doilies. "Sit down, won't you?"

"Thank you, ma'am." I sat down with Ed on my right. Connerly stood near the radiator, his hands behind his back.

Ed took out his pad, and cleared his throat. I took that as my cue and said, "Can you tell us exactly what happened, ma'am?"

"Well, I . . . I don't really know, exactly. You see, I was in the kitchen baking. This is Wednesday, and I usually bake on Wednesdays. The boys . . ." She hesitated and bit her lip. "The boys like pie, and I try to bake one at least once a week."

"Yes, ma'm."

"I . . . I was putting the pie into the oven when I heard this . . . this noise from the attic. I knew the boys were up there playing so I didn't think anything of it."

"What are the boys' names, ma'm?"

"Jeffrey. He's my oldest. And . . . and . . ."

"Yes, ma'm?"

"Ronald."

"Was Ronald the boy who was shot, ma'm?"

She didn't answer. She simply nodded her head. I got up because I was embarrassed as hell, and I began walking around the room. On top of the upright piano, four photos in silver frames beamed up at me. One was of an older man, obviously the dead Mr. Owens. A second was of a young man in an Army uniform, with infantry rifles crossed on his lapel. The other two were of the younger boys.

Mrs. Owens blew her nose in a small handkerchief and looked up.

"Which one is Jeffrey?" I asked.

"The . . . the blond boy."

I looked at the photo. He seemed like a nice kid, with a pleasant smile, and his mother's dark eyes. "Is he in the house?"

"Yes. He's upstairs in his room."

"I'd like to talk to him, ma'm."

"All right."

"If you don't mind, I'd like to see the attic first."

She seemed about to refuse, and then she nodded, "Certainly."

"You needn't come up, Mrs. Owens," Ed said. "The patrolman can show us the way."

"Thank you," she said.

We followed Connerly up the steps, and he whispered, "See what I mean? Jesus, this is a rotten business."

"Well, what are you gonna do?" Ed philosophized.

The attic had been fixed as a playroom, with plasterboard walls and ceiling. An electric train layout covered one half of the room. In the other half, covered with a sheet, lay young Ronald Owens, I walked over and lifted the sheet, looking down at the boy. He resembled the older Jeffrey a great deal, except that his hair was brown. He had the same dark eyes, though, staring up at me now, sightless. There was a neat hole between his eyes, and his face was an ugly mixture of blood and powder burns. I put the sheet back.

"Where's the gun?" I asked Connerly.

"Right here, sir."

He fished into his pocket and produced the Luger wrapped carefully in his handkerchief. I opened the handkerchief and stared at the German gun.

"Did you break it open, Connerly?"

"Why, no, sir. A patrolman isn't allowed to . . ."

"Can it," I said. "If you broke it open, you'll save me the trouble." Connerly looked abashed. "Yes, sir, I did."

"Any shells in it?"

"No, sir."

"Not even in the firing chamber?"

"No, sir."

"One bullet, then. That's strange."

"What's so strange about it?" Ed wanted to know.

"A Luger's magazine fed, that's all," I said. "Eight slugs in a clip. Strange to find only one." I shrugged, handing the pistol back to Connerly. "Let's see what else is around here."

We started rummaging around the attic, not really looking for anything in particular. I think I was just postponing the talk I had to have with the young kid who'd shot his own brother.

"Bunch of books," Ed said.

"Mmmm?"

"Yeah. Few old newspaper clippings."

"Here's something," Connerly cut in.

"What have you got?"

"Looks like a box of clips, sir."

"Yeah? For the Luger?"

"Looks that way, sir."

I walked over to where Connerly was standing, and took the box from the shelf. He had carefully refrained from touching it. The box was covered with a fine layer of dust. There were two clips in the open box, and they too were covered with dust. I lifted one of the clips out, running my eyes over the cartridges. Eight. The second clip had only seven cartridges in it.

"Only seven here," I said.

"Yeah," Connerly said, nodding. "That's where the bullet came from, all right."

"Anything else there, Ed?" I turned to where Ed squatted on the floor.

"Just these loose newspaper clippings. Nothing really . . . hey!"

"What've you got?"

"That's strange as hell," Ed said.

"What? What's so strange?"

He got to his feet and walked over to me, holding a clipping in his big hand. "Take a look at this, Art."

The clipping was scissored from one of the tabloids. It was simply the story of a boy and a girl who'd been playing in their back yard. Playing with a Colt .45 that was a war souvenir. The .45 had gone off, blowing half the girl's head away. There was a picture of the boy in tears, and a story of the fatal accident.

"Some coincidence, huh, Art?"

"Yeah," I said. "Some coincidence."

I put the box of clips back on the shelf. "I think I'd better talk to the kid now," I said.

We left the attic, and Connerly whispered something about the way fate sometimes works. He called Mrs. Owens, and she came up to lead me to the boy's room on the second floor of the house.

She rapped on the door and softly called, "Jeffrey?"

I could hear sobbing beyond the door, and then a muffled, "Yes?"

"Some gentlemen would like to talk to you," she said.

The sobbing stopped, and I heard the sound of bare feet padding to the door. The door opened and Jeffrey stood there, drying his face. He was thinner than the photograph had shown him, with bright brown eyes and narrow lips. His hair hung over his forehead in unruly strands, and there were streaks under his eyes and down his cheeks.

"You're policemen, aren't you?" he said.

"Yes, son."

"We just want to ask a few questions," Ed said.

"Come in."

We walked into the room. There were two beds in it, one on either side of the large window. There was one dresser, and I imagined the two boys shared this. Toys were packed neatly in a carton on one side of the room. A high school pennant, and several college pennants decorated the walls, and a model airplane hung from the ceiling.

Mrs. Owens started into the room and Ed said gently, "If we can talk to him alone . . ."

Her hand went to her mouth, and she said, "Oh. Oh, all right."

Jeffrey walked to his bed and sat on it, one leg tucked under him. He stared out of the window, not looking at us.

"Want to tell us how it happened, son?"

"It was an accident," he said. "I didn't mean to do it, honest."

"We know," Ed said. "We just want to know how it happened."

"Well, we were upstairs playing with the trains, and then we got sort of tired. We started kidding around, and then I found Perry's . . . that's my older brother, who was killed in the war . . . I found Perry's Luger and we started foolin' around with that."

"Is that the first time you saw the gun, son?"

"No, no." He turned to look me full in the face. "Perry sent it home a long time ago. Before he was killed, even. One of his buddies brought it to us."

"Uh-huh. Go on, son."

"Well, then we found the bullets in the box. I . . ."

"You didn't know the bullets were there before this?"

"No." Again, Jeffrey stared at me. "No, we just found them today."

"Did you know where the gun was?"

"Well . . . yes."

"You said you found it, though. You didn't mean that, did you, son?"

"Well, I knew it was in the attic someplace because that's where Mom put it. I didn't know just where until I found it today."

"Oh, I see. Go on, please." Ed looked at me curiously, and then returned his interest to the boy.

"We found the bullets, and I took one from one of the magazines, just to fool around. I stuck it in the gun and then all at once the gun went off and . . . and . . . Ronnie . . . Ronnie . . ."

The kid turned his face away, then threw himself onto the pillow.

"I didn't mean to do it. Honest, honest. The gun just went off. I didn't know it would go off. It just did. I loved my brother. I didn't want it to happen. I didn't!"

"Sure, son," I said. I walked to the bed and sat down beside him. "You liked your brother a lot. I know. I have a brother, too."

Ed gave me another curious look, but I continued to pat the kid's shoulder.

"Yes," Jeffrey said, "I did like him. I liked Perry, too, and he was killed. And now . . . now this. Now there's just me and Mom.

They're all gone. Dad, and Perry, and . . . and . . . Ronnie. Now we're all alone." He started bawling again. "It's my fault. If I hadn't wanted to play with that old gun . . ."

"It's not your fault," I said. "Accidents happen. They happen all the time. No one could possibly blame you for it."

His tears ebbed slowly, and he finally sat up again. "You know it's not my fault, don't you?" he asked solemnly.

"Yes," I said. "We know."

He tried to smile, but failed. "It was just an accident," he repeated.

"Sure," I said. I picked myself off the bed and said, "Let's go, Ed. Nothing more for us here."

At the door, I turned to look at Jeffrey once more. He seemed immensely relieved, and he smiled when I winked at him. The smile was still on his mouth and in his eyes when we left him.

It was cold in the Merc, even with the heater going.

We drove in silence for a long time, and finally Ed asked, "All right, what was all that business about?"

"What business?"

"First of all, that brother routine. You know damn well you're a lousy, spoiled only child."

"Sure," I said. "I wanted to hear the kid tell me how much he loved all his brothers."

"That's another thing. Why the hell did you cross-examine the kid? Jesus, he had enough trouble without your . . ."

"I was just wondering about a few things," I said. "That's all."

"What kind of things?"

"Well, the clipping about the little boy who accidentally killed that girl, for one. Now why do you suppose any kid would save a clipping like that?"

"Hell," Ed said, "you know how kids are. It probably caught his fancy, that's all."

"Probably. Maybe the Luger magazines caught his fancy, too."

"What do you mean?"

"The kid said he found those magazines for the first time today. He said he took a cartridge from one of the clips and stuck it into the gun. Tell me how he managed to handle a dust-covered magazine without smearing any of the dust?"

"Well, maybe he . . ."

"He didn't, that's the answer. He took that bullet from the clip a long time ago, Ed. Long enough ago for the box and the magazine to acquire a new coat of dust. This was no spur-of-the-minute job. No, sir, not at all."

"Hey," Ed said suddenly. "What the hell are you trying to say? You mean the kid did this on purpose? You mean he actually killed his brother? *Murdered* him?"

"Just him and Mom now, Ed. Just the two of them. No more Dad, no more big brother, and now no more little brother." I shook my head, and stared at my own breath as it clouded the windshield.

"But just take it to a judge," I added. "Just take the whole fantastic thing to a judge and see how fast he kicks you out of court."

Ed glanced at me quickly, and then turned his eyes back to the road.

"We'll have to watch that kid," I said, "Maybe get him psychiatric care. I hate to think what would happen if he suddenly builds up a dislike for his mother."

I didn't say anything after that, but it was a cold ride back to the station.

Damned cold.

Death Flight

Squak Mountain was cold at this time of the year. The wind groaned around Davis, and the trees trembled bare limbs, and even at this distance he could hear the low rumble of planes letting down at Boeing and Renton. He found the tree about a half-mile east of the summit. The DC-4 had struck the tree and then continued flying. He looked at the jagged, splintered wood and then his eyes covered the surrounding terrain. Parts of the DC-4 were scattered all over the ridge in a fifteen-hundred-foot radius. He saw the upper portion of the plane's vertical fin, the number-two propeller, and a major portion of the rudder. He examined these very briefly, and then he began walking toward the canyon into which the plane had finally dropped.

Davis turned his head sharply once, thinking he had heard a sound. He stood stock-still, listening, but the only sounds that came to him were the sullen moan of the wind and the muted hum of aircraft in the distant sky.

He continued walking.

When he found the plane, it made him a little sick. The Civil Aeronautics Board report had told him that the plane was demolished by fire. The crash was what had obviously caused the real demolition. But the report had only been typed words. He saw *impact* now, and *causing fire*, and even though the plane had been moved by the investigating board, he could imagine something of what had happened.

It had been in nearly vertical position when it struck the ground, and the engines and cockpit had bedded deep in soft, muddy loam. Wreckage had been scattered like shrapnel from a hand grenade burst, and fire had consumed most of the plane, leaving a ghostlike skeleton that confronted him mutely. He stood watching it for a time, then made his way down to the charred ruins.

The landing gear was fully retracted, as the report had said. The wings' flaps were in the twenty-five-degree down position.

He studied these briefly and then climbed up to the cockpit. The plane still stank of scorched skin and blistered paint. When he entered the cockpit, he was faced with complete havoc. It was impossible to obtain a control setting or an instrument reading from the demolished instrument panel. The seats were twisted and tangled. Metal jutted into the cockpit and cabin at grotesque angles. The windshield had shattered into a million jagged shards.

He shook his head and continued looking through the plane, the stench becoming more overpowering. He was silently grateful that he had not been here when the bodies were still in the plane, and he still wondered what he was doing here anyway, even now.

He knew that the report had proved indication of an explosion prior to the crash. There had been no structural failure or malfunctioning of the aircraft itself. The explosion had occurred in the cabin, and the remnants of the bomb had shown it to be a home-made job. He'd learned all this in the past few days, with the co-operation of the CAB. He also knew that the Federal Bureau of Investigation and the Military Police were investigating the accident, and the knowledge had convinced him that this was not a job for him. Yet here he was.

Five people had been killed. Three pilots, the stewardess, and Janet Carruthers, the married daughter of his client, George Ellison. It could not have been a pleasant death.

Davis climbed out of the plane and started toward the ridge. The sun was high on the mountain, and it cast a feeble, pale yellow tint on the white pine and spruce. There was a hard grey winter sky overhead. He walked swiftly, with his head bent against the wind.

When the shots came, they were hard and brittle, shattering the stillness as effectively as twin-mortar explosions.

He dropped to the ground, wriggling sideways toward a high outcropping of quartz. The echo of the shots hung on the air and then the wind carried it toward the canyon and he waited and listened, with his own breathing the loudest sound on the mountain.

I'm out of my league, he thought. *I'm way out of my league. I'm just a small-time detective, and this is something big . . .*

The third shot came abruptly. It came from some high-powered rifle, and he heard the sharp *twang* of the bullet when it struck the quartz and ricocheted into the trees.

He pressed his cheek to the ground, and he kept very still, and he could feel the hammering of his heart against the hard earth. His hands trembled and he waited for the next shot.

The next shot never came. He waited for a half-hour, and then he bundled his coat and thrust it up over the rock, hoping to draw fire if the sniper was still with him. He waited for several minutes after that, and then he backed away from the rock on his belly, not venturing to get to his feet until he was well into the trees.

Slowly, he made his way down the mountain.

"You say you want to know more about the accident?" Arthur Porchek said. "I thought it was all covered in the CAB report."

"It was," Davis said. "I'm checking further. I'm trying to find out who set that bomb."

Porchek drew in on his cigarette. He leaned against the wall and the busy hum of radios in Seattle Approach Control was loud around them. "I've only told this story a dozen times already."

"I'd appreciate it if you could tell it once more," Davis said.

"Well," Porchek said heavily, "it was about twenty-thirty-six or so." He paused. "All our time is based on a twenty-four-hour check, like the Army."

"Go ahead."

The flight had been cleared to maintain seven thousand feet. When they contacted us, we told them to make a standard range approach to Boeing Field and requested that they report leaving each one-thousand-foot level during the descent. That's standard, you know."

"Were you doing all the talking to the plane?" Davis asked.

"Yes."

"All right, what happened?"

"First I gave them the weather."

"And what was that?"

Porchek shrugged, a man weary of repeating information over and over again. "Boeing Field," he said by rote. "Eighteen hundred scattered, twenty-two hundred overcast, eight-miles, wind south-southeast, gusts to thirty, altimeter twenty-nine, twenty-five; Seattle-Tacoma, measured nineteen hundred broken with thirty-one hundred overcast."

"Did the flight acknowledge?"

"Yes, it did. And it reported leaving seven thousand feet at twenty-forty. About two minutes later, it reported being over the outer marker and leaving the six-thousand-foot level."

"Go on." Davis said.

"Well, it didn't report leaving five thousand and then at twenty-forty-five, it reported leaving four thousand feet. I acknowledged that and told them what to do. I said, "If you're not VFR by the time you reach the range you can shuttle on the northwest course at two thousand feet. It's possible you'll break out in the vicinity of Boeing Field for a south landing.' "

"What's VFR?" Davis asked, once again feeling his inadequacy to cope with the job.

"Visual Flight Rules. You see, it was overcast at twenty-two hundred feet. The flight was on instruments above that. They've got to report to us whether they're on IFR or VFR."

"I see. What happened next?"

"The aircraft reported at twenty-fifty that it was leaving three thousand feet, and I told them they were to contact Boeing Tower on one eighteen, point three for landing instructions. They acknowledged with 'Roger,' and that's the last I heard of them."

"Did you hear the explosion?"

"I heard something, but I figured it for static. Ground witnesses heard it, though."

"But everything was normal and routine before the explosion, is that right?"

Porchek nodded his head emphatically. "Yes, sir. A routine letdown."

"Almost," Davis said. He thanked Porchek for his time, and then left.

He called George Ellison from a pay phone. When the old man came on the line, Davis said, "This is Milt Davis, Mr. Ellison."

Ellison's voice sounded gruff and heavy, even over the phone. "Hello, Davis," he said. "How are you doing?"

"I'll be honest with you, Mr. Ellison. I'd like out."

"Why?" He could feel the old man's hackles rising.

"Because the FBI and the MPs are already onto this one. They'll crack it for you, and it'll probably turn out to be some nut with a grudge against the government. Either that, or a plain case of sabotage. This really doesn't call for a private investigation."

"Look, Davis," Ellison said. "I'll decide whether this calls for . . ."

"All right, you'll decide. I'm just trying to be frank with you. This kind of stuff is way out of my line. I'm used to trailing wayward husbands, or skip tracing, or an occasional bodyguard stint. When you drag in bombed planes, I'm in over my head."

"I heard you were a good man," Ellison said. "You stick with it. I'm satisfied you'll do a good job."

Davis sighed. "Whatever you say," he said. "Incidentally, did you tell anyone you'd hired me?"

"Yes, I did. As a matter of fact . . ."

"Who'd you tell?"

"Several of my employees. The word got to a local reporter somehow, though, and he came to my home yesterday. I gave him the story. I didn't think it would do any harm."

"Has it reached print yet?"

"Yes," Ellison said. "It was in this morning's paper. A small item. Why?"

"I was shot at today, Mr. Ellison. At the scene of the crash. Three times."

There was a dead silence on the line. Then Ellison said, "I'm sorry, Davis, I should have realized." It was a hard thing for a man like Ellison to say.

"That's all right," Davis assured him. "They missed."

"Do you think—do you think whoever set the bomb shot at you?"

"Possibly. I'm not going to start worrying about it now."

Ellison digested this and then said, "Where are you going now, Davis?"

"To visit your son-in-law, Nicholas Carruthers. I'll call in again."

"Fine, Davis."

Davis hung up, jotting down the cost of the call, and then made reservations on the next plane to Burbank. Nicholas Carruthers was chief pilot of Intercoastal Airways' Burbank Division. The fatal flight had been made in two segments; the first from Burbank to San Francisco, and the second from Frisco to Seattle. The DC-4 was to let down at Boeing, with Seattle-Tacoma designated as an alternate field. It was a simple ferry flight, and the plane was to pick up military personnel in Seattle, in accordance with the company's contract with the Department of National Defense.

Quite curiously, Carruthers had been along on the Burbank-to-Frisco segment of the hop, as company observer. He'd disembarked at Frisco, and his wife, Janet, had boarded the plane there as a non-revenue passenger. She was bound for a cabin up in Washington, or so old man Ellison had told Davis. He'd also said that Janet had been looking forward to the trip for a long time.

When Davis found Captain Nicholas Carruthers in the airport restaurant, he was sitting with a blonde in a black cocktail dress, and he had his arm around her waist. They lifted their martini glasses and clinked them together, the girl laughing. Davis studied the pair from the doorway and reflected that the case was turning into something he knew a little more about.

He hesitated inside the doorway for just a moment and then walked directly to the bar, taking the stool on Carruthers' left. He waited until Carruthers had drained his glass and then he said, "Captain Carruthers?"

Carruthers turned abruptly, a frown distorting his features. He was a man of thirty-eight or so, with prematurely graying temples and sharp gray eyes. He had thin lips and a thin straight nose that divided his face like an immaculate stone wall. He wore civilian clothing.

"Yes," he said curtly.

"Milton Davis. Your father-in-law has hired me to look into the DC-4 accident." Davis showed his identification. "I wonder if I might ask you a few questions?"

Carruthers hesitated, and then glanced at the blonde, apparently realizing the situation was slightly compromising. The blonde leaned over, pressing her breasts against the bar top, looking past Carruthers to Davis.

"Take a walk, Beth," Carruthers said.

The blonde drained her martini glass, pouted, lifted her purse from the bar, and slid off the stool. Davis watched the exaggerated swing of her hips across the room and then said, "I'm sorry if . . ."

"Ask your questions," Carruthers said.

Davis studied him for a moment. "All right, Captain," he said mildly. "I understand you were aboard the crashed DC-4 on the flight segment from Burbank to San Francisco. Is that right?"

"That's right," Carruthers said. "I was aboard as observer."

"Did you notice anything out of the ordinary on the trip?"

"If you mean did I see anyone with a goddamn bomb, no."

"I didn't—"

"And if you're referring to the false alarm, Mister Whatever-the-Hell-Your-Name-Is, you can just start asking your questions straight. You know all about the false alarm."

Davis felt his fists tighten on the bar top. "You tell me about it again."

"Sure," Carruthers said testily. "Shortly after take-off from Burbank, we observed a fire-warning signal in the cockpit. From number three engine."

"I'm listening," Davis said.

"As it turned out, it was a false warning. When we got to Frisco, the mechanics there checked and found no evidence of a fire having occurred. Mason told the mechanics—"

"Was Mason pilot in command?"

"Yes." A little of Carruthers' anger seemed to be wearing off. "Mason told the mechanics he was satisfied from the inspection that no danger of fire was present. He did not delay the flight."

"Were *you* satisfied with the inspection?" Davis asked.

"It was Mason's command."

"Yes, but your wife boarded the plane in Frisco. Were you satisfied there was no danger of fire?"

"Yes, I was."

"Did your wife seem worried about it?" Davis asked.

"I didn't get a chance to talk to Janet in Frisco," Carruthers said.

Davis was silent for a moment. Then he asked, "How come?"

"I had to take another pilot up almost the moment I arrived."

"I don't understand."

"For a hood test. I had to check him out. I'm chief pilot, you know. That's one of my jobs."

"And there wasn't even enough time to stop and say hello to your wife?"

"No. We were a little ahead of schedule. Janet wasn't there when we landed."

"I see."

"I hung around while the mechanics checked the fire-warning system, and Janet still hadn't arrived. This other pilot was waiting to go up, so I left."

"Then you didn't see your wife at all," Davis said.

"Well, that's not what I meant. I meant I hadn't spoken to her. As we were taxiing for take-off, I saw her come onto the field."

"Alone?"

"No," Carruthers said. "She was with a man." The announcement did not seem to disturb him.

"Do you know who he was?"

"No. They were rather far from me, and I was in a moving ship. I recognized Janet's red hair immediately, of course, but I couldn't make out the man with her. I waved, but I guess she didn't see me."

"She didn't wave back?"

"No. She went directly to the DC-4. The man helped her aboard, and then the plane was behind us and I couldn't see any more."

"What do you mean, helped her aboard?"

"Took her elbow, you know. Helped her up the ladder."

"I see. Was she carrying luggage?"

"A suitcase, yes. She was bound for our cabin, you know."

"Yes," Davis said. "I understand she was on a company pass. What does that mean exactly, Captain?"

"We ride for a buck and a half," Carruthers said. "Normally, any pilot applies to his chief pilot for written permission for his wife to ride and then presents the permission at the ticket window. He then pays one-fifty for the ticket. Since I'm chief pilot, I simply got the ticket for Janet when she told me she was going up to the cabin."

"Mmm," Davis said. "Did you know all the pilots on the ship?"

"I knew one of them. Mason. The other two were new on the route. That's why I was along as observer."

"Did you know Mason socially?"

"No. Just business."

"And the stewardess?"

"Yes, I knew her. Business, of course."

"Of course," Davis said, remembering the blonde in the cocktail dress. He stood up and moved his jacket cuff off his wrist-watch. "Well, I've got to catch a plane, Captain. Thanks for your help."

"Not at all," Carruthers said. "When you report in to Dad, give him my regards, won't you?"

"I'll do that," Davis said. He thanked Carruthers again, and then went out to catch his return plane.

He bought twenty-five thousand dollars' worth of insurance for fifty cents from one of the machines in the waiting room, and then got aboard the plane at about five minutes before take-off. He browsed through the magazine he'd picked up at the newsstand, and when the fat fellow plopped down into the seat beside him, he just glanced up and then turned back to his magazine again. The plane left the ground and began climbing, and Davis looked back through the window and saw the field drop away below him.

"First time flying?" the fellow asked.

Davis looked up from the magazine into a pair of smiling green eyes. The eyes were embedded deep in soft, ruddy flesh. The man owned a nose like the handle of a machete, and a mouth with thick, blubbery lips. He wore an orange sports shirt against which the color of his complexion seemed even more fiery.

"No," Davis said. "I've been off the ground before."

"Always gives me a thrill," the man said. "No matter how many times I do it." He chuckled and added, "An airplane ride is just like a woman. Lots of ups and downs, and not always too smooth—but guaranteed to keep a man up in the air."

Davis smiled politely, and the fat man chuckled a bit more and then thrust a beefy hand at him. "MacGregor," he said. "Charlie or Chuck or just plain Mac, if you like."

Davis took his hand and said, "Milt Davis."

"Glad to know you, Milt," MacGregor said. "You down here on business?"

"Yes," he said briefly.

"Me, too," MacGregor said. "Business mostly." He grinned slyly. " 'Course, what the wife don't know won't hurt her, eh?"

"I'm not married," Davis told him.

"A wonderful institution," MacGregor said. He laughed aloud, and then added, "But who likes being in an institution?"

Davis hoped he hadn't winced. He wondered if he was to be treated to MacGregor's full repertoire of wornout gags before the trip was over. To discourage any further attempts at misdirected wit, he turned back to the magazine as politely as he could, smiling once to let MacGregor know he wasn't being purposely rude.

"Go right ahead," MacGregor said genially. "Don't mind me."

That was easy, Davis thought. *If it lasts.*

He was surprised that it did last. MacGregor stretched out in the seat beside him, closing his eyes. He did not speak again until the plane was ten minutes out of San Francisco.

"Let's walk to the john, eh, Milt?" he said.

Davis lifted his head and smiled. "Thanks, but—"

"This is a .38 here under my overcoat, Milt," MacGregor said softly.

For a second, Davis thought it was another of the fat man's tired jokes. He turned to look at MacGregor's lap. The overcoat was folded over his chunky left arm, and Davis could barely see the blunt muzzle of a pistol poking from beneath the folds.

He lifted his eyebrows a little. "What are you going to do after you shoot me, MacGregor? Vanish into thin air?"

MacGregor smiled. "Now who mentioned anything about shooting, Milt? Eh? Let's go back, shall we, boy?"

Davis rose and moved past MacGregor into the aisle. MacGregor stood up behind him, the coat over his arm, the gun completely hidden now. Together, they began walking toward the rear of the plane, past the food buffet on their right, and past the twin facing seats behind the buffet. An emergency window was set in the cabin wall there, and Davis sighed in relief when he saw that the seats were occupied.

When they reached the men's room, MacGregor flipped open the door and nudged Davis inside. Then he crowded in behind him, putting his wide back to the door. He reached up with one heavy fist, rammed Davis against the sink, and then ran his free hand over Davis' body.

"Well," he said pleasantly. "No gun."

"My name is Davis, not Spade," Davis told him.

MacGregor lifted the .38, pointing it at Davis' throat. "All right, Miltie, now give a listen. I want you to forget all about that crashed DC-4, I want you to forget there are even such things as airplanes, Miltie. Now, I know you're a smart boy, and so I'm not even going to mark you up, Miltie. I could mark you up nice with the sight and butt of this thing." He gestured with the .38 in his hand. "I'm not going to do that. Not now. I'm just telling you, nice-like, to lay off. Just lay off and go back to skip-tracing, Miltie boy, or you're going to get hurt. Next time, I'm not going to be so considerate."

"Look . . ." Davis started.

"So let's not have a next time, Miltie. Let's call it off now. You give your client a ring and tell him you're dropping it, Miltie boy. Have you got that?"

Davis didn't answer.

"Fine," MacGregor said. He reached up suddenly with his left hand, almost as if he were reaching up for a light cord. At the same time, he grasped Davis' shoulder with his right hand and spun him around, bringing the hand with the gun down in a fast motion, flipping it butt-end up.

The walnut stock caught Davis at the base of his skull. He stumbled forward, his hands grasping the sink in front of him. He felt the second blow at the back of his head, and then his hands dropped from the sink, and the aluminum deck of the plane came up to meet him suddenly, all too fast . . .

Someone said, "He's coming around now," and he idly thought, *Coming around where?*

"How do you feel, Mr. Davis?" a second voice asked.

He looked up at the ring of faces. He did not recognize any of them. "Where am I?" he asked.

"San Francisco," the second voice said. The voice belonged to a tall man with a salt-and-pepper mustache and friendly blue eyes. MacGregor had owned friendly green eyes, Davis remembered.

"We found you in the men's room after all the passengers had disembarked," the voice went on. "You've had a nasty fall, Mr. Davis. Nothing serious, however. I've dressed the cut, and I'm sure there'll be no complications."

"Thank you," Davis said. "I wonder . . . did you say all the passengers have already gone?"

"Why, yes."

"I wonder if I might see the passenger list? There was a fellow aboard I promised to look up, and I'm darned if I haven't forgotten his name."

"I'll ask the stewardess," the man said. "By the way, I'm Doctor Burke."

"How do you do?" Davis said. He reached for a cigarette and lighted it. When the stewardess brought the passenger list, he scanned it hurriedly.

There was no MacGregor listed, Charles or otherwise. This fact did not surprise him greatly. He looked down the list to see if there were any names with the initials C.M., knowing that when a person assumes an alias, he will usually choose a name with the same initials as his real name. There were no C.M.s on the list, either.

"Does that help?" the stewardess asked.

"Oh, yes. Thank you. I'll find him now."

The doctor shook Davis' hand, and then asked if he'd sign a release stating he had received medical treatment and absolving the airline. Davis felt the back of his head, and then signed the paper.

He walked outside and leaned against the building, puffing idly on his cigarette. The night was a nest of lights. He watched the lights and listened to the hum of aircraft all around him. It wasn't until he had finished his cigarette that he remembered he was in San Francisco.

He dropped the cigarette to the concrete and ground it out beneath his heel. Quite curiously, he found himself ignoring MacGregor's warning. He was a little surprised at himself, but he was also pleased. And more curious, he found himself wishing that he and MacGregor would meet again.

He walked briskly to the cyclone fence that hemmed in the runway area. Quickly, he showed the uniformed guard at the gate his credentials and then asked where he could find the hangars belonging to Intercoastal Airways. The guard pointed them out.

Davis walked through the gate and towards the hangars the guard had indicated, stopping at the first one. Two mechanics in greasy coveralls were leaning against a work bench, chatting idly. One was smoking, and the other tilted a Coke bottle to his lips, draining half of it in one pull. Davis walked over to them.

"I'm looking for the mechanics who serviced the DC-4 that crashed up in Seattle," he said.

They looked at him blankly for a few seconds, and then the one with the Coke bottle asked, "You from the CAB?"

"No," Davis said. "I'm investigating privately."

The mechanic with the bottle was short, with black hair curling over his forehead, and quick brown eyes that silently appraised Davis now. "If you're thinking about that fire warning," he said, "it had nothing to do with the crash. There was a bomb aboard."

"I know," Davis said. "Were you one of the mechanics?"

"I was one of them," he said.

"Good." Davis smiled and said, "I didn't catch your name."

"Jerry," the man said. "Mangione." His black brows pulled together suspiciously. "Who you investigating for?"

"A private client. The father of the girl who was a passenger."

"Oh. Carruthers' wife, huh?"

"Yes. Did you know her?"

"No. I just heard it was his wife. He's chief pilot down Burbank, ain't he?"

"Yes," Davis said.

Mangione paused and studied Davis intently. "What'd you want to know?"

"First, was the fire-warning system okay?"

"Yeah. We checked it out. Just one of those things, you know. False alarm."

"Did you go into the plane?"

"Yeah, sure. I had to check the signal in the cockpit. Why?"

"I'm just asking."

"You don't think *I* put that damn bomb on the plane, do you?"

"Somebody did," Davis said.

"That's for sure. But not me. There were a lot of people on that plane, mister. Any one of 'em could've done it."

"Be a little silly to bring a bomb onto a plane you were going to fly."

"I guess so. But don't drag me into this. I just checked the fire-warning system, that's all."

"Were you around when Mrs. Carruthers boarded the plane?"

"The redhead? Yeah, I was there."

"What'd she look like?"

Mangione shrugged. "A broad, just like any other broad. Red hair."

"Was she pretty?"

"The red hair was the only thing gave her any flash. In fact, I was a little surprised."

"Surprised? What about?"

"That Tony would bother, you know."

"Who? Who would bother?"

"Tony. Tony Radner. He brought her out to the plane."

"What?" Davis said.

"Yeah, Tony. He used to sell tickets inside. He brought her out to the plane and helped her get aboard."

"Are you sure about that? Sure you know who the man with her was?"

Mangione made an exasperated gesture with his hairy hands. "Hell, ain't I been working here for three years? Don't I know Tony when I see him? It was him, all right. He took the broad right to her seat. Listen, it was him, all right. I guess maybe . . . well, I was surprised, anyway."

"Why?"

"Tony's a good-looking guy. And this Mrs. Carruthers, well, she wasn't much. I'm surprised he went out of his way. But I guess maybe she wasn't feeling so hot. Tony's a gent that way."

"Wasn't feeling so hot?"

"Well, I don't like to talk about anybody's dead, but she looked like she had a snootful to me. Either that, or she was pretty damn sick."

"What makes you say that?"

"Hell, Tony had to help her up the ladder, and he practically carried her to her seat. Yeah, she musta been looped."

"You said Radner used to work here. Has he quit?"

"Yeah, he quit."

"Do you know where I can find him?"

Mangione shrugged. "Maybe you can get his address from the office in the morning. But, mister, I wouldn't bother him right now, if I was you."

"Why not?"

Mangione smiled. "Because he's on his honeymoon," he said.

He slept the night through and when he awoke in the morning, the back of his head hardly hurt at all. He shaved and washed quickly, downed a breakfast of orange juice and coffee, and then went to the San Francisco office of Intercoastal Airways.

Radner, they told him, was no longer with them. But they did have his last address, and they parted with it willingly. He grabbed a cab, and then sat back while the driver fought with the California traffic. When he reached Radner's address, he paid and tipped the cabbie, and listed the expenditure in his book.

The rooming house was not in a good section of the city. It was red brick, with a brown front stoop. There was an old-fashioned bell pull set in the wide, wooden door jamb. He pulled this and heard the sound inside, and then he waited for footsteps. They came sooner than he expected.

The woman who opened the door couldn't have been more than fifty. Her face was still greasy with cold cream, and her hair was tied up in rags. "Yes?"

"I'm looking for Tony Radner," Davis said. "I'm an old friend of his, knew him in the Army. I went out to Intercoastal, but they told me he doesn't work for them any more. I wonder if you know where I can reach him."

The landlady regarded him suspiciously for a moment. "He doesn't live here anymore," she said.

"Darn," Davis said. He shook his head and assumed a false smile. "Isn't that always the way? I came all the way from New York, and now I can't locate him."

"That's too bad," the landlady agreed.

"Did he leave any forwarding address?" Davis asked.

"No. He left because he was getting married."

"Married!" Davis said. "Well, I'll be darned! Old Tony getting married!"

The landlady continued to watch Davis, her small eyes staring fixedly.

"You wouldn't know who he married, would you?"

"Yes," she said guardedly. "I guess I would."

"Who?" he asked.

"Trimble," the landlady said. "A girl named Alice Trimble."

"Alice Trimble," Davis said reflectively. "You wouldn't have her phone number, would you?"

"Come on in," the landlady said, finally accepting Davis at face value. She led him into the foyer of the house, and Davis followed her to the pay phone on the wall.

"They all scribble numbers here," she said. "I keep washing them off, but they keep putting them back again."

"Shame," Davis said sympathetically.

"Hers is up there, too. You just wait a second, and I'll tell you which one." She stepped close to the phone and examined the scribbled numbers on the wall. She stood very close to the wall, moving her head whenever she wanted to move her eyes. She stepped back at last and placed a long white finger on one of the numbers. "This one. This is the one he always called."

Davis jotted down the number hastily, and then said, "Well, gee, thanks a million. You don't know how much I appreciate this."

"I hope you find him," the landlady said. "Nice fellow, Mr. Radner."

"One of the best," Davis said.

He called the number from the first pay phone he found. He listened to the phone ring four times on the other end, and then a voice said, "Hello?"

"Hello," he said, "May I speak to Miss Trimble, please?"

"This is Miss Trimble," the voice said.

"My name is Davis," he said. "I'm an old friend of Tony Radner's. He asked me to look him up if ever I was in town . . ." He paused and forced himself to laugh in embarrassment. "Trouble is, I can't seem to find him. His landlady said you and Tony . . ."

"Oh," the girl said. "You must want my sister. This is *Anne* Trimble."

"Oh," he said. "I'm sorry. I didn't realize . . ." He paused. "Is your sister there?"

"No, she doesn't live with me any more. She and Tony got married."

"Well, now, that's wonderful," Davis said. "Know where I can find them?"

"They're still on their honeymoon."

"Oh, that's too bad." He thought for a few seconds, and then said, "I've got to catch a plane back tonight. I wonder . . . I wonder if I might come over and . . . well, you could fill me in on what Tony's been doing and all. Hate like the devil to go back without knowing *something* about him."

The girl hesitated, and he could sense her reluctance.

"I promise I'll make it a very short visit. I've still got some business to attend to here. Besides . . . well, Tony loaned me a little money once, and I thought . . . well, if you don't mind, I'd like to leave it with you."

"I . . . I suppose it would be all right," she said.

"Fine. May I have the address?"

She gave it to him, and he told her he'd be up in about an hour, if that was all right with her. He went to the coffee counter, ordered coffee and a toasted English, and browsed over them until it was time to go. He bought a plain white envelope on the way out, slipped twenty dollars into it, and sealed it. Then he hailed a cab.

He found the mailbox marked *A. Trimble,* and he realized the initial sufficed for both Alice and Anne. He walked up two flights, stopped outside apartment 22, and thumbed the ivory stud in the door jamb. A series of chimes floated from beyond the door, and then the peephole flap was thrown back.

"I'm Mr. Davis," he said to the flap. "I called about—"

"Oh, yes," Anne Trimble said. The flap descended, and the door swung wide.

She was a tall brunette, and her costume emphasized her height. She was wearing tightly tailored toreador slacks. A starched white blouse with a wide collar and long sleeves was tucked firmly into the band of the slacks. A bird in flight, captured in sterling, rested on the blouse just below the left breast pocket.

"Come in," she said, "won't you?" She had green eyes and black eyebrows, and she smiled pleasantly now.

Davis stepped into the cool apartment, and she closed the door behind him.

"I'm sorry if I seemed rude when you called me," she said. "I'm afraid you woke me."

"Then I should be the one to apologize," Davis said.

He followed her into a sunken living room furnished in Swedish modern. She walked to a long, low coffee table and took a cigarette from a box there, offering the box to him first. Davis shook his head and watched her as she lighted the cigarette. Her hair was cut close to her head, ringing her face with ebony wisps. She wore only lipstick, and Davis reflected that this was the first truly beautiful woman he had ever met. Two large, silver hoop earrings hung from her ears. She lifted her head, and the earrings caught the rays of the sun streaming through the blinds.

"Now," she said. "You're a friend of Tony's, are you?"

"Yes," he answered. He reached into his jacket pocket and took out the sealed envelope. "First, let me get this off my mind. Please tell Tony I sincerely appreciate the loan, won't you?"

She took the envelope without comment, dropping it on the coffee table.

This is a very cool one, Davis thought.

"I was really surprised to learn that Tony was married," he said.

"It was a little sudden, yes," she said.

"Oh? Hadn't he known your sister long?"

"Three months, four months."

Davis shook his head. "I still can't get over it. How'd he happen to meet your sister?"

"Like that," Anne said. "How do people meet? A concert, a club, a soda fountain." She shrugged. "You know, people meet."

"Don't you like Tony?" he asked suddenly.

She seemed surprised. "Me? Yes, as a matter of fact, I do. I think he'll be very good for Alice. He has a strong personality, and she needs someone like him. Yes, I like Tony."

"Well, that's good," Davis said.

"When we came to Frisco, you see, Alice was sort of at loose ends. We'd lived in L.A. all our lives, and Alice depended on Mom a good deal, I suppose. When Mom passed away, and this job opening came for me . . . well, the change affected her. Moving and all. It was a good thing Tony came along."

"You live here alone then, just the two of you?"

Anne Trimble smiled and sucked in a deep cloud of smoke. "Just two little gals from Little Rock," she said.

Davis smiled with her. "L.A., you mean."

"The same thing. We're all alone in the world. Just Alice and me. Dad died when we were both little girls. Now, of course, Alice is married. Don't misunderstand me. I'm very happy for her."

"When were they married?"

"January 6th," she answered. "It's been a long honeymoon."

January 6th, Davis thought. *The day the DC-4 crashed.*

"Where are they now?" he asked.

"Las Vegas."

"Where in Las Vegas?"

Anne Trimble smiled again. "You're not planning on visiting a pair of honeymooners, are you, Mr. Davis?"

"God, no," he said. "I'm just curious."

"Fact is," Anne said, "I don't know where they're staying. I've only had a wire from them since they were married. I don't imagine they're thinking much about me. Not on their honeymoon."

"No, I guess not," Davis said. "I understand Tony left his job. Is that right?"

"Yes. It didn't pay much, and Tony is really a brilliant person. He and Alice said they'd look around after the honeymoon and settle wherever he could get located."

"When did he quit?"

"A few days before they were married, I think. No, wait, it was on New Year's Eve, that's right. He quit then."

"Then he wasn't selling tickets on the day of . . ."

Anne looked at him strangely. "The day of what?"

"The day he was married," Davis said quickly.

"No, he wasn't." She continued looking at him, and then asked, "How do you happen to know Tony, Mr. Davis?"

"Oh, the Army," Davis said. "The last war, you know."

"That's quite a feat," Anne said.

"Huh?" Davis looked up.

"Tony was in the Navy."

Once again, he felt like a damn fool. He cursed the crashed plane, and he cursed George Ellison, and he cursed the stupidity that had led him to take the job in the first place. He sighed deeply.

"Well," he said. "I guess I pulled a bloomer."

Anne Trimble stared at him coldly. "Maybe you'd better get out, Mr. Davis. If that's your name."

"It's my name. Look," he said, "I'm a private eye. I'm investigating the crash for my client. I thought . . ."

"*What* crash?"

"A DC-4 took a dive in Seattle. My client's daughter was aboard her when she went down. There was a bomb aboard."

"Is this another one of your stories?"

Davis lifted his right hand. "God's truth, s'help me. I'm trying to find whoever put the bomb aboard."

"And you think Tony did?"

"No, I didn't say that. But I've got to investigate all the possibilities."

Anne suddenly smiled. "Are you new at this business?"

"No, I've been at it a long time now. This case is a little out of my usual line."

"You called yourself a private eye. Do private eyes really call themselves that? I thought that was just for the paperback trade."

"I'm afraid we really do," Davis said. "Private Investigator, shortened to Private I, and then naturally to private eye."

"It must be exciting."

"Well, I'm afraid it's usually deadly dull." He rose and said, "Thanks very much for your time, Miss Trimble. I'm sorry I got to see you on a ruse, but . . ."

"You should have just asked. I'm always willing to help the cause of justice." She smiled. "And I think you'd better take this money back."

"Well, thanks again," he said, taking the envelope.

"Not at all," she said. She led him to the door, and shook his hand, and her grip was firm and warm. "Good luck."

The door whispered shut behind him. He stood in the hallway for a few moments, sighed, and then made his way down to the courtyard and the street.

The time has come, he thought, *to replenish the bank account. If Ellison expects me to chase hither and yon, then Ellison should also realize that I'm a poor boy, raised by the side of a railroad car. And if a trip to Vegas is in the offing . . . the time has come to replenish the bank account.*

He thought no more about it. He hailed a cab for which Ellison would pay, and headed for the old man's estate.

The butler opened the door and announced, "Mr. Davis, sir,"

Davis smiled at the butler and entered the room. It was full of plates and pitchers and cups and saucers and mugs and jugs and platters. For a moment Davis thought he'd wandered into the pantry by error, but then he saw Ellison seated behind a large desk.

Ellison did not look old, even though Davis knew he was somewhere in his seventies. He had led an easy life, and the rich are expert at conserving their youth. The only signs of age on Ellison were in his face. It was perhaps a bit too ruddy for good health, and it reminded him of MacGregor's complexion—but Ellison was not a fat man. He had steel-gray hair cropped close to his head. His brows were black, in direct contrast to the hair on his head, and his eyes were a penetrating pale blue. Davis wondered from whom Janet had inherited her red hair, then let the thought drop when Ellison rose and extended his hand.

"Ah, Davis, come in, come in."

Davis walked to the desk, and Ellison took his hand in a tight grip.

"Hope you don't mind talking in here," he said. "I've got a new piece of porcelain, and I wanted to mount it."

"Not at all," Davis said.

"Know anything about porcelain?" Ellison asked.

"Not a thing, sir."

"Pity. Volkstedt wouldn't mean anything to you then, would it?"

"No, sir."

"Or Rudolstadt? It's more generally known as that."

"I'm afraid not, sir," Davis said.

"Here now," Ellison said. "Look at this sauce boat."

Davis looked.

"This dates back to 1783, Davis. Here, look." He turned over the sauce boat, but he did not let it out of his hands. "See the crossed hayforks? That's the mark, you know, shows it's genuine stuff. Funny thing about this. The mark so resembles the Meissen crossed swords . . ." He seemed suddenly to remember that he was not talking to a fellow connoisseur. He put the sauce boat down swiftly but gently. "Have you learned anything yet, Davis?"

"A little, Mr. Ellison. I'm here mainly for money."

Ellison looked up sharply and then began chuckling. "You're a frank man, aren't you?"

"I try to be," Davis said, "When it concerns money."

"How much will you need?"

"A thousand will do it. I'll probably be flying to Vegas and back, and I may have to spread a little money for information while I'm there."

Ellison nodded briefly. "I'll give you a check before you leave. What progress have you made, Davis?"

"Not very much. Do you know a Tony Radner?"

Ellison looked up swiftly. "Why?"

"He put your daughter on the DC-4, sir. Do you know him?"

Ellison's mouth lengthened, and he tightened his fists on the desk top. "Has that son of a bitch got something to do with this?" he asked.

"Do you know him, sir?"

"Of course I do! How do you know he put Janet on that plane?"

"An eyewitness, sir."

"I'll kill that bastard!" Ellison shouted. "If he had anything to do with . . ."

"How do you know him, Mr. Ellison?"

Ellison's rage subsided for a moment. "Janet was seeing him," he said.

"What do you mean, seeing him?"

"She fancied herself to be in love with him," Ellison said. "He's a no-good, Davis, a plain . . ."

"You mean she wanted to marry him, rather than Carruthers?"

"No, that's not what I mean. I mean she was seeing Radner. *After* she and Nick were married. She . . . she had the supreme gall to tell me she wanted a divorce from Nick." Ellison clenched his hands and then relaxed them again. "You don't know Nick, Davis. He's a fine boy, one of the best. I feel toward him the way I'd feel toward my own son. I never had any boys, Davis, and Janet wasn't much of a daughter." He paused. "I'm grateful I've still got Nick," he said.

"Your daughter wanted to divorce Carruthers?"

"Yes," Ellison said.

"Did she tell Carruthers?"

"Yes, she did. But I told *her* I'd cut her off without a penny if she did any such damn-fool thing. She changed her mind mighty fast after that. Janet was used to money, Davis. The idea of marrying a ticket seller didn't appeal to her when she knew she'd have to do without it."

"So she broke it off with him?"

"On the spot."

"When was this?"

"About six months ago," Ellison said.

"And she hadn't seen him since?"

"Not that I knew of. Now you tell me he put her on that plane. I don't know what to think."

Davis nodded. "It *is* a little confusing."

"Do you suppose she was going to keep a rendezvous in Washington with Radner?" Ellison shook his head. "Dammit, I wouldn't put it past her."

"I don't think so. At least . . . well, I should think they'd have left together if that were the case."

"Not if she didn't want to be seen. She was travelling on a company pass, you know."

"That seems odd," Davis said. "I mean—"

"You mean, with all my money, why should she travel on a pass?" Ellison smiled. "I like to help Nick out, Davis. I keep him living well; did it when Janet was alive, and still do it. But he's a proud boy, and I've got to be careful with my methods of seeing to his welfare. Getting Janet her ticket was one of the things that kept his pride going."

"I see." Davis washed his hand over his face. "Well, I'll talk to Radner. Did you know he was married now?"

"No, I didn't."

"Yes. On the day of the crash."

"On the day . . . then what on earth was he doing with Janet?"

"That's a good question," Davis said. He paused, and then added, "Can I have that check now?"

It was not until after supper that evening that Nicholas Carruthers showed up. Davis had eaten lightly, and after a hasty cigarette he had begun packing a small bag for the Vegas trip. When the knock sounded on the door to his apartment, he dropped a pair of shorts into the suitcase and called, "Who is it?"

"Me. Carruthers."

"Second," Davis said. He went to the door rapidly, wondering what had occasioned this visit from the pilot. He threw back the night latch, and then unlocked the door.

Carruthers was in uniform this time. He wore a white shirt and black tie, together with the pale blue trousers and jacket of the airline, and a peaked cap.

"Surprised to see you, Carruthers," Davis said. "Come on in."

"Thanks," Carruthers said. He glanced around the simply furnished apartment noncommittally, then stepped inside and took off his cap, keeping it in his hands.

"Something to drink?" Davis asked. "Scotch okay?"

"Please," Carruthers replied.

Davis poured, and when Carruthers had downed the drink, he refilled the glass. "What's on your mind, Carruthers?"

Carruthers looked into the depths of his glass, sipped a bit of the scotch, and then looked up. "Janet," he said.

"What about her?"

"Let it lie. Tell the old man you're dropping it. Let it lie."

"Why?"

"How much is the old man paying you?" Carruthers asked, avoiding Davis' question.

"That's between the old man and myself."

"I'll match it," Carruthers said. "And then some. Just let's drop the whole damn thing."

Davis thought back to the genial Mr. MacGregor. "You remind me of someone else I know," he said.

Carruthers did not seem interested. "Look, Davis, what does this mean to you, anyway? Nothing. You're getting paid for a job. All right, I'm willing to pay you what you would have made. So why are you being difficult?"

"Am I being difficult? I didn't say I *wouldn't* drop it, did I?"

"Will you?"

"It depends. I'd like to know why you want it dropped."

"Let's just say I'd like it better if the whole thing were forgotten."

"A lot of people would like it better that way. Including the person who put that bomb on the plane."

Carruthers opened his eyes wide. "You don't think I did that, do you?"

"You were aboard the plane. You could have."

"Why would I do a thing like that?"

"I can think of several reasons," Davis said.

"Like what?" Carruthers sipped at the scotch again.

"Maybe you didn't like the idea of Janet playing around with Tony Radner."

Carruthers laughed a short, brittle laugh. "You think that bothered me? That two-bit punk? Don't be ridiculous." He drank some more scotch and then said, "I was used to Janet's excursions. Radner didn't bother me at all."

"You mean there were others?"

"Others? Janet collected them the way the old man collects porcelain. A hobby, you know."

"Did the old man know this?"

"I doubt it. He knew his daughter was a bitch, but I think Radner was the first time it came into the open. He squelched that pretty damn fast, you can bet."

"But you knew about it? And it didn't bother you?"

"Not in the least. I'm no angel myself, Davis. If Janet wanted to roam, fine. If she thought of leaving me, that was another thing."

"That you didn't like," Davis said.

"That I didn't like at all." Carruthers paused. "Look, Davis,

I like money. The old man has a lot of it. Janet was my wife, and the old man saw to it that we lived in style. I could have left the airline any time I wanted to, and he'd have set me up for life. Fact is, I like flying, so I stayed on. But I sure as hell wasn't going to let my meal ticket walk out."

"That's not the way I heard it," Davis said.

"What do you mean?"

"Janet's gone, and the old man is still feeding the kitty."

"Sure, but I didn't know it would work that way."

"Didn't you?"

Carruthers swallowed the remainder of his scotch. "I don't get you, Davis."

"Look at it this way, Carruthers. Janet's a handy thing to have around. She comes and goes, and you come and go, and the old man sees to it that you come and go in Cadillacs. A smart man may begin wondering why he needs Janet at all. If he can be subsidized even after she's gone, why not get rid of her? Why not give her a bomb to play with?"

"Why not?" Carruthers asked. "But I didn't."

"That's what they all say," Davis told him. "Right up to the gas chamber."

"You're forgetting that I didn't know what the old man's reactions would be. Still don't know. It's early in the game yet, and he's still crossing my palm, but that may change. Look, Davis, when a man takes out accident insurance, it's not because he hopes he'll get into an accident. The same thing with Janet. I needed her. She was my insurance. As long as she was around, my father-in-law saw to it that I wasn't needing." Carruthers shook his head. "No, Davis, I couldn't take a chance on my insurance lapsing."

"Perhaps not. Why do you want me to drop the case?"

"Because I want a status quo. The memory of Janet is fresh in the old man's mind. I'm coupled with the memory. That means he keeps my Cadillac full of gas. Suppose you crack this damned thing? Suppose you find out who set that bomb? It becomes something that's resolved. There's a conclusion, and the old man can file it away like a piece of rare porcelain. He loses interest—and maybe my Cadillac stops running."

"You know something, Carruthers? I don't think I like you very much."

Carruthers smiled. "Why? Because I'm trying to protect an investment? Because I don't give a damn that Janet is gone? Look, Davis, let's get this thing straight. We hated each other's guts. I stayed with her because I like the old man's money. And she stayed with me because she knew she'd be cut off penniless if she didn't. A very simple arrangement." He paused. "What do you say, Davis?"

"I say get the hell out of here."

"Be sensible, Davis. Look at it . . ."

"Take a walk, Carruthers. Take a long walk and don't come back."

Carruthers stared at Davis for a long time. He said nothing, and there was no emnity in his eyes. At last he rose and settled his cap on his head.

At the door, he turned and said, "You're not being smart, Davis."

Davis didn't answer him.

Maybe he *wasn't* being smart. Maybe Carruthers was right.

It would have been so much easier to have said no, right from the start. No, Mr. Ellison, I'm sorry. I won't take the case. Sorry.

That would have been the easy way. He had not taken the easy way. The money had appealed to him, yes, and so he'd stepped into something that was really far too big for him, something that still made very little sense to him. A bomb seemed an awfully elaborate way of killing someone, assuming the death of Janet Carruthers was, in fact, the reason for the bomb. It would have been so much easier to have used a knife, or a gun, or a rope, or even poison.

Unless the destruction of the plane was an important factor in the killing.

Did the killer have a grudge against the airline as well?

Carruthers worked for the airline, but he was apparently well satisfied with his job. Liked flying, he'd said. Besides, to hear him tell it, he'd never even considered killing his wife. Sort of killing the goose, you know. She was too valuable to him. She was—what had he alluded to?—insurance, yes, insurance.

Which, in a way, was true. Carruthers had no way of knowing how Ellison would react to his daughter's death. He could just as easily have washed his hands of Carruthers, and a man couldn't take a chance on . . .

"I'll be goddamned!" Davis said aloud.

He glanced at his watch quickly. It was too late now. He would have to wait until morning.

"I'll be goddamned," he said again.

It would be a long night.

Mr. Schlemmer was a balding man in his early fifties. A pair of rimless glasses perched on his nose, and his blue eyes were genial behind them.

"I can only speak for Aircraft Insurance Association of America, you understand," he said. "Other companies may operate on a different basis, though I think it unlikely."

"I understand," Davis said.

"First, you wanted to know how much insurance can be

obtained from our machines at the San Francisco airport." Schlemmer paused. "We sell it at fifty cents for twenty-five thousand dollars' worth. Costs you two quarters in the machine."

"And what's the maximum insurance for any one person?"

"Two hundred thousand," Schlemmer said. "The premium is four dollars."

"Is there anything in your policy that excludes a woman travelling on a company pass?" Davis asked.

"No," Schlemmer said. "Our airline trip policy states 'travelling on ticket or pass.' No, this woman would not be excluded."

"Suppose the plane's accident occurred because of a bomb explosion aboard the plane while it was in flight? Would that invalidate a beneficiary's claim?"

"I should hardly think so. Just a moment, I'll read you the exclusions." He dug into his desk drawer and came out with a policy which he placed on the desk top, leafing through it rapidly. "No," he said. "The exclusions are disease, suicide, war, and of course, we will not insure the pilot or any active member of the crew."

"I see," Davis said. "Can I get down to brass tacks now?"

"By all means, do," Schlemmer said.

"How long does it take to pay?"

"Well, the claim must be filed within twenty days after the occurrence. Upon receipt of the claim, and within fifteen days, we must supply proof-of-loss forms to the claimant. As soon as these are completed and presented to us, we pay. We've paid within hours on some occasions. Sometimes it takes days, and sometimes weeks. It depends on how rapidly the claim is made, the proof of loss submitted—and all that. You understand?"

"Yes," Davis said. He took a deep breath. "A DC-4 crashed near Seattle on January 6th. Was anyone on that plane insured with your company?"

Schlemmer smiled, and a knowing look crossed his face. "I had a suspicion you were driving at that, Mr. Davis. That was the reason for your 'bomb' question, wasn't it?"

"Yes. Was anyone insured?"

"There was only one passenger," Schlemmer said. "We would not, of course, insure the crew."

"The passenger was Janet Carruthers," Davis said. "Was she insured?"

"Yes."

"For how much?"

Schlemmer paused. "Two hundred thousand dollars, Mr. Davis." He wiped his lips and said, "You know how it works, of course. You purchase your insurance from a machine at the airport. An envelope is supplied for the policy, and you mail this directly to your beneficiary or beneficiaries as the case may be, before you board the flight."

"Yes, I've taken insurance," Davis said.

"A simple matter," Schlemmer assured him, "and well worth the investment. In this case, the beneficiaries have already received a check for two hundred thousand dollars."

"They have?"

"Yes. The claim was made almost instantly, proof of loss filed, the entire works. We paid at once."

"I see," Davis said. "I wonder . . . could you tell me . . . you mentioned suicide in your excluding clause. Was there any thought about Mrs. Carruthers' death being suicide?"

"We considered it," Schlemmer said. "But quite frankly, it seemed a bit absurd. An accident like this one is hardly conceivable as suicide. I mean, a person would have to be seriously unbalanced to take a plane and its crew with her when she chose to kill herself. Mrs. Carruthers' medical history showed no signs of mental instability. In fact, she was in amazingly good health all through her life. No, suicide was out. We paid."

Davis nodded. "Can you tell me who the beneficiaries were?" he asked.

"Certainly," Schlemmer said. "Mr. and Mrs. Anthony Radner."

He asked her to meet him in front of DiAngelo's and they lingered on the wharf awhile, watching the small boats before entering the restaurant. When they were seated, Anne Trimble asked, "Have you ever been here before?"

"I followed a delinquent husband as far as the door once," he answered.

"Then it's your first time."

"Yes."

"Mine, too." She rounded her mouth in mock surprise. "Goodness, we're sharing a first."

"That calls for a drink," he said.

She ordered a daiquiri, and he settled for scotch on the rocks, and he sipped his drink slowly, thinking, *I wish I didn't suspect her sister of complicity in murder.*

They made small talk while they ate, and Davis felt he'd known her for a long time, and that made his job even harder. When they were on their coffee, she said, "I'm a silly girl, I know. But not silly enough to believe this is strictly social."

"I'm an honest man," he said. "It isn't."

She laughed. "Well, what is it then?"

"I want to know more about your sister."

"Alice? For heaven's sake, why?" Her brow furrowed, and she said, "I really should be offended, you know. You take me out and then want to know more about my sister."

"You've no cause for worry," he said very softly. He was not even sure she heard him. She lifted her coffee cup, and her eyes were wide over the brim.

"Will you tell me about her?" he asked.

"Do you think she put the bomb on the plane?"

He was not prepared for the question. He blinked his eyes in confusion.

"Do you?" she repeated. "Remember, you're an honest man."

"Maybe she did," he said.

Anne considered this, and then took another sip of coffee. "What do you want to know?" she asked.

"I want to . . ."

"Understand, Mr. Davis . . ."

"Milt," he corrected.

"All right. Understand that I don't go along with you, not at all. Not knowing my sister. But I'll answer any of your questions because that's the only way you'll see she had nothing to do with it."

"That's fair enough," he said.

"All right, Milt. Fire away."

"First, what kind of a girl is she?"

"A simple girl. Shy, often awkward. Honest, Milt, very honest. Innocent. I think Tony Radner is the first man she ever kissed."

"Do you come from a wealthy family, Anne?"

"No."

"How does your sister feel about—"

"About not having a tremendous amount of money?" Anne shrugged. "All right, I suppose. We weren't destitute, even after Dad died. We always got along very nicely, and I don't think she ever yearned for anything. What are you driving at, Milt?"

"Would two hundred thousand dollars seem like a lot of money to Alice?"

"Yes," Anne answered without hesitation. "Two hundred thousand would seem like a lot of money to anyone."

"Is she easily persuaded? Can she be talked into doing things?"

"Perhaps. I know damn well she couldn't be talked into putting a bomb on a plane, though."

"No. But could she be talked into sharing two hundred thousand that was come by through devious means?"

"Why all this concentration on two hundred thousand dollars? Is that an arbitrary sum, or has a bank been robbed in addition to the plane crash?"

"Could she be talked," Davis persisted, "into drugging another woman?"

"No," Anne said firmly.

"Could she be talked into forging another woman's signature on an insurance policy?"

"Alice wouldn't do anything like that. Not in a million years."

"But she married Radner. A man without money, a man without a job. Doesn't that seem like a shaky foundation upon which to build a marriage?"

"Not if the two people are in love."

"Or unless the two people were going to come into a lot of money shortly."

Anne said, "You're making me angry. And just when I was beginning to like you."

"Then please don't be angry. I'm just digging, believe me."

"Well, dig a little more gently, please."

"What does your sister look like?"

"Fairly pretty, I suppose. Well, not really. I suppose she isn't pretty, in fact. I never appraised her looks."

"Do you have a picture of her?"

"Yes, I do."

She put her purse on the table and unclasped it. She pulled out a red leather wallet, unsnapped it, and then removed one of the pictures from the gatefold. "It's not a good shot," she apologized.

The girl was not what Davis would have termed pretty. He was surprised, in fact, that she could be Anne's sister. He studied the black-and-white photograph of a fair-haired girl with a wide forehead, her nose a bit too long, her lips thin. He studied the eyes, but they held the vacuous smile common to all posed snapshots.

"She doesn't look like your sister," he said.

"Don't you think so?"

"No, not at all. You're much prettier."

Anne screwed up her eyebrows and studied Davis seriously. "You have blundered upon my secret, Mr. Davis," she said with mock exaggeration.

"You wear a mask, Miss Trimble," he said, pointing his finger at her like a prosecuting attorney.

"Almost, but not quite. I visit a remarkable magician known as Antoine. He operates a beauty salon and fender-repair shop. He is responsible for the midnight of my hair and the ripe apple of my lips. He made me what I am today, and now you won't love me any more." She brushed away an imaginary tear.

"I'd love you if you were bald and had green lips," he said, hoping his voice sounded light enough.

"Goodness!" she said, and then she laughed suddenly, a rich, full laugh he enjoyed hearing. "I may very well be bald after a few more tinting sessions with Antoine."

"May I keep the picture?" he asked.

"Certainly," she said. "Why?"

"I'm going up to Vegas. I want to find your sister and Radner."

"Then you're serious about all this," she said softly.

"Yes, I am. At least, until I'm convinced otherwise. Anne . . ."

"Yes?"

"It's just a job. I . . ."

"I'm not really worried, you understand. I know you're wrong about Alice, and Tony, too. So I won't worry."

"Good," he said. "I hope I *am* wrong."

She lifted one raven brow, and there was no coyness or archness in the motion. "Will you call me when you get back?"

"Yes," he said, "Definitely."

"If I'm out when you call, you can call my next-door neighbor, Freida. She'll take the message." She scribbled the number on a sheet of paper. "You will call, won't you, Milt?"

He covered her hand with his and said, "Try and stop me."

He went to City Hall right after he left her. He checked on marriage certificates issued on January 6th, and he was not surprised to find that one had been issued to Anthony Louis Radner and Alice May Trimble. He left there and went directly to the airport, making a reservation on the next plane for Las Vegas. Then he headed back for his apartment to pick up his bag.

The door was locked, just as he had left it. He put his key into the lock, twisted it, and then swung the door wide.

"Close it," MacGregor said.

MacGregor was sitting in the armchair to the left of the door. One hand rested across his wide middle and the other held the familiar .38, and this time it was pointed at Davis' head. Davis closed the door, and MacGregor said, "Better lock it, Miltie."

"You're a bad penny, MacGregor," Davis said, locking the door.

MacGregor chuckled. "Ain't it the truth, Miltie?"

"Why are you back, MacGregor? Three strikes and I'm out, is that it?"

"Three . . ." MacGregor cut himself short, and then grinned broadly. "So you figured the mountain, huh, Miltie?"

"I figured it."

"I wasn't aiming at you, you know. I just wanted to scare you off. You don't scare too easy, Miltie."

"Who's paying you, MacGregor?"

"Now, now," MacGregor said chidingly, waving the gun like an extended forefinger. "That's a secret now, ain't it?" Davis watched the way MacGregor moved the gun, and he wondered if he'd repeat the gesture again. It might be worth remembering, for later.

"So what do we do?" he asked.

"We take a little ride, Miltie."

"Like in the movies, huh? Real melodrama."

MacGregor scratched his head. "Is a pleasant little ride melodrama?"

"Come on, MacGregor, who hired you?" He poised himself on the balls of his feet, ready to jump the moment MacGregor started wagging the gun again. MacGregor's hand did not move.

"Don't let's be silly, Miltie boy," he said.

"Do you know *why* you were hired?"

"I was told to see that you dropped the case. That's enough instructions for me."

"Do you know that two hundred grand is involved? How much are you getting for handling the sloppy end of the stick?"

MacGregor lifted his eyebrows and then nodded his head. "Two hundred grand, huh?"

"Sure. Do you know there's a murder involved, MacGregor? Five murders, if you want to get technical. Do you know what it means to be accessory after?"

"Can it, Davis. I've been in the game longer than you're walking."

"Then you know the score. And you know I can go down to R and I, and identify you from a mug shot. Think about that, MacGregor. It adds up to rock-chopping."

"Maybe you'll never get to see a mug shot."

"Maybe not. But that adds another murder to it. Are they paying you enough for a homicide rap, MacGregor?"

"Little Miltie, we've talked enough."

"Maybe we haven't talked enough yet. Maybe you don't know that the Feds are in on this thing, and that the Army . . ."

"Oh, come on, Miltie. Come on now, boy. You're reaching."

"Am I? Check around, MacGregor. Find out what happens when sabotage is suspected, especially on a plane headed to pick up military personnel. Find out if the Feds aren't on the scene. And find out what happens when a big-time fools with the government."

"I never done a state pen," MacGregor said, seemingly hurt. "Don't call me a big-time."

"Then why are you juggling a potato as hot as this one? Do you yearn for Quentin, MacGregor? Wise up, friend. You've been conned. The gravy is all on the other end of the line. You're getting all the cold beans, and when it comes time to hang a frame, guess who'll be it? Give a good guess, MacGregor."

MacGregor said seriously, "You're a fast talker."

"What do you say, MacGregor? How do you feel, playing the boob in a big ante deal? How much are you getting?"

"Four G's," MacGregor said. "Plus."

"Plus what?"

MacGregor smiled the age-old smile of a man who has known a woman and is reluctant to admit it. "Just plus," he said.

"All right, keep the dough and forget you were hired. You've already had the 'plus', and you can keep that as a memory."

"I've only been paid half the dough," MacGregor said.

"When's the rest due?"

"When you drop the case."

"I can't match it, MacGregor, but I'll give you a thou for your trouble. You're getting off easy, believe me. If I don't crack this, the Feds will, and then you'll really be in hot water."

"Yeah," MacGregor said, nodding.

"You'll forget it then?"

"Where's the G-note?"

Davis reached for his wallet on the dresser. "Who hired you, MacGregor?" He looked up, and MacGregor's smile had widened now.

"I'll take it all, Miltie."

"Huh?"

"All of it." MacGregor waved the gun. "Everything in the wallet. Come on."

"You *are* a jackass, aren't you?" Davis said. He fanned out the money in the wallet, and then held it out to MacGregor. MacGregor reached for it, and Davis loosened his grip, and the bills began fluttering towards the floor.

MacGregor grabbed for them with his free hand, turning sideways at the same time, taking the gun off Davis.

It had to be then, and it had to be right, because the talking game was over and MacGregor wasn't buying anything.

Davis leaped, ramming his shoulder against the fat man's chest. MacGregor staggered back, and then swung his arm around just as Davis' fingers clamped on his wrist. He did not fire, and Davis knew he probably didn't want to bring the apartment house down around his ears.

They staggered across the room in a clumsy embrace, like partners at a dance school for beginners. Davis had both hands on

MacGregor's gun wrist now, and the fat man swung his arm violently, trying to shake the grip. They didn't speak or curse. MacGregor grunted loudly each time he swung his arm, and Davis' breath was audible as it rushed through his parted lips. He did not loosen his grip. He forced MacGregor across the room, and when the fat man's back was against the wall Davis began methodically smashing the gun hand against the plaster.

"Drop it," he said through clenched teeth. "Drop it."

He hit the wall with MacGregor's hand again, and this time the fingers opened and the gun clattered to the floor. Davis stepped back for just an instant, kicking the gun across the room, and then rushed forward with his fist clenched.

He felt his fist sink into the flesh around MacGregor's middle. The fat man's face went white, and then he buckled over, his arms embracing his stomach. Davis dropped his fist and then brought it up from his shoe-laces, catching MacGregor on the point of his jaw. MacGregor lurched backward, slamming into the wall, knocking a picture to the floor. Davis hit him once more, and MacGregor pitched forward onto his face. He wriggled once, and was still.

Davis stood over him, breathing hard. He waited until he caught his breath, and then he glanced at his watch.

Quickly, he picked up the .38 from where it lay on the floor. He broke it open, checked the load, and then brought it to his suitcase, laying it on top of his shirts.

He snapped the suitcase shut, called the police to tell them he'd just subdued a burglar in his apartment, and then left to catch his Las Vegas plane.

He started with the hotels. He started with the biggest ones.

"Mr. and Mrs. Anthony Radner," he said. "Are they registered here?"

The clerks all looked the same.

"Radner, Radner. The name doesn't sound familiar, but I'll check, sir."

Then the shifting of the ledger, the turning of pages, the signatures, largely scrawled, and usually illegible.

"No, sir, I'm sorry. No Radner."

"Perhaps you'd recognize the woman, if I showed you her picture?"

"Well . . ." The apologetic cough. "Well, we get an awful lot of guests, sir."

And the fair-haired girl emerging from the wallet. The black and white, stereotyped photograph of Alice Trimble, and the explanation, "She's a newlywed—with her husband."

"We get a lot of newlyweds, sir."

The careful scrutiny of the head shot, the tilting of one eyebrow, the picture held at arm's length, then closer.

"No, I'm sorry. I don't recognize her. Why don't you try . . . ?"

He tried them all, all the hotels, and then all the rooming houses, and then all the motor courts. They were all very sorry. They had no Radners registered, and couldn't identify the photograph.

So he started making the rounds then. He lingered at the machines, feeding quarters into the slots, watching the oranges and lemons and cherries whirl before his eyes, but never watching them too closely, always watching the place instead, looking for the elusive woman named Alice Trimble Radner.

Or he sat at the bars, nursing along endless scotches, his eyes fastened to the mirrors that commanded the entrance doorways. He was bored, and he was tired, but he kept watching, and he began making the rounds again as dusk tinted the sky, and the lights of the city flicked their siren song on the air.

He picked up the newspaper by chance. He flipped through it idly, and he almost turned the page, even after he'd read the small head: FATAL ACCIDENT.

The item was a very small one. It told of a Pontiac convertible with defective brakes which had crashed through the guard rail on the highway, killing its occupant instantly. The occupant's name was Anthony Radner. There was no mention of Alice in the article.

Little Alice Trimble, Davis thought. *A simple girl. Shy, often awkward. Honest.*

Murder is a simple thing. All it involves is killing another person or persons. You can be shy and awkward, and even honest—but that doesn't mean you can't be a murderer besides. So what is it that takes a simple girl like Alice Trimble and transforms her into a murderess?

Figure it this way. Figure a louse named Tony Radner who sees a way of striking back at the girl who jilted him and coming into a goodly chunk of dough besides. Figure a lot of secret conversation, a pile of carefully planned moves. Figure a wedding, planned to coincide with the day of the plotted murder, so the murderers can be far away when the bomb they planted explodes.

Radner gets to see Janet Carruthers on some pretext, perhaps a farewell drink to show there are no hard feelings. This is his wedding day, and he introduces her to his bride, Alice Trimble. They share a drink, perhaps, but the drink is loaded and Janet suddenly feels very woozy. They help her to the airport, and they stow the bomb in her valise. None of the pilots know Radner. The only bad piece of luck is the fact that the fire-warning system is acting up, and a mechanic named Mangione recognizes him. But that's part of the game.

He helps her aboard and then goes back to his loving wife,

Alice. They hop the next plane for Vegas, and when the bomb explodes they're far, far away. They get the news from the papers, file claim, and come into two hundred thousand bucks.

Just like falling off Pier 8.

Except that it begins to get sour about there. Except that maybe Alice Trimble likes the big time now. Two hundred G's is a nice little pile. Why share it?

So Tony Radner meets with an accident. If he's not insured, the two hundred grand is still Alice's. If he is insured, there's more for her.

The little girl has made her debut. The shy, awkward thing has emerged.

Portrait of a killer.

Davis went back to the newsstand, bought copies of all the local newspapers and then went back to the hotel.

When he was in his room, he called room service and asked for a tall scotch, easy on the ice. He took off his shoes and threw himself on the bed.

The drink came, and he went back to the bed again.

The easy part was over, of course. The hard part was still ahead. He still had to tell Anne about it, and he'd give his right arm not to have that task ahead of him. Alice Trimble? The police would find her. She'd probably left Vegas the moment Radner piled up the Pontiac. She was an amateur, and it wouldn't be too hard to find her. But telling Anne, that was the difficult thing.

Davis sat upright, took a long swallow of the scotch, and then swung his stockinged feet to the floor. He walked to the pile of newspapers on the dresser, picked them up, and carried them back to the bed.

He thumbed through the first one until he found the item about Radner's accident. It was a small notice, and it was basically the same as the one he'd read. It did add that Alice Trimble was on her honeymoon, and that she had come from San Francisco where she lived with her sister.

He leafed through the second newspaper, scanning the story quickly. Again, basically the same facts. Radner had taken the car for a spin. Alice hadn't gone along because of a headache. The accident had been attributed to faulty brakes, and there was speculation that Alice might have grounds for suit, if she cared to press charges, against the dealer who'd sold them the car.

The third newspaper really did a bang-up job. They treated the accident as a human-interest piece, playing up the newly-wed angle. They gave it the tearful head, "FATE CHEATS BRIDE," and then went on to wring the incident dry. There was also a picture of Alice Trimble leaving the coroner's office. She was raising her hand to cover her face when the picture had been taken. It was a good shot, close up, clear. The caption read: *Tearful Alice Radner, leaving the coroner's office after identifying the body of her husband, Anthony Radner.*

Davis did not notice any tears on Alice Trimble's face.

He looked at the photograph again.

He sat erect and took a long gulp of his scotch, and then he brought the newspaper closer to his face and stared at the picture for a long time.

And he suddenly remembered something important he'd forgotten to ask Anne about her sister. Something damned important. So important he nearly broke his neck getting to the phone.

He asked long distance for Anne's number, and then let the phone ring for fifteen minutes before he gave up. He remembered the alternate number she'd given him then, the one belonging to Freida, the girl next door. He fished the scrap of paper out of his wallet, studying the number in Anne's handwriting, recalling their conversation in the restaurant. He got long distance to work again, and the phone was picked up on the fourth ring.

"Hello?"

"Hello, Freida?"

"Yes?"

"My name is Milt Davis. You don't know me, but Anne said I could leave a message here if . . ."

"Oh, yes. Anne's told me all about you, Mr. Davis."

"Well, good, good. I just tried to phone her, and there was no answer. I wonder if you know where I can reach her?"

"Why, yes," Freida said. "She's in Las Vegas."

"What!"

"Yes. Her brother-in-law was killed in a car crash there. She . . ."

"You mean she's here? Now?"

"Well, I suppose so. She caught a plane early this evening. Yes, I'm sure she's there by now. Her sister called, you see. Alice. She called and asked Anne to come right away. Terrible thing, her husband getting killed like . . ."

"Oh, Christ!" Davis said. He thought for a moment and then asked, "Did she say where I could reach her?"

"Yes. Just a moment."

Freida put the phone down with a clatter, and Davis waited impatiently. By the time she returned, he was ready to start chewing the mouthpiece.

"What's the address?" he asked.

"It's outside of Las Vegas. A rooming house. Alice and Tony were lucky to get such a nice . . ."

"Please, the address!"

"Well, all right," Freida said, a little miffed. She read off the address and Davis scribbled it quickly. He said goodbye, and hung up immediately. There was no time for checking plane schedules now. No time for finding out which plane Anne had caught out of Frisco, nor for finding out what time it had arrived in Vegas.

There was only time to tuck MacGregor's .38 into the waistband of his trousers and then run like hell down to the street. He caught a cab and reeled off the address, and then sat on the edge of his seat while the lights of Vegas dimmed behind him.

When the cabbie pulled up in front of the clapboard structure, he gave him a fiver and then leaped out of the car. He ran up the front steps and pulled the door pull, listening to steps approaching inside. A white-haired woman opened the door, and Davis said, "Alice Radner. Where?"

"Upstairs, but who . . . ?"

Davis shoved the woman aside and started up the flight of steps, not looking back. There was a door at the top of the stairwell, and he rapped on it loudly. When he received no answer, he shouted, "I know you're in there! Open the goddamn door!"

The door opened instantly, and Davis found himself looking into the bore of a .22.

"Come in," a woman's voice said softly.

"Where is she?" she asked.

"I'm afraid I had to tie her and gag her. She raised a bit of a fuss when she got here."

He stepped into the room, and she closed the door behind him. Anne was lying on the bed, her hands tied behind her, a scarf stuffed in her mouth. He made a move toward her and the voice came from the doorway, cool and crisp.

"Leave her alone."

"Why?" Davis said. "It's all over now, anyway."

She smiled, but there was no mirth in her eyes. "You should have stayed out of it. From the very beginning."

"Everybody's been telling me that," Davis said. "Right from go."

"You should have paid more attention to them, Mr. Davis. All this might have been avoided then."

"All what?"

She did not answer. She opened the door again, and called, "It's all right, Mrs. Mulready. He's a friend of mine." Then she slammed the door and bolted it.

"That takes care of her," she said, the .22 steady in her hand. She was a beautiful woman with a pale complexion and blue eyes set against the ivory of her skin. She stared at Davis solemnly.

"It all seemed out of whack," Davis said, "but I didn't know just where. It all pointed to Tony Radner and Alice Trimble, but I couldn't conceive of her as a murderess. Sure, I figured Tony led her into it. A woman in love can be talked into anything. But when I learned about Tony's accident here, a new Alice Trimble took shape. Not the gal who was talked into anything, and not the gal who'd do anything for love. This new Alice Trimble was a cold-blooded killer, a murderess who . . ."

Davis saw Anne's eyes widen. She struggled to speak.

"Anne," he said, "tell me something. Was your sister a red-head?"

Anne nodded dumbly, and he saw the confused look that stabbed her eyes. It was then that he realized he'd unconsciously used the past tense in talking about her sister.

"I'm sorry," he said. "I'm sorry as hell, Anne." He paused and drew a deep breath. "Alice is dead."

It was almost as if he'd struck her. She flinched, and then a strangled cry tried to shove its way past the gag.

"Believe me," he said, "I'm sorry. I . . ." He wiped his hand across his lips and then said, "I never thought to ask. About her hair, I mean. Hell, I had her picture and that was all I needed to identify her. I'm . . . I'm sorry, Anne."

He saw the tears spring into her eyes, and he went to her in spite of the .22 that was still pointed at him. He ripped the gag from her mouth, and she said, "I don't understand. I . . . what . . . what do you mean?"

"Alice left you on the sixth," he said, "to meet Tony Radner, allegedly to marry him. She didn't know about the trap that had been planned by Tony and Janet Carruthers."

Anne took her eyes from Davis and looked at the .22 in the woman's hand. "Is . . . is that who . . ."

"Janet Carruthers," Davis said, "who wanted to be free of her husband more than anything else in the world. But not at the expense of cutting herself off without a cent. So she and Tony figured it all out, and they started looking for a redhead who would take the hook. Your sister came along, starry-eyed and innocent, and Radner led her to the chopping block."

Davis paused and turned to the redhead with the gun. "I can fill it in, if you like. A lot of guessing, but I think I'm right."

"Go ahead," Janet said. "Fill it in."

"Sure. Alice met Tony as scheduled on the day they were to be married. He probably suggested a drink in celebration, drugged her, and then took her someplace to get her into some of your clothes. He drove her to the airport because your signature was necessary on the insurance policy. You insured Alice, who was now in Janet Carruthers' clothing, with Janet Carruthers' identification in case anything was left of her after the crash, for two hundred thousand dollars. And Janet Carruthers' beneficiaries were Mr. and Mrs. Anthony Radner. You knew that Nick would be on the DC-4, but outside of him, no one else on the plane knew what you looked like. It would be simple to substitute Alice for you. You left the airport, probably to go directly to City Hall to wait for Tony. Tony waited until Nick took a pilot up on a test, and then he brought Alice to the plane, dumped her into her seat, with the bomb in her suitcase, and left to meet you. You got married shortly after the DC-4 took off. You used Alice Trimble's name, and most likely the identification—if it was needed—that Tony had taken from her. The switch had been completed, and you were now Mrs. Radner. You flew together to Las Vegas, and as soon as the DC-4 crashed, you made your claim for the two hundred G's."

"You're right except for the drug, Mr. Davis. That would have been overdoing it a bit."

"All right, granted. What'd Tony do, just get her too damned drunk to walk or know what was going on?"

"Exactly. Her wedding day, you know. It wasn't difficult."

Davis heard a sob catch in Anne's throat. He glanced at her briefly and then said to Janet, "Did Tony know he was going to be driving into a pile of rocks?"

Janet smiled. "Poor Tony. No, I'm afraid he didn't know. That part was all my idea. Even down to stripping the brakes. Tony never knew what hit him."

"Neither did all the people on that DC-4. It was a long way to go for a lousy hunk of cash," Davis said. "Was Tony insured, too?"

"Yes," Janet said, "but not for much." She smiled. "Enough, though."

Davis nodded. "One after the other, right down the line. And then you sent for Anne because she was the only living person who could know you were *not* Alice Trimble. And it had to be fast, especially after that picture appeared in the Las Vegas paper."

"Was that how you found out?" she asked.

"Exactly how. The picture was captioned *Alice Radner* but the girl didn't match the one in the photo I had. Then I began thinking about the color of Alice's hair, which I knew was light, and it got clear as a bell." He shook his head sadly. "I still don't know how you hoped to swing it. You obviously sent for Anne because you were afraid someone would recognize you in Frisco. Hell, someone would have recognized you sooner or later, anyway."

"In Mexico?" Janet asked. "Or South America? I doubt it. Two hundred thousand can do a lot outside of this country, Mr. Davis. Plus what I'll get on Tony's death. I'll manage nicely, don't you worry." She smiled pleasantly.

Davis smiled back. "Go ahead," he said. "Shoot. And then try to explain the shots to your landlady."

Janet Carruthers walked to the dresser, keeping the gun on Davis. "I hadn't wanted to do it here," she said, shrugging. "I was going to take Miss Trimble away after everyone was asleep. You're forcing my hand, though." She opened a drawer and came out with a long, narrow cylinder. The cylinder had holes punched into its sides, and Davis knew a silencer when he saw one. He saw Janet fitting the silencer to the end of the .22 and he saw the dull gleam in her eyes and knew it was time to move. He threw back his coat and reached for the .38 in his waistband. The .22 went off with a sharp *pouff*, and he felt the small bullet rip into his shoulder. But he'd squeezed the trigger of the .38 and he saw her arm jerk as his larger bullet tore flesh and bone. Her fingers opened, and the silenced gun fell to the floor.

Her face twisted in pain. She closed her eyes, and he kicked the gun away, and then she began swearing. She kept swearing when he took her good arm and twisted it behind her back.

He heard footsteps rushing up the stairs, and then the landlady shouted. "What is it? *What is it?*"

"Get the police!" he yelled through the closed door. "Get them fast."

"You don't know what you're doing," Janet said. "This will kill my father."

Davis looked over to where Anne sat sobbing on the bed. He wanted to go to her and clasp her into his arms, but there would be time for that later.

"My father . . ." Janet started.

"Your father still has Nick." Davis said, "and his porcelain." His shoulder ached, and the trickle of blood down his jacket front was not pleasant to watch. He paused and lifted his eyes to Janet's. "That's all your father ever had."

The Confession

I said Look, all I want is the truth, Liz. I just want to know what the hell's going on. I can't walk in that squadroom tomorrow and not be able to take a stand on this. It's been going on too long up there, the guys talking behind my back. I got to be able to tell them they're wrong. Whatever you done or didn't do, that's *our* business. If it's true what they're saying, well then we'll have to talk it over. I don't know what we'll do if it's true, Liz, I just don't know. I know I love you. So if it's true, I guess we'll have to talk it over, find out how we can patch things up. I hope it isn't true, Liz. I love you so much, I . . . I just hope it isn't true. What I'm hoping is I can go in there tomorrow and tell the guys Look, I know what the rumble's been around here, I wasn't born yesterday. And I talked to my wife last night, and I've got the straight goods now, and if I ever hear anybody around here even *hinting* she's playing around, I'll personally break his arms and legs. That's what I'm hoping I can do tomorrow, Liz. But if it's true what they're saying, then I got to know that, too, so I can figure some way of handling it. You understand me, Liz? We been married twelve years now, we never had any trouble talking about anything before. I want to talk about it now. I want your side of it. So you want to tell me about it, or what?

So she sat on the edge of the bed there, this was in our bedroom. I'd been home maybe ten minutes, I was still wearing the shoulder holster. I was in my shirt-sleeves and wearing the harness. So I took it off and hung it on the back of the chair, and still she didn't say anything, just sat on the edge of the bed there and stared at me. This was maybe a little after midnight, I'd been sitting that liquor store on Twelfth with O'Neill; the guy closed at eleven and I went straight home. She sat there staring at me, not saying anything, and then she took off her shoes, and stood up and walked barefooted to where I was standing by the dresser, and turned her back to me so I could lower the zipper on her dress. Then she said, "All you want is a confession."

I said. "No, I don't want a confession, Liz. I just want to set things straight between us."

She took off the dress, and carried it to the closet and hung it up. Then she went to the dresser in her bra and panties, and shook a cigarette loose from the package there, and searched around for a match, and got the cigarette going. She took an ashtray to the bed with her, and sat on the edge again, and let out a stream of smoke, and crossed her legs and said, "Tell me exactly what they're saying."

I told her I'd pieced the thing together little by little—that was another thing, Liz. A detective isn't supposed to spend half his working day putting together facts on whether or not his wife is playing around behind his back. That liquor store, for one thing, it's been held up four times in the past six months, and we still ain't got a hint who's doing it. I'm supposed to be working on *crimes,* and not acting like a private eye looking for proof in a divorce action. Not that I'm talking divorce, Liz, I swear to God I'm not even *thinking* divorce. If this is true, what they're saying, then we'll work it out someway, there's nothing we haven't yet been able to work out, we'll work this out, too.

So she said again, "Tell me exactly what they're saying."

I told her I'd first got wind of it in the locker room one night. I was changing into my long johns because we had a stakeout later on, and I expected to be outside on a street corner. This wasn't the liquor store, this was that numbers runner we finally busted; this must've been last month sometime, when I first got wind of it. There were these two guys on the squad talking behind the lockers. They were talking about Harris, who'd got a court order to put in a wire downtown, and he was getting some very juicy conversations on that phone, conversations that had nothing to do with narcotics. The reason the wire was in there, I told her, was because the guy was suspected of running a dope factory, cutting and packaging shit for sale on the street. Now you either *know* all this, Liz, or you don't, I told her. Because if it's true what they're saying, then you've *got* to know the guy is in narcotics. He's a cheap gangster in narcotics. I don't know how you could've got involved with somebody like that, if it's true, but that's not the point. I don't care about that. If it's true, then we'll talk about it, and work it out. The point is that the guy was getting phone calls all day long from this woman, and it didn't take Harris long to figure out the woman's husband is a cop. This had nothing to do with Harris's case; he was just being *entertained* by all these conversations. Because here's a guy he's setting up for a bust if he gets anything good on the wire, and at the same time the guy is getting calls from a woman who's married to a cop, and who he's banging regularly when the cop's working. That was the first I heard of it, Liz. In the locker room there. The two guys talking about it while I changed into my long johns. The only name mentioned was Harris's, who was sitting the wire. At the time, I didn't know the narcotics bum was a guy named Anthony Laguna, that's not his real name, that's what he goes by on the street, I guess you know his name, if the stories are true. I looked up his B-sheet, Liz, he's got a record going back to when he was seventeen, including one arrest for rape, which he got off with. Just the idea of your having anything to do with somebody like him, though I can't imagine how'd you'd ever have met a guy like him, well, just the idea . . . though I swear to God it never crossed my mind that first time I heard them talking in the locker room. All I knew was it was a cop's wife involved with this Laguna bum. That's what I told her.

She put out the cigarette then, and carried the ashtray back to the dresser, and then she unclasped her bra and put it on the chair where the gun was hanging, and then she slipped out of her panties and walked naked to the bed. She fluffed up a pair of pillows against the headboard, and then she got on the bed and leaned back against the pillows and said, "What else did you hear?"

I told her the next thing I heard was that the cop with the horns was working out of our precinct. I figured at the time it was a patrolman; a guy with fixed shifts, you know, his wife could easily be playing around while he was on the four-to-midnight, or the graveyard or whatever. I mean, it was a perfect setup for a patrolman's wife, because while the poor stiff was out there walking his beat, he couldn't be checking up on her at the same time. So I figured it was a patrolman. There was, in fact, a lot of joking in the squadroom. About the guy being a patrolman, you know. Harris is giving us detailed reports on the juicy conversations Laguna and his broad are having, and by now we all know it's a cop in the precinct, and we figure it's a patrolman, it *has* to be a patrolman. Harris is complaining about he's not getting anything on the wire but sex talk. He's supposed to be setting up a narcotics bust, and nobody's talking about dope, all they're talking about is screwing. This girl has got to be a nympho, Harris says, she calls the guy every ten minutes, describes in detail what she wants him to do to her next time she sees him. We're all feeling pretty sorry for the patrolman, whoever he is. But at the same time, we're making jokes about him. You know the kind of jokes go on in a squadroom, Liz, it's like the Army. It's like when I was in the Army.

Well, this goes on for a week or two, I forget how long, and then I figured either Laguna and the girl broke up, or else all the jokes are going stale because all at once nobody's talking about it anymore. Not even Jefferson, who used to be with Vice and who's got nothing but sex on his mind all the time, not even Jefferson is mentioning Harris and that hot wire he's sitting. Then I hear someplace, I forget where, I think it's in the john, I'm sitting in there and I hear two guys out at the sinks and one of them is saying the broad's name is Liz—Laguna's broad. They're saying whoever that patrolman is out there, he's got a wife named Liz who's putting the horns on him with a cheap thief. I still didn't, I swear to God, I *still* didn't make a connection, I never for a minute thought this was maybe *my* Liz. This was still some patrolman out there married to a Liz.

"Yes, some patrolman's wife," she said.

Yes, I told her, that's what I thought at the time, that's what I thought when I first heard the name Liz mentioned, but then I put that together with the fact that nobody's talking about it in the squadroom anymore, leastways not when I'm around. So I singled out Harris one day, I found him there in the swing room, I said Hey there, Charlie, how's that wire doing? Harris said Oh, it's coming along, Duke, slow, but it's coming along. And I said You still getting those hot flashes from Laguna's broad? And Harris said Oh, you know how it is with these wires, you get all kinds of shit on them except what you're looking for. So I told him about a wire I was sitting one time, where we had a phone booth on Third Avenue bugged because we knew it was a booth this torch used all the time—we were investigating an arson at the time. But we got all different kinds of people making calls in that booth, people besides the torch. And one time I was sitting the wire, and I heard a guy telling his wife he was calling from the office and he'd be working late that night, this is a call he's making from a *booth* on Third Avenue! And his wife says That's okay, darling, I'll look for you later, and he hangs up and the next minute places a call to his girlfriend and sets up a date. Harris and I had a good laugh over that one, and then I asked him whether it was true Laguna's broad was named Liz, and Harris said Yeah, he guessed that was true, and I said Liz *what?* Harris turned his eyes away and said he hadn't heard the girl using her last name.

Well, what I did then, I went into Clerical and checked out the records for all the uniformed cops in the precinct, where it lists their home addresses, you know, and the names of spouses and kids and so on. And I found out there are three guys whose wives' names are Elizabeth. Patrolmen, these guys. None of the detectives on the squad got a wife named Elizabeth. And then I checked the patrolmen's duty chart, this was last week, I checked the chart and found out which shifts these three patrolmen were working, and I began staking out their houses while they were working, and following around their wives wherever they went. I made excuses to O'Neill, I told him I was clearing up some deadwood in the files, following up on some burglaries, talking to witnesses again, stuff like that. He bought it because we're so backlogged now, he figured anything I could do to put a case in the open file, anything like that would give us a chance to catch up. So what I did was follow these women around and, well, I guess you know I'm an experienced cop, I told her, and by the end of the week if any of those women were fooling around with a cheap hood, why then they were doing it at the laundromat or the supermarket because that's the kind of places they went to while their husbands were on the job. Or a movie with a girlfriend, if the guy was working nights. Or one of them went to a Bingo game at the church. They were clean, I told her. So it wasn't a patrolman's wife, Liz, it just wasn't. So it had to be somebody else.

Then tonight, O'Neill and I were heading out to the liquor store, we're riding in his old Chevy, and I said to him straight out, I said Johnny, you got to tell me what they're saying. Is it Liz they're talking about? Is it *my* wife who's playing around with this Laguna? And first O'Neill said it was all a bunch of bullshit, Harris was probably making the whole thing up to keep the squadroom clowns amused. I told him I didn't think Harris was making it up, and he said Well, even it it's true, there must be ten thousand women named Liz in this city, and I said Yeah, Johnny, but not all of them are married to a cop in our precinct. So he told me it was probably some poor fucking patrolman, and I said Johnny, it's not a patrolman, I checked. And he looked at me, he was driving the car, he just turned his head slightly to the side and looked at me, and I said Johnny, I think it's *me*. He turned his head back to the road then, and he said Well, Duke, I guess that's what they're saying.

She was still sitting there on the bed, propped up against the pillows, but there was a smile on her face now, as if I'd said some-thing very comical, something she was going to deny in the next minute, set the whole thing straight by simply saying Well, this is ridiculous, Duke, you know I love you and would never in a mil-lion years get involved with another man. That's what I wanted to hear from her, and I guess I began feeling a little better the minute

I saw that smile. So I said Liz, all I'm asking for now is the truth. If it's as terrible as maybe it looks to be, we'll work it out. And if it's true, I don't know what, maybe I'll ask for a transfer, I just don't know what. But if it's a lie, then I've got to be able to go in there and face those guys down. That's all I'm asking, Liz. I'm asking you to help me with this thing, one way or another. I love you, Liz, and whatever the truth is, it's better we get it out in the open and deal with it. Now that's it Liz, and I'd appreciate it if you'd tell me now.

"You want a confession, right?" she said. She was still smiling.

"No," I said, "I don't want a confession, I want to be able to talk about this, I want to be able to set things stright."

"Okay," she said, "you'll get a confession, if that's what you want. Okay?"

"I'm listening," I said.

"It's true," she said. "All of it is true."

She was still smiling, I thought for a minute she was putting me on, I thought she couldn't be saying this was true, while smiling at the same time—it had to be a put-on. "I met him downtown six months ago," she said. "It was raining. He offered me a lift in his car, and I got in. It was as simple as that."

"Liz," I said.

"I've been seeing him ever since."

"Liz," I said, "the man is a bum."

"I love him," she said.

I think that was what did it, her saying she loved him. I think I really *would* have been willing to talk it over, the way I'd promised her, if only she'd hadn't said she loved him. Because, you see, the man was a bum, the man was everything I'd learned to despise, the man was a bum. So I went to the chair where I'd hung the shoulder holster, and I took the .38 from it without even thinking what I was doing, I just took the gun out of the clamshell, and I turned to where she was sitting there on the bed, still smiling, and I fired four shots into her chest and then I went to the bed and fired another shot into her head.

I make this confession freely and voluntarily in the presence of Detective-Lieutenant Alfred Laber and Detective 2nd/Grade John O'Neill and Detective 1st/Grade Charles Harris, having been duly warned of my rights, and having waived my privilege to remain silent.

The Last Spin

The boy sitting opposite him was his enemy.

The boy sitting opposite him was called Tigo, and he wore a green silk jacket with an orange stripe on each sleeve. The jacket told Dave that Tigo was his enemy. The jacket shrieked "Enemy, enemy!"

"This is a good piece," Tigo said, indicating the gun on the table. "This runs you close to forty-five bucks, you try to buy it in a store."

The gun on the table was a Smith & Wesson .38 Police Special.

It rested exactly in the center of the table, its sawed-off two-inch barrel abruptly terminating the otherwise lethal grace of the weapon. There was a checked walnut stock on the gun, and the gun was finished in a flat blue. Alongside the gun were three .38 Special cartridges.

Dave looked at the gun disinterestedly. He was nervous and apprehensive, but he kept tight control of his face. He could not show Tigo what he was feeling. Tigo was the enemy, and so he presented a mask to the enemy, cocking one eyebrow and saying, "I seen pieces before. There's nothing special about this one."

"Except what we got to do with it," Tigo said. Tigo was studying him with large brown eyes. The eyes were moist-looking. He was not a bad-looking kid, Tigo, with thick black hair and maybe a nose that was too long, but his mouth and chin were good. You could usually tell a cat by his mouth and his chin. Tigo would not turkey out of this particular rumble. Of that, Dave was sure.

"Why don't we start?" Dave asked. He wet his lips and looked across at Tigo.

"You understand," Tigo said. "I got no bad blood for you."

"I understand."

"This is what the club said. This is how the club said we should settle it. Without a big street diddlebop, you dig? But I want you to know I don't know you from a hole in the wall—except you wear a blue and gold jacket."

"And you wear a green and orange one," Dave said, "and that's enough for me."

"Sure, but what I was trying to say . . ."

"We going to sit and talk all night, or we going to get this rolling?" Dave asked.

"What I'm trying to say," Tigo went on, "is that I just happened to be picked for this, you know? Like to settle this thing that's between the two clubs. I mean, you got to admit your boys shouldn't have come in our territory last night."

"I got to admit nothing," Dave said flatly.

"Well, anyway, they shot at the candy store. That wasn't right. There's supposed to be a truce on."

"Okay, okay," Dave said.

"So like . . . like this is the way we agreed to settle it. I mean, one of us and . . . and one of you. Fair and square. Without any street boppin', and without any Law trouble."

"Let's get on with it," Dave said.

"I'm trying to say, I never even seen you on the street before this. So this ain't nothin' personal with me. Whichever way it turns out, like . . ."

"I never seen you neither," Dave said.

Tigo stared at him for a long time. "That's 'cause you're new around here. Where you from originally?"

"My people come down from the Bronx."

"You got a big family?"

"A sister and two brothers, that's all."

"Yeah, I only got a sister," Tigo shrugged. "Well." He sighed. "So." He sighed again. "Let's make it, huh?"

"I'm waitin'," Dave said.

Tigo picked up the gun, and then he took one of the cartridges from the table top. He broke open the gun, slid the cartridge into the cylinder, and then snapped the gun shut and twirled the cylinder. "Round and round she goes," he said, "and where she stops, nobody knows. There's six chambers in the cylinder, and only one cartridge. That makes the odds five-to-one that the cartridge'll be in firing position when the cylinder stops twirling. You dig?"

"I dig."

"I'll go first," Tigo said.

Dave looked at him suspiciously. "Why?"

"You want to go first?"

"I don't know."

"I'm giving you a break." Tigo grinned. "I may blow my head off first time out."

"Why you giving me a break?" Dave asked.

Tigo shrugged. "What the hell's the difference?" He gave the cylinder a fast twirl.

"The Russians invented this, huh?" Dave asked.

"Yeah."

"I always said they was crazy bastards."

"Yeah, I always . . ." Tigo stopped talking. The cylinder was still now. He took a deep breath, put the barrel of the .38 to his temple, and then squeezed the trigger.

The firing pin clicked on an empty chamber.

"Well, that was easy, wasn't it?" he asked. He shoved the gun across the table. "Your turn, Dave."

Dave reached for the gun. It was cold in the basement room, but he was sweating now. He pulled the gun toward him, then left it on the table while he dried his palms on his trousers. He picked up the gun then and stared at it.

"It's a nifty piece," Tigo said. "I like a good piece."

"Yeah, I do too," Dave said. "You can tell a good piece just by the way it feels in your hand."

Tigo looked surprised. "I mentioned that to one of the guys yesterday, and he thought I was nuts."

"Lots of guys don't know about pieces," Dave said, shrugging.

"I was thinking," Tigo said, "when I get old enough, I'll join the Army, you know? I'd like to work around pieces."

"I thought of that, too. I'd join now, only my old lady won't give me permission. She's got to sign if I join now."

"Yeah, they're all the same," Tigo said, smiling. "Your old lady born here or the island?"

"The island," Dave said.

"Yeah, well, you know they got these old-fashioned ideas."

"I better spin," Dave said.

"Yeah," Tigo agreed.

Dave slapped the cylinder with his left hand. The cylinder whirled, whirled and then stopped. Slowly, Dave put the gun to his head. He wanted to close his eyes, but he didn't dare. Tigo, the enemy, was watching him. He returned Tigo's stare, and then he squeezed the trigger.

His heart skipped a beat, and then over the roar of his blood he heard the empty click. Hastily, he put the gun down on the table.

"Makes you sweat, don't it?" Tigo said.

Dave nodded, saying nothing. He watched Tigo. Tigo was looking at the gun.

"Me now, huh?" he said. He took a deep breath, then picked up the .38.

He shrugged. "Well." He twirled the cylinder, waited for it to stop, and then put the gun to his head.

"Bang!" he said, and then he squeezed the trigger. Again, the firing pin clicked on an empty chamber. Tigo let out his breath and put the gun down.

"I thought I was dead that time," he said.

"I could hear the harps," Dave said.

"This is a good way to lose weight, you know that?" He laughed nervously, and then his laugh became honest when he saw that Dave was laughing with him. "Ain't it the truth? You could lose ten pounds this way."

"My old lady's like a house," Dave said, laughing. "She ought to try this kind of a diet." He laughed at his own humor, pleased when Tigo joined him.

"That's the trouble," Tigo said. "You see a nice deb in the street, you think it's crazy, you know? Then they get to be our people's age, and they turn to fat." He shook his head.

"You got a chick?" Dave asked.

"Yeah, I got one."

"What's her name?"

"Aw, you don't know her."

"Maybe I do," Dave said.

"Her name is Juana." Tigo watched him. "She's about five-two, got these brown eyes . . ."

"I think I know her," Dave said. He nodded. "Yeah, I think I know her."

"She's nice, ain't she?" Tigo asked. He leaned forward, as if Dave's answer was of great importance to him.

"Yeah, she's nice," Dave said.

"The guys rib me about her. You know, all they're after—well, you know—they don't understand something like Juana."

"I got a chick, too," Dave said.

"Yeah? Hey, maybe sometime we could . . ." Tigo cut himself short. He looked down at the gun, and his sudden enthusiasm seemed to ebb completely. "It's your turn," he said.

"Here goes nothing," Dave said. He twirled the cylinder, sucked in his breath, and then fired.

The empty click was loud in the stillness of the room.

"Man!" Dave said.

"We're pretty lucky, you know?" Tigo said.

"So far."

"We better lower the odds. The boys won't like it if we . . ." He stopped himself again, and then reached for one of the cartridges on the table. He broke open the gun again, and slipped the second cartridge into the cylinder. "Now we got two cartridges in here," he said. "Two cartridges, six chambers. That's four-to-two. Divide it, and you get two-to-one." He paused. "You game?"

"That's . . . that's what we're here for, ain't it?"

"Sure."

"Okay then."

"Gone," Tigo said, nodding his head. "You got courage, Dave."

"You're the one needs the courage," Dave said gently. "It's your spin."

Tigo lifted the gun. Idly, he began spinning the cylinder.

"You live on the next block, don't you?" Dave asked.

"Yeah." Tigo kept slapping the cylinder. It spun with a gently whirring sound.

"That's how come we never crossed paths, I guess. Also I'm new on the scene."

"Yeah, well you know, you get hooked up with one club, that's the way it is."

"You like the guys on your club?" Dave asked, wondering why he was asking such a stupid question, listening to the whirring of the cylinder at the same time.

"They're okay." Tigo shrugged. "None of them really send me, but that's the club on my block, so what're you gonna do, huh?" His hand left the cylinder. It stopped spinning. He put the gun to his head.

"Wait!" Dave said.

Tigo looked puzzled. "What's the matter?"

"Nothing. I just wanted to say . . . I mean . . ." Dave frowned. "I don't dig too many of the guys on my club, either."

Tigo nodded. For a moment, their eyes locked. Then Tigo shrugged, and fired.

The empty click filled the basement room.

"Phew," Tigo said.

"Man, you can say that again."

Tigo slid the gun across the table.

Dave hesitated an instant. He did not want to pick up the gun. He felt sure that this time the firing pin would strike the percussion cap of one of the cartridges. He was sure that this time he would shoot himself.

"Sometimes I think I'm turkey," he said to Tigo, surprised that his thoughts had found voice.

"I feel that way sometimes, too," Tigo said.

"I never told that to nobody," Dave said. "The guys on my club would laugh at me, I ever told them that."

"Some things you got to keep to yourself. There ain't nobody you can trust in this world."

"There should be somebody you can trust," Dave said. "Hell, you can't tell nothing to your people. They don't understand."

Tigo laughed. "That's an old story. But that's the way things are. What're you gonna do?"

"Yeah. Still, sometimes I think I'm turkey."

"Sure, sure," Tigo said. "It ain't only that, though. Like sometimes . . . well, don't you wonder what you're doing stomping some guy in the street? Like . . . you know what I mean? Like . . . who's the guy to you? What you got to beat him up for? 'Cause he messed with somebody else's girl?" Tigo shook his head. "It gets complicated sometimes."

"Yeah, but . . ." Dave frowned again. "You got to stick with the club. Don't you?"

"Sure, sure . . . no question." Again, their eyes locked.

"Well, here goes," Dave said. He lifted the gun. "It's just . . ." He shook his head, and then twirled the cylinder. The cylinder spun, and then stopped. He studied the gun, wondering if one of the cartridges would roar from the barrel when he squeezed the trigger.

Then he fired.

Click.

"I didn't think you was going through with it," Tigo said.

"I didn't neither."

"You got heart, Dave," Tigo said. He looked at the gun. He picked it up and broke it open.

"What are you doing?" Dave asked.

"Another cartridge," Tigo said. "Six chambers, *three* cartridges. That makes it even money. You game?"

"You?"

"The boys said . . ." Tigo stopped talking. "Yeah, I'm game," he added, his voice curiously low.

"It's your turn, you know."

"I know."

Dave watched as Tigo picked up the gun.

"You ever been rowboating on the lake?"

Tigo looked across the table at him, his eyes wide. "Once," he said. "I went with Juana."

"Is it . . . is it any kicks?"

"Yeah. Yeah, it's grand kicks. You mean you never been?"

"No," Dave said.

"Hey, you got to try it, man," Tigo said excitedly. "You'll like it. Hey, you try it."

"Yeah, I was thinking maybe this Sunday I'd . . ." He did not complete the sentence.

"My spin," Tigo said wearily. He twirled the cylinder. "Here goes a good man," he said, and he put the revolver to his head and squeezed the trigger.

Click.

Dave smiled nervously. "No rest for the weary," he said. "But, Jesus, you got heart. I don't know if I can go through with it."

"Sure, you can," Tigo assured him. "Listen, what's there to be afraid of?" He slid the gun across the table.

"We keep this up all night?" Dave asked.

"They said . . . you know . . ."

"Well, it ain't so bad. I mean, hell, we didn't have this operation, we wouldn'ta got a chance to talk, huh?" He grinned feebly.

"Yeah," Tigo said, his face splitting in a wide grin. "It ain't been so bad, huh?"

"No, it's been . . . well, you know, these guys on the club, who can talk to them?"

He picked up the gun.

"We could . . ." Tigo started.

"What?"

"We could say . . . well . . . like we kept shootin' an' nothing happened, so . . ." Tigo shrugged. "What the hell! We can't do this all night, can we?"

"I don't know."

"Let's make this the last spin. Listen, they don't like it, they can take a flying leap, you know?"

"I don't think they'll like it. We supposed to settle this for the clubs."

"Screw the clubs!" Tigo said vehemently. "Can't we pick our own . . ." The word was hard coming. When it came, he said it softly, and his eyes did not leave Dave's face." . . . friends?"

"Sure we can," Dave said fervently. "Sure we can! Why not?"

"The last spin," Tigo said. "Come on, the last spin."

"Gone," Dave said. "Hey, you know, I'm *glad* they got this idea. You know that? I'm actually glad!" He twirled the cylinder. "Look you want to go on the lake this Sunday? I mean, with your girl and mine? We could get two boats. Or even one if you want."

"Yeah, one boat," Tigo said. "Hey, your girl'll like Juana, I mean it. She's a swell chick."

The cylinder stopped. Dave put the gun to his head quickly.

"Here's to Sunday," he said. He grinned at Tigo, and Tigo grinned back, and then Dave fired.

The explosion rocked the small basement room, ripping away half of Dave's head, shattering his face. A small sharp cry escaped Tigo's throat, and a look of incredulous shock knifed his eyes. Then he put his head on the table and began weeping.

About the Author

ED McBAIN was one of several pen names for Evan Hunter, whose writing career spanned more than five decades, from his first novel, *The Blackboard Jungle*, in 1954, to the screenplay for Alfred Hitchcock's *The Birds*, to *Candyland*, to his last novel, *Fiddlers*. He was the first American ever to receive the Diamond Dagger, the British Crime Writers Association's highest award. He also held the Mystery Writers of America's prestigious Grand Master Award. The author of more than 130 novels and story collections, he died in 2005.